The Widow

Dennis Edward Hurley

Chapter 1

Jessica watched as the lariat loop drifted almost sleepily through the dusty air until it settled around the Hereford bull's horns. Clint's roping horse, Mickey, automatically veered to the side then started to back straight away from the bull as Clint dallied the rope around the saddle horn. The bull fought the rope, head high at first, then twisted as a little bit of slack showed itself. The slack gave the animal enough freedom to try to break away. It bolted until the bull slammed into the end of the now taut rope. The clear snap sliced through the thick air, and the rope end came hissing back at high speed. Clint never had time to duck. The rope end hit him directly between the eyes. He dropped from the saddle as if he had been shot landing head first, his neck at an impossible angle.

...

They had spent the day gathering cattle from the rugged hill country on their one-man spread west of Seligman, Arizona. The March day was unusually warm, and with no rain through late winter and most of the early Spring, the dust had risen with every hoof strike until they moved in a tan cloud that settled over them and their mounts and created a hazy, dreamlike quality. The horses snorted to clear their nostrils. Clint and Jessica had worked hard to keep the herd bunched and moving back toward the branding pen.

Their cattle were a ragtag conglomeration of Herefords and mixed breed beef cattle, wild as the mule deer that often grazed with them. It took all of Clint's cow sense, Jessica's riding skills, and their Blue Heeler cattle dog, Blue, to keep the herd together and moving slowly but steadily forward. They had funneled the cattle down through a twisting valley until it opened up on a brushy flat. A quarter-mile ahead lay their branding pen, a rough circle of mesquite and twisted cedar wired together to create a circular enclosure 100 feet across. Clint rode point to lead the herd down to the pen. Jessica rode drag, and she had had her hands full with a Brahma bull that kept wanting to challenge her. Suddenly, a cow made a break for freedom on the west side. She didn't see the escapee until she heard Clint's raspy voice echo off the rock face to her right.

"Jess, what the hell? Get your head out of your ass, and get on that cow before we lose the whole damned herd. How many times I have to tell you to pay attention back there. Damn it! Get your bony ass after her!"

Jessica had cringed at the sound of his voice. When she looked up, she saw the Hereford, tail-high, breaking for a little draw a few hundred yards to the south. She spun her filly on its hindquarters and took off at a full gallop to cut the cow off before it could slip back up into the high country. Her pony, Faith, broke out of the dust cloud, ran loose and free under her, and in these wild chase moments, Jessica felt that looseness, that freedom travel up through her pony's body until she and the horse became one. She felt then that the freedom belonged to them both.

For Jess, her life all came down to this, a trained horse anybody could trust to do its job, to go where it was directed, to keep its rider safe. Their horses had those qualities because she knew horses, understood them better than Clint, better than most horsemen really. Clint would never admit that, never give her credit for all she did for him, credit for her part in making the ranch successful. She didn't care really. She felt a satisfaction inside where no one could touch it, where she felt her own sense of accomplishment. Her long dark hair, tied back in a pony tail, flagged out behind her as she rode, so she appeared to be what she had always felt herself to be, an extension of the horse.

"Jess, get your ass over to the north side of the herd. It's starting to loosen up over there. Pack 'em in so they got no place else to go but into the chute."

Clint had drifted back along the south side of the herd, and the tension in the herd had increased along with the veil of dust that hid them. The cattle moved as one now, the babies bawling for their mamas as they became separated. The cattle crowded through the gate, and Clint maneuvered the gate shut just as Jessica slipped through. He slipped the wire latch over the gate post, rode to a free-standing post, swung down and tied his horse. Jessica edged her horse past the herd, then stepped off and tied Faith next to Mickey. Clint had already turned on the propane and lit the torch in its steel tube where their branding iron rested. He stepped into the stirrup and swung up into the saddle again, undid his rope and built a loop.

"You ought to know what to do by now, so what do you say you do it, so I don't have to keep jumpin' off my horse to help you."

Jessica shook her head. Fear and anger had roiled through her gut, but she moved into position, pigging strings tucked into her belt where she could pull them out easily. Clint nosed Mickey into the herd and settled on the first calf to be roped, a small brown and white yearling that cut in front of him, frantically trying to find its mama. Clint's rope snaked out and caught the calf around the hind legs. He dallied, turned, and dragged the baby out of the herd and over to Jess. She grabbed a front leg, rolled her knees into the calf, and dropped it on its side where she pinned it. She quickly wrapped the pigging string around the legs and went over to the now heated branding iron

After she had burned in their brand, she set the iron back in the heater, ear notched and tagged the calf, then quickly castrated it with her pocket knife, and tossed the prairie oysters to Blue. She pulled off the pigging string, and the calf jumped to its feet as Clint eased off the rope on the hind legs.

She always hated the violence of the branding ritual, the fear, the blood, the burning hair smell. She hadn't grown up with it, had married into it. She had to learn to deal with the painful reality of it once she and Clint were a team. The physical skills needed had become almost second nature to her now, but she never got over the sick feeling at the pit of her stomach when she had to come to terms with the actual doing.

She stood. Sweat had formed little rivulets through the dust on her deeply tanned face. She took out a bandana and wiped at the mixture to clean it away. Her dark complexion came from her Italian father, her tall, slim, almost boyish figure from her mother. Even in the dirt and manure of the stock pen, she moved with a certain elegance, a certain grace. She had fallen into this alien place by chance it seemed. She had been raised in Boston, gone to good schools, and learned to ride in indoor arenas on $30,000 horses. Her course had been set almost at birth by her domineering father. She would attend Harvard as he had, get a law degree eventually, and become part of the family business. She had always done what he told her to despite his constant criticism. The catch had come just before her high school graduation in 2007. The plan was for her to enter Harvard in the fall but a chance summer job as a wrangler on a dude ranch came up. Her father fought the idea when she brought it up. He had wanted her to work as an intern at his office instead, but she wore him down. Eventually, he had let her go with the caveat to not fall in love with any cowboys out there.

The head wrangler was Clint, tall and muscular and blond and 100% cowboy. He had wooed her through the summer until by September, she had fallen hopelessly for the man she thought he was. By then he had convinced her to marry him and move to a ranch he was leasing along the stretch of highway between Kingman and Seligman. Parts of the ranch were already being split off into small parcels, but Arizona was still an open range state so, they would be able to run their cattle within the original ranch boundaries. He made it sound far more romantic than it would actually turn out to be.

The homestead was a ramshackle stone structure with no indoor plumbing and a leak in the roof over the bed, which only evidenced itself during the middle of winter when fixing it didn't fit in with Clint's plans. For a while, he treated her like a queen, patient as he taught her the business of ranching. Despite the misery of their primitive living conditions, she was madly in love with him. Gradually, all of that changed. At first, he started to blame her for things that went wrong around the ranch even when she clearly had nothing to do with those things. She felt irritated and talked back to him, but then he berated her so much that she found her life was easier if she just kept quiet. She convinced herself that he was just stressed by the pressure of the ranching business. She didn't want to make things any harder on him than necessary.

She had a cell phone when they married and used it to stay in contact with her mom back home. Her dad had disowned her when she married Clint, but her mom was her touchstone, and Jess had talked to her almost every day. One day the phone was gone when she got up. She searched frantically for it but found nothing. She asked Clint if he had seen it.

"We can't afford for you to have a cell phone, Jess. Our bills are piling up, and we haven't even sold our first steer yet to pay them."

"My mom will send me the money to cover that bill then. I haven't asked them for anything, and she will help us out with this. I know she will."

I don't want to be beholdin' to them for nothin'. No. It's time you cut ties with them anyway. You got enough to keep you busy here without them distractin' you."

"But, Clint. What harm is a cell phone going to do? We might need it in an emergency if nothing else."

"I said no. End of discussion. Don't say nothin' more about it! You got that, little missy? I'm in charge here, not you. Let it go."

It had been six years since that had happened, but it had been a pivotal moment for her. Caught between her growing fear of Clint and her fear of returning home, she chose to stay. Six years that had felt like a lifetime now ended with the snap of a rope.

Chapter 2

Clint lay still, face down in the dirt and manure of the corral. At first, the cattle milled around him like he was the center of a pinwheel. The Hereford bull moved off to the far corner of the pen, and as Jessica stood in stunned silence, the pen full of stock settled into its own stillness with Clint lying at center stage, his rope in a tangle around him. The dust cloud drifted away. She moved, trance-like through the herd toward him, squatted next to him. Jess rolled him onto his side, laid her fingers along his neck. No pulse. Supporting his neck as best she could, she rolled him the rest of the way onto his back and began to do CPR. She had no training in it, but had seen it performed once before by the gym teacher on a classmate from high school, and she had a vague idea of what needed to be done. She wanted to call for help, but they had no phone.

She was surprised to find herself crying now. She heard her own voice as if it came from a distance as if it belonged to someone else as she begged him to wake up, to come back. Nothing. No amount of pounding on his chest or tears or supplications would bring him back, and, after a while, she knew that to be true. She stood up, feeling like she was in a dream as she looked down on the man she had once loved but had grown to fear, now nothing but a lifeless bit of flesh and bone. She knew she had to get help, but also knew she couldn't just leave him there to be trampled over by the herd. She just didn't know how she was going to move him. He was a big man, two twenty and solid muscle, and she knew she wouldn't be able to drag him out of the pen on her own.

She settled on the only solution she could think of. She led her little filly over to him. Faith was skittish, nervous as Jessica undid the rope from her saddle and struggled to work the loop under his shoulders. She lifted each of the limp, heavy arms and slid the rope so that it circled Clint across his chest and through his armpits. She tightened the rope by hand, then tied the end off around her saddle horn. She led her horse toward the gate, felt the rope gain tension, then heard the sound of his body sliding over the dirt as it began to move across the rough ground. The sound made her want to vomit, and she wretched a little bit but fought it off.

When she had him outside the gate, she closed and secured it. It was a good mile back to the ranch house, then she would have to get in the pickup and drive five miles to the nearest neighbor to call for help. She undid her rope, dropped it on the ground, and swung up into the saddle. She turned and took one last look at him lying there, head now twisted awkwardly to the side, and was surprised again when a sob caught in her throat. Blue was sniffing at the body. She managed to whistle him to her as she spurred her mare into a long lope as she rode back to the ranch. Blue trailed reluctantly behind.

As she rode across the bunch grass and fringed bromegrass flats, she puzzled over her reaction. Clint had been probably the worst decision she could have ever made. On top of everything else he had been a drinker, and when he got shit-faced, he looked for her to beat her up whenever he could. She had taken to grabbing her horse and going for long rides when she saw it coming. For the past six years, she had lived a life where she had to stay constantly alert just to protect herself. So, why did she feel upset now that he no longer was a problem, she wondered. Maybe it was remembering now that he was gone what he had been like in those first few months, the one happy time in her marriage. She couldn't puzzle it out just then, and so she settled into the rhythm of the ride. Their house came into sight within minutes, its dark, stone exterior with the low, covered porch across the front, nestled against a steep, rocky hill to the south. A shear, bare-rock bluff to the east rose up and bracketed the homestead.

The rest of the day seemed like a blur. She drove the dirt ranch road to the nearest house, the Webster place, and the Websters made the calls. At first, she didn't even know who to have them call. There was little point in calling for medical help even though that seemed like something she should do. She settled on the sheriff. She sat in the pickup in the Webster's driveway to wait for him to arrive, and when the patrol car pulled into the driveway behind her, she stepped out of the truck to greet him. The officer, tall and dark complected, got out of the cruiser.

"He's about three miles east of here. I think the best way to go though is to drive on down to our spread, and go from there," she said. "Pretty level and open so you should be able to drive there."

She felt weak and leaned back against the door of her pickup then slid down until she was squatting in the driveway. Tears filled her eyes, rolled down her cheeks. She covered her face with both hands.

"I'm sorry for your loss, Mrs. Oliver. I'm Deputy Contreras." He paused and looked closely at her then stepped away. "Let me give you a minute. I know this is hard for you, but I need you to take me down there. You think you can do that?" His tone soft, almost as if he was talking with a child. She nodded. He helped her to her feet, guided her to his cruiser, opened the door, and helped her get in. Then he walked over to the Websters who were standing, watching everything. He touched the brim of his Stetson as he got close.

"Afternoon, folks. Can you tell me anything about what Mrs. Oliver said when she got here?"

Cal Webster nodded, looked at his wife. "Molly, you talked to her first. What did she tell you?"

"She just said Clint had an accident and that he had died out at their branding pen."

"Nothing else? She say how it happened?"

"Nope. She was pretty upset. Just said she needed help. Didn't even know who to call really. When she said he was dead, we figured to call you. Figured that was probably the right thing to do."

"You did fine. Just tryin' to get a feel for the situation is all. I may have to call you in to make a statement before this is all over. I won't trouble you anymore right now." He turned and went back to the cruiser.

It took them a half hour of slow driving to get back out to the pen. By that time, the buzzards had discovered the body and were circling when they pulled up. The deputy had already called for the coroner to come out and for a team from the state police, crime lab to secure and assess the scene. He asked Jessica to stay in the cruiser while he got out to take a look at the situation.

Clint's body had already started to stiffen, and deputy Contreras walked around it carefully trying not to disturb anything. Clint's horse was still in the pen with the cattle, the broken rope dragging behind it like a question mark. The deputy took out a small pad and made some notes. He went to the cruiser, opened the trunk, and took out a blue tarp, walked over, and covered the body to protect it from the vultures circling above.

When he got back to the cruiser, Jessica had her face buried in her hands again still crying. He opened the door and got in. "Mrs. Oliver, I can't take you back to your place right now. We have to wait for the state troopers to get here. Do you have anybody who can stay with you when I do take you back?"

She shook her head without looking up. "Not really. Clint never wanted to have any friends over. The Websters I guess were as close as we came to that. I don't really know them though. Officer Contreras, can I get Clint's horse? I need to get him back home, get him grained and watered. He's been working all day"

"I'm sorry, Mrs. Oliver. Things will have to stay pretty much as they are for a while until the State Police team gets here. Shouldn't be much longer." His eyes, soft, his voice, gentle.

There was an emptiness in her that she couldn't put into words. She also felt a looming sense of catastrophe if she didn't get the branding done soon. The pen was not set up for the cattle to stay there long. She worried that she would lose some if they stayed penned up much longer without food or water. At the same time, she didn't want to let them out because that meant she would have to re-gather them by herself, and that felt overwhelming. But above all, she harbored a sense of guilt because she realized that she felt almost nothing about Clint's death.

Actually, that wasn't completely true, but what she felt just didn't seem really appropriate. She felt a sense of relief that she couldn't completely admit even to herself. For most of the past six years she had lived in a constant state of tension, fear really, and suddenly that burden had been lifted from her. It felt odd, frightening because it had been the center of her focus for so long that she wasn't sure she knew how to live without it. As she thought about that, it occurred to her that it had actually been the same with her dad. Oh, not so much physically afraid as she had been with Clint, but afraid of failing, afraid of his constant criticism, his disdain when she didn't perform as well in school as he would have liked. She always felt less around him, inferior and unworthy.

The only place she felt she could be herself had always been at the barn. She knew she was good with horses, understood them, connected with them, even the ones that others had given up on. Other people recognized her skill. Soon she had found herself working with the problem horses when they needed her. She had had few friends in school, as she was too shy and insecure to try to join any group, so, her riding, her work with the horses had been her salvation. With the horses, she felt a connection. The horses took her for who she was, and her quiet way with them had made it easy for them to respond to her. When she heard about the wrangler's summer job at the Bar X dude ranch in northern Arizona, she had used every last chip of hers to get her father to say yes, and by some miracle, he had relented. Six years ago. Six years of doing whatever Clint demanded. Six years of not being her own person except with the horses. As she sat there, the realization began to creep over that for the first time in her life she was on her own with all that the realization implied.

Two state police cruisers pulled up behind the sheriff's car. Another car, a black sedan followed in the cloud of dust they had raised. Everyone else got out of their vehicles. Jessica tried to join them but found the cruiser's door locked. Deputy Contreras saw her trying to open the door, and through the closed window motioned for her to stay in the car.

It killed her to wait because all she could think of was Clint's horse without any food or water and trailing that rope that might tangle his legs at any time. She had to get it home, and then she had to get back and finish with the cattle. Dressed only in the T-shirt she had put on that morning and her jeans, the unaccustomed air conditioning chilled her. She shivered and wrapped her arms around herself trying to stay warm.

The state police completed their investigation of the scene. A tall dark-haired officer and a short, chubby, blond officer came over to the cruiser to talk with her. Officer Contreras unlocked the door. She stepped out into the heat as they approached and waited impatiently as they sipped from their water bottles and wiped at the sweat on their foreheads. The shorter officer seemed to be in charge.

He began the questioning. Jess repeated everything she had told the sheriff's deputy although the state police questioning seemed more thorough, more pointed. At last, she couldn't hold it in any longer.

"Do you think I had something to do with this? Why am I being questioned? It was an accident. Can we speed this up? I have stock that absolutely has to be taken care of as soon as possible. Otherwise, I'm going to lose them."

"Take it easy, Mrs. Oliver. You aren't a suspect. We just need to get all of the facts straight for the report. How did the rope hit him again?"

"It snapped by the honda. I told him he needed to replace that rope, but he said it was his favorite, and he damn well wasn't going to replace it if he didn't have to. Now, look at him. If he had only listened." She began to cry again. The two officers stood self-consciously and waited for her to regain control.

"I'm sorry. This is just so overwhelming. I don't know what I'm going to do."

"Is there anybody you can call to stay with you, help you?"

"Not really. I have to get this done myself, and I have to get it done by tomorrow morning."

She began to tear up again. The afternoon had settled into the special quiet that the high desert held as the shadows began to lengthen. Her voice barely audible now, "I just need to get my horse home and figure out what I'm going to do. I hope you understand." She searched their faces for a sign that they knew what she was going through but found little there to encourage her.

The dark-haired officer turned away and walked back to their cruiser while talking on his shoulder mic. The blond fixed her with a steady stare. "What was your marriage like, Mrs. Oliver? Were you happy?"

Jessica wasn't sure how to answer. She could tell that the officer was trying to bait her into something, but she didn't want to lie either. "It was a marriage like all marriages, I guess. Some good and some bad." She had a hard time remembering the good right then, but she felt there must have been something there at the beginning, so it wasn't a lie.

"No arguments, fights today?"

"No, not at all. We had too much to do to fight about anything." She hesitated. "I still have too much to do."

"Okay. Just one last thing. Please don't leave the area for a couple weeks until the investigation is wrapped up. We will be in touch to let you know when you can leave." He handed her a card. "If anything else comes up, give me a call. I'm really sorry for your loss, Ma'am. You are free to go now."

"Can I take my horse now? I need to get him home and fed and watered."

"Yes, Ma'am. We're done here."

Jessica turned and headed for the enclosure. Clint's horse was tied to a mesquite branch in a corner where the shade had lengthened into deep pools as the afternoon sun dropped lower on the horizon. He stood, one hind foot cocked as he slept. He seemed no worse for wear. The state troopers had taken Clint's rope and stored it in an evidence bag. She undid the single rein that had

Mickey tied to the enclosure and swung up into the saddle. She let her feet hang free because the stirrup leathers were set for Clint, too long for her. She didn't feel like changing them right then. She would deal with that later. All she wanted to do now was get Mickey home, then get some rest. She felt unbelievably tired and wanted to have a quick meal then just go to bed. She would have to have a plan for tomorrow, but for now, she just needed to rest.

She took a quick round of the herd to assess the condition of the cattle and found nothing for her to be immediately concerned about. She rode up to the gate, moved Mickey over next to it and slipped the wire loop free, swung the gate open, and then side-passed to shut it again after she rode out.

Officer Contreras came up to her and handed her his card. "We will have the body at the morgue in Kingman, Mrs. Oliver. You should be able to make arrangements to have him picked up in a couple days. You take care now"

Jess took the card and looked down at the deputy. She realized in that moment how kindly he had treated her and how rare that had been in her life. She managed a half smile then nudged Mickey forward. All she could think of was, ten minutes and she would be home. Ten minutes and she would have the house to herself. Ten minutes and maybe it would totally sink in that she didn't have to deal with Clint ever again.

She set off at an easy lope and was home in less than the ten minutes she had anticipated. Faith called to them as they approached, head high, running the fence line. Jess jumped down from the saddle when she got to the barn door, loosened the girth, and led Mickey inside to untack him. She put him in a stall long enough for him to eat the grain she gave him and then set him out with Faith and a pile of hay big enough to keep them busy most of the night. As she left the barn, deputy Contreras pulled her pickup into the yard. He turned the engine off and stepped out of the truck, A sheriff's cruiser pulled in behind him.

"Thought you might need this, so we brought it over for you."

She nodded and thanked him, and once again she felt the tears begin to form, but now it was because no one had done anything that thoughtful for her in a long time. He hesitated as if he wanted to say something more, but then backed away and turned to go. She watched him get into the cruiser with the other officer. As they pulled out of the yard, she watched them disappear in the dust as they headed back to the Webster's place

In the house, for the first time, she allowed herself to feel the emptiness that had been gnawing at her since the accident. The house, with its two rooms, the main room which included the kitchen, and a small bedroom, was stark under the best of circumstances, but now it felt almost like a tomb. Clint hadn't wanted any decorations, so the walls were bare, their stone surface rough and blackened from years of cooking grease and woodstove soot. As she stood in the main room, she felt a chill run along her spine and visibly shook for a moment before going into the kitchen area. Hardly better there, but at least she felt the comfort of the food that she had.

She took some eggs from the refrigerator, whipped four of them up in a bowl, heated a cast iron fry pan, and poured the eggs in to cook. She chopped some chive cuttings from a plant on the window sill and sprinkled the cuttings over the eggs then began to work the mixture with a spatula. She stopped long enough to put a couple slices of bread in the toaster, and when the eggs were done, she spooned them onto a plate, buttered the toast, and poured herself a glass of milk. The food felt good going down, comforting somehow, and it at least seemed to ease the emptiness she had felt from the moment she knew Clint had died. She ate half of the eggs, and she put the rest in the refrigerator for her lunch tomorrow.

Full darkness had descended by the time she had washed the dishes and put everything away. She went out to the outhouse, and when she came back in, washed her face at the sink and lay on her side on top of the old quilt that she had found at a garage sale that first year. She had loved it at first sight, and after making a fuss about the price, Clint had actually let her buy it. Now she closed her eyes and fell into a fitful sleep.

By midnight the moon had risen and its brilliance came through the filter of the ragged Venetian blinds as through a sieve. When the light awakened her, she looked down at her hand lying on the quilt. Shattered fragments of moonlight formed a pattern there, and suddenly, they seemed a metaphor for her own life, fragmented and in pieces. She hardly knew how to begin to assess all she had to do, where her life might take her. The only thing she knew for sure was that she had a certain freedom now, that she had never had before, and with it came both a release and a nagging fear that she wasn't up to the decision-making that accompanied it. She closed her eyes and when she opened them again, the pattern was different, more cohesive. She opened and closed her hand, watched the shards of light appear, disappear. She broke down again and the tears came steadily, no stopping them. By the time she had cried herself out, she had fallen asleep and the moonlight now lay softly on her face.

Chapter 3

The early morning sunlight cut a bright sliver along her cheek. She awoke to its warmth and to the sound of the desert wind picking up and rattling along the house's open eaves. She washed her face, dressed quickly, made two egg sandwiches from last night's leftovers, filled two canteens, fed Blue, and hurried out to the barn to feed Faith and get Mickey ready. When she had him tacked up and the stirrup leathers shortened, she grabbed her rope off her saddle, loaded saddlebags with her lunch and the canteens, swung up onto Mickey, whistled for Blue, and headed out at a long, ground-eating trot. She could hear the calves bawling a quarter-mile away. Working alone it would take her more than twice as long to get the job done, and with all the time the calves had spent with no water, she was worried she would lose some of them in the process.

They were bunched together in a spot shaded by some redberry juniper growing just outside the pen. She felt grateful for those trees since the sun had already started to heat up the pen. She got off, ground tied Mickey inside the enclosure, and started the propane burner to heat the branding iron. When she had everything set, she climbed back on Mickey, and she cut out the first calf she needed to work on, a rough-coated little Hereford cross.

It tried to run back into the herd, but Mickey raced to cut it off, and Jess, roped its hind legs and tied it off as Mickey backed to keep the rope taut. She jumped down. She had a pigging string clutched in her teeth as she put her knees into the calf's side and flipped it onto the ground. She quickly bound the front legs with the pigging string and set about branding, castrating, and ear-notching, the calf. When she finished, she undid the strings, beckoned Mickey forward, and slipped the rope off the calf's hind legs. The calf jumped up and went bawling to its mama.

She had repeated the procedure on the next two calves when Blue started barking. She was coiling up her rope and was surprised to see a rider top the horizon, thread his way through a patch of prickly pear cactus, and head on down to the catch pen. She didn't recognize him, but that wasn't unusual. Clint hadn't let her socialize with anybody, so she knew almost no one from the area. Short and stocky, he brushed at his longish brown hair, trying to shove it back under the headband of his Stetson. He was maybe in his early thirties and rode a flashy blue, roan quarter horse. He wore well-worn chinks over his jeans. The rider touched the brim of his hat as he approached.

"Howdy."

Jess nodded at him.

"The Websters called me. Told me you might need a hand. Name's Casey. What say, you let me do the ropin,' little missy, and you can stay on the ground and do the brandin' and cuttin'."

Jess eyed him warily through the hair that hung across her left eye. "Little missy." Clint's voice echoed through this stranger's words. She looked more closely at him. Her voice, tentative, barely audible, "I'm sorry, but they were wrong. You'll have to ride on back and find other work."

"Well, it 'ppears to me like you are workin' alone. Be a lot easier if two of us was to do this. You can ask anybody. I make a hand. You won't be disappointed." He said it in a way that seemed to imply something besides his roping ability. She turned away and swung up into the saddle. Something about the situation made her want to be on the same level as he was. She brushed the hair away from her eye.

"Look, Casey is it?"

He nodded.

"I don't have two cents to rub together right now, so there's no way I can afford to hire you. Best look someplace else. I'm sorry."

"I think we can make some arrangement on that, Ma'am. I don't need to be paid until you sell your stock. Go a lot easier if I were to give you a hand."

More deferential now. Maybe not as bad a guy as she had thought. Jess took off her hat and, using her sleeve, rubbed the sweat from her forehead. It would go a lot quicker with a second set of hands, that was for sure, and it would mean less stress on her stock. She knew she should probably ask more questions, but she didn't know what to ask. References would make no difference because she really didn't know anybody in the area. She decided to take a chance.

"All right. If you are willing to work for free until I get paid, I can use the help. I'll pay day wages for all the hours you work. If you want to do the roping, that probably works best for now, but after you see what I'm doing, we'll switch off every few head."

Somehow, saying that made her feel empowered like she never had felt before. She didn't have to do the job some man wanted her to do. She could call her own shots for a change.

Casey nodded. "Whatever you say, boss." He smiled at her.

She couldn't help herself and smiled back. "Let's get started."

They worked together through the morning and into the noon heat. They took a short break for lunch. She shared her lunch with him since he hadn't brought any food. She studied him now. Not a bad-looking guy, really. His hair was a bit too long, but he seemed generally to take some pride in the way he looked. Good face with sharp, dark brown eyes set wide. He had worked hard and efficiently all through the morning without complaining, and despite his stocky frame, he was quick, agile. She decided she felt glad she had hired him.

By midafternoon they had finished all the branding and tagging. "We'll split off the mommas, and the babies and heifers, and the bulls and send them on their way. The two-year-old steers are going back to the ranch to be shipped, so we will keep them separated until we are ready to move them. Do you want to cut or work the gate?"

"I'll work the gate. You sort out what you want to let go. Kind of surprised you aren't just sellin' the whole lock, stock, and barrel of them though what with your husband dyin' and all."

Jess turned away, tears starting to form in her eyes again. "I haven't decided what I'm going to do yet. For now, I'm sticking with Clint's original plan which is to move these two-year-olds to the shipping pen to be sold." She turned Mickey into the herd and called to Blue to join her.

They sorted and released for the better part of an hour until all that was left was the steers for shipping. Blue kept them cornered in the furthest part of the pen while Jess checked over the herd to make sure she hadn't missed anything. When she was ready, she opened the gate and took point as they began to move the steers toward the ranch. She felt a certain satisfaction in what she had accomplished as the herd of thirty-five moved out with Casey riding drag and her leading the way back to the pen.

This herd represented so much for her now. This was her money walking behind her, and she knew she desperately needed it to start whatever kind of life she would choose. Right now, all she knew was ranching. She felt totally disconnected from her previous life of relative luxury back in Boston. She knew she could never go back to that. Besides her dad had disowned her, and she had no idea what her mom felt since they hadn't talked in so long.

They worked the cattle all the way down to the holding pen and didn't lose one of them. She guessed Casey was right. He did make a hand. When the cattle funneled into the pen and she slammed the gate, she felt like crying again. This had been Clint's dream, and he never got to see it. For the life of her, she didn't know why that mattered to her, but somehow, she felt an unexpected emptiness that seemed to come in waves and overwhelmed her.

She turned Mickey to face Casey. "You might as well head out. Nothing really left to do now until tomorrow. I can handle the loading myself. If you want to leave me your name and address. I'll send you a check when I get the sale completed. Or if you want, you can swing by in a few days, and I'll pay you in cash if that works better for you."

"The cash thing works best, so I'll see you in a few days?" He stated it like a question instead of a statement. He smiled that easy smile of his, and Jess once again couldn't help but smile back.

"Yep. See you then."

Casey touched the brim of his hat. "See you then, Boss." He spun his horse and took off at a lope. Jess watched him go. For six years now, she had interactions with only one man, Clint. Now she had to deal with Casey, and her need for his help and at the same time, her feelings of distrust confused her.

After taking care of the horses, she spent the next half hour putting out hay and making sure the stock tanks were full. By the time she had finished, it was after three. She realized she had a couple of hours before stores closed and decided she had to at the very least get a cell phone, so she could contact the stock haulers. She had never been exactly sure how Clint did that since they hadn't had a phone, but she had seen the invoice and knew the name of the company. She also needed some food in the house, and though, after a search of the house, she had found only a small amount of cash in Clint's extra boots under the bed, she figured she could get what food she needed for a few days anyway. She washed up, combed her hair, and put on a clean t-shirt. She didn't really have any "going-to-

town clothes." This was the best she could do. She headed out in the pickup to Seligman, the closest town.

Seligman didn't have much to offer in the way of amenities, but there was a phone store. By the time she got to the store, she only had an hour before everything closed up. She made a decision quickly and within a half-hour, they had set up an account and gotten the phone charging. The salesman said he would stay open until she got back so that she could pick up the phone before she left town. She hurried to the Seligman Mart to get a few groceries to tide her over until she got a check.

When she returned to the phone store, the salesman had her phone charged and ready, gave her a quick lesson on it, and hurried her to the door. The groceries and the phone had taken the last of her cash, but nonetheless, she felt an unaccustomed sense of empowerment.

The drive home gave her time to think. So many changes so fast had been really overwhelmed her. She still had to take care of some kind of funeral arrangements for Clint when they released the body. He had no relatives that she knew of, so she had pretty much decided on cremating him and not holding a service. Who would be there after all? She had to be careful with the money she spent now. Tomorrow she would do a serious examination of the important papers that Clint had kept in a fireproof box in the desk. She needed to find what bank he had been using. He had kept the financial matters, like most of his life, a secret. She also thought about possibly getting a lawyer to settle whatever estate there was to settle. For now, though, all she wanted to do was go home, go to bed, and get a good night's sleep.

By the time she pulled into the drive, she could barely keep her eyes open. She fed Blue and once back in the house, settled for a quick Spam sandwich and some orange juice for herself. After supper, she crawled into bed, exhausted. She fell asleep with the shade open and the full moon clear and bright and lighting her bed in a soft light.

Chapter 4

The next day dawned bright and warm with the temperature already hovering in the 90's at six o'clock. Jess got up and washed her face, and then got the stock hauler's number from the invoice lying on Clint's desk. She called at eight. They were making a run in her direction that day, and, yes, they could pick up her stock. First job done.

She fed her horses and Blue and returned to the house to look through the fireproof box. The box was packed with a variety of papers and old receipts but after a half-hour of looking at everything in there, she had learned next to nothing. No bank account, nothing to tell her where the money had gone or if there even was any. At last, she resigned herself to the fact that she would be starting from scratch.

She dressed and walked out to the hen house to gather some eggs for breakfast. Before she went in to search the nests, she stood for a minute listening to the soft, dry wind as it coursed through the branches of the old desert willow tree that hung over the ranch house. Like everything right now, it seemed to intensify the emptiness she had been feeling since the accident. She shook her head, opened the hen house door, and hunted through the nests for the eggs she knew would be there.

The next thing on her list had to be to contact the sheriff and find out when Clint's body would be released and then make arrangements at the funeral home for it to be picked up. She decided it would be easier to just go into town and take care of it. There was no point in waiting around for the stock hauler. Better to keep busy, to distract herself.

After breakfast, she checked to be sure Blue had plenty of water and then climbed into the pickup and headed to Kingman. The road was quiet and empty until she got to the freeway, and then the morning traffic became intense, frightening at first because she had hardly driven since they were married. She held the wheel in a death grip, and tried to keep up with the flow of trucks and cars as they made their way steadily west toward Kingman. By nine, she had pulled into the sheriff's office parking lot and found a parking spot. She sat for a minute listening to the ticking of the hot engine, then stepped out of the truck into the stifling heat.

The office itself didn't appear to be much from the outside, a no-nonsense brick building with a glass door and a small lobby as she entered. To her left, behind a thick glass window, a secretary sat talking on the phone. Jess walked up to the window. The secretary glanced up, signaled that it would be a minute before she could help her, and gestured toward some straight back chairs along the wall.

Jess sat on the chair nearest the door and studied the room. On the longest wall, a display case held framed pictures of deputies receiving awards and several pictures of the civilian, mounted posse. There was also an antique revolver in a holster. Beyond that case, there was nothing else in the room. She waited impatiently until the secretary beckoned her up to the window.

"What can I help you with, ma'am?"

"I'm here to see Deputy Contreras. My husband died in an accident a couple of days ago, and I'm here to find out when I can have his body taken to the funeral home." She was surprised that she choked up a bit as she said the last part.

"Are you okay, ma'am? Can I get you a water or some coffee?"

"No, I'm fine. I just would like to get this done and make arrangements at the funeral home."

"Okay. Your name please?"

"Jessica Oliver."

"I'll call Mike and have him come up to get you." The receptionist turned back to her phone, dialed a number, and then quietly talked into the receiver with her back to Jess.

Jess turned and sat back down on the edge of her chair. A minute later the double click of the lock on the door between the reception area and the offices startled her. The door swung open and Officer Contreras stepped into the room and held the door open.

"Hi, Mrs. Oliver? Please come in."

Jess studied his face as she stood up and made her way to the door. His brown eyes seemed to miss nothing as they swept the room and then riveted on hers. He held the door as she passed through, and she could feel a sense of calm about him that she hadn't felt from anyone for a very long time. She immediately felt more comfortable, didn't feel the need to put her guard up which both relaxed and frightened her. He directed her to a cubicle with a desk and a pair of chairs. He pulled out one of the chairs for her and held it as she sat down. He sat down opposite her and leafed through a stack of papers until he pulled out the one he was looking for.

"I'm really sorry for your loss, Mrs. Oliver. I know that was tough being right there when it happened." He looked up at her, and from the look in his eyes, she felt like he really meant what he was saying.

She looked down at her hands folded in her lap, then looked up at him. She wanted to say something, to respond, but no words came out, and the tears started to form again.

"I'm sorry. I didn't mean to upset you."

"No, it's okay. It's just so new and kind of raw. I don't even know how to respond to it. I just end up crying."

"Okay. I just have a few questions for you, and we'll get you on your way."

He looked down at his notes. The questions were short and dealt with the time frame and a quick recap of the events on the day of the accident. He gave her a release form for the funeral home to pick up the body from the coroner's office. When he finished, he stood up and took her hand to help her stand. "If there is anything I can do, please, don't hesitate to call." He handed her his card, then took it back.

He took out a pen and flipped the card over. "Here, I'm going to give you my cell number. Call me any time if I can be of help." He wrote the number on the back of the card and gave it back to her.

He walked her to the door to the lobby, and she turned to him as she reached for the door handle. "Thank you. You've been very kind." He smiled a sad smile at her, and she opened the door and went into the lobby and then out into the heat of the day.

She drove rather aimlessly around town for a while until she spotted a funeral home. The Fieldcrest Funeral Home sounded like something fancy, but in reality, it was a low, single-story building that butted up to a parking lot of crack-filled asphalt. An older model black hearse sat in the driveway next door. She pulled into the parking lot, slid out of the pickup onto the hot asphalt and made her way to the front door. Inside, the temperature dropped drastically. Not being used to air conditioning anymore, it felt like a refrigerator to her. Everything was dark except for a light coming from a door down a short hall. She called down the hall.

Immediately, a head popped out the door and then disappeared only to instantly reappear attached to the body of a short, rather rotund, middle-aged man.

"Can I help you?

"Yes. I need to have my husband's body picked up from the morgue and cremated."

"Come in, come in." He waved her into his office and pointed her to a straight back chair with a seat covered in purple plush material. She sat. He asked a few questions, took the release form from the sheriff's office, and leaned back in his chair, his fingers steepled on his chest. "You don't want any kind of showing or wake?"

She felt a little guilty. It had sounded so accusatory. She shook her head. "No, we really don't know anybody around here, and there is no family. I just want the cremation."

He nodded his head, leaned forward, and pulled some papers from his desk for her to sign, and then asked for a check. She suddenly realized she didn't even have any way to pay him.

"I'm sorry. My husband handled all the money. I won't have the money for a few days until I get paid for the latest shipment of steers that I'm sending out today. Is there any way I could pay you later?" She felt the tears coming again, but this time they were tears of frustration.

"We can make arrangements. I will hold the body until you are ready to have him cremated."

"Ok. I should have a check by the end of the week. I will contact you as soon as I'm ready." She stood up, and he hurriedly jumped to his feet.

"Let me give you my card." He reached for a card display on his desk, fumbled, and sent some of the cards spilling onto the floor before picking one up and handing it to her.

"I'll pick the body up this afternoon," he said as she made her way to the door.

Once again in the street and back into the heat, she felt lost as to what she needed to do next. She climbed into the truck and sat for a minute staring down the street. A woman crossed the street with a child, and suddenly, she knew what she wanted to do. She wanted to talk with her mother. She still had her mother's cell phone number memorized, had wanted to call it many times over the past six years but couldn't. She took out her new phone and punched in the numbers and listened to the sound of the ringing nearly three thousand miles away.

Chapter 5

"Hello." The voice was hesitant, unsure.

"Mom? It's Jess."

A pause and then, "Jess? Oh, Jess! Is it this really you? Oh, God, how I've missed your voice, missed you. I tried calling you so many times, but for a while, it kept saying that the number was no longer in service and then nothing. What happened? Why haven't you called? I've been so worried. I wanted to come out there and look for you. I was so afraid something had happened. Your dad wouldn't hear of it. He just kept saying, 'She made her choice.' He wouldn't let me come out there. Are you okay? Where are you?"

"I'm still in Arizona, Mom. Clint took my phone a long time ago. I had no way to contact you to let you know what happened, but things have changed. Clint died in an accident a couple of days ago."

"What? How?"

"It was a roping accident. It's a long story, but he's gone now."

"Oh, Jess. I'm so sorry. I never even got the chance to meet him. That has to have been so tough for you. Is there anything I can do?"

"No, it's okay. I hate to say it, but it's really a good thing. Things have been pretty bad here. I'm fine. I just have a lot to take care of. I still have 300 head of cattle that need to be worked. I haven't really thought about what I'm going to do beyond that, but, Mom, how are you? It seems like a lifetime since we talked."

"I'm fine, especially now that I know that you're alright." Her mom hesitated then, "But things have changed here too, Jess. I'm not exactly sure how to tell you this, but your dad and I are in the process of getting a divorce now, and I've just moved into my own apartment."

"Really? Wow. I never thought that would happen. Your choice or his?"

"Mine, actually. It really started when he disowned you and wouldn't let me come to visit. I've been so passive this whole marriage, but that was the beginning of the end for me. I started to look at all the things in my life and yours that he had controlled, and it's made me reassess who I was and what I wanted in this last segment of my life. Most of all it made me sick to my stomach when I thought about the way he had treated you--the put-downs, the yelling, the slaps, and I just knew I couldn't go on living with a man like that. The first thing I wanted to do was come out there and find you. I made plane reservations to come out there yesterday in fact."

"Oh, Mom. I'm sad that you went through all that, but I'm so happy you were able to break away. I know this must have been hard, and he probably made you feel like shit. I know he always made me feel that way. I hope this is a wonderful new chapter in your life. Hold off on visiting right now though. When you get settled, and I get things squared away here, then come out and visit. So much has happened, and we have so much catching up to do."

"Honey, are you sure you want to stay out there? From what you told me about the routine when you first moved in there, it sounded like an incredible amount of work, and now without a husband, how will you manage it all? I have a two-bedroom apartment. You could come here and stay with me as long as you wanted or needed to."

Jess didn't hesitate. She thought of the desert as it started its spring bloom with the lavender of Desert Sand Verbena and the pale yellows of Rayless Goldenhead. She pictured the blue mountains ranged across endless sky and the immense sweep of stars at night, the freedom she felt when she rode across the rough and rocky hills, and knew she couldn't leave, never wanted to go back to the stuffy cities and crowds of the east.

"No, Mom. This is my home now. I don't know exactly what my plans are going to be, but I do know this is where I belong. You get settled, and when you do, you'll have to come out and visit. We have so much to talk about. I have to go now though. I'm sitting in the sun in my pickup with its busted air conditioning, and I'm about roasted. I'll call you soon when I'm in a better place. I miss you, and love you."

"Oh, Jess, I miss you so much. Is this the number I can reach you at? I'll call soon and work out a time to visit."

"Yes, it is. Oh, Mom, I can't tell you how good it is to hear your voice again. You take care, and hopefully, I'll see you soon."

After she disconnected the call, Jess sat staring down the street. She really wasn't sure what to do next, but she knew that she had to get another batch of cattle rounded up and worked, and she wasn't sure she was going to be able to do that by herself. She started the truck and rolled away from the curb and headed out to the highway to home. She would stop at the Webster's place and see what they could tell her about Casey.

The heat mirages swirled off the pavement as she headed east to the Webster's place. It was going to be brutal today, and she hadn't been able to get the early start she should have to avoid the worst of it. She didn't want to put her horses through this. Instead, she decided after she met with the Websters it was best to just go out and work on the holding pen, patch a couple of the places she knew were weak. Tomorrow she would start the round-up again she thought as she pulled into the Websters' drive.

The dogs greeted her as she came to a stop, two cattle dogs and an older German Shepherd, barking and swirling around the truck. She waited a moment to get out until they settled down and Molly Webster opened the door to the house. Molly was short and a bit overweight, her brown hair cut short, almost boyish. She had a warm, welcoming smile when she opened the door, and instantly Jess felt comfortable. Molly waved to Jess and called the dogs off as Jess got out of the truck.

"Come in, come in. They won't hurt you. They just have to make their fuss over anybody who pulls in here. Come on in and have a cup of coffee with me."

The invitation brought tears to Jess' eyes. She hadn't really been able to connect with another woman-- anybody really-- since she married Clint, and the loneliness she had suppressed for so long, overwhelmed her now. She nodded her head. "I would really love that."

Molly held the screen door open for her as she came up the porch steps. "I just put on a fresh pot, and I have some chocolate chip cookies I made yesterday. I was able to save a few from Cal so we would get a second day out of the batch. He'd eat everything I baked in one sitting if I didn't squirrel some away each time. I swear that man can inhale cookies." She smiled and shook her head in mock aggravation.

On the outside, the house was a copy of a traditional adobe although made from poured concrete. As Jess entered, she could see that the entry opened onto a modest living area that carried the southwest themed style inside as well. Navajo blankets hung on at least two of the walls and southwestern prints decorated the area over the fireplace. The smell of the freshly brewed coffee added to the cozy atmosphere. Jess ran her hand along a sheepskin laid over the back of the couch and the softness against her fingers had a soothing effect.

Molly Webster called from the small kitchen just off the main living area." What do you like in your coffee? I don't have any real cream, but I do have half and half. Do you want sugar?"

"Half and half would be fine and a spoonful of sugar, thanks. Your home is lovely. Clint would never let me do much with our place. It feels good to be in a place that has a homey feeling to it." She stood taking in the room, savoring it. She realized now how much she missed what she had taken for granted growing up; the sense of warmth and comfort a real home could have, her mom's special touches.

She turned toward the kitchen just as Molly came out of the door with a tray with two steaming mugs of coffee, a half dozen cookies, and some paper napkins. She set them carefully on the low coffee table in front of the couch and gestured to Jess to have a seat.

"I'm so glad you came by. I hardly ever get visitors out here, and I get hungry for something other than man talk all the time." She took one of the cups and sipped a little of it and then set it down.

"Cal and I are really sorry about your loss. We didn't really know your husband-- Clint, right? -- but I know this has to be hard for you. No offense, but he was always so standoffish, we never felt comfortable stopping by for a visit." She looked away, uncomfortable with what she had said.

"You're right about that. He never wanted any friends out here at all. I have hardly talked with anybody since I married him six years ago." She stared intently at her cup, unsure what more to say.

"Oh, you poor thing. I got the feeling that was the way it was. I wish you would've stopped over a long time ago. Obviously, we both needed somebody to talk with."

Tears were streaming down Jess' cheeks. She buried her face in her hands, and Molly got up and came over to sit next to her and wrap her arm around her shoulders. They sat that way for what seemed a long time to Jess while she wept, this time not for the loss of Clint, but for the loss of herself over the past several years.

Molly gave a last squeeze and sat up. "I'm here to listen any time, Jess. I might not be a psychiatrist, but I'm a good listener, so any time you are ready, you have a friend here to listen to whatever you have to say."

Jess looked up, used one of the paper napkins to wipe her eyes and blow her nose. "I'm sorry. I don't know what came over me. I'm not really a crier, or at least I didn't think I was until the past few days." She dabbed at her eyes again and then turned to face Molly. "I really appreciate the offer. I am kind of at a loss right now. I don't know exactly what to do except put one foot in front of the other each day and try to keep some semblance of normal."

"Cal and I wondered if you were going to try to keep running the ranch. Seems like a pretty big job for one person."

Jess was grateful that Molly hadn't said "one woman". "I know. That's actually why I stopped by, or at least it was the reason I told myself I was stopping by." She smiled. "I wanted to find out what you knew about Casey. He said you had recommended him. I'm going to need a hand at least during the Spring round up and probably the Fall too. By then I hope I know what I'm going to do with the ranch."

"Casey Parker. Well, I'm not sure what I can tell you. He came by here about six months ago looking for work and for a place to board, so we let him board his horse here. He takes good care of his horse. Says he's a ranch hand, and he does seem to take his horse in his trailer and go off for a week or two at a time. We kind of assume he's doing some kind of ranch work somewhere. He generally pays his board costs on time. Occasionally, he goes on a bender, and we won't see him for a couple of days. I don't know whether he has any family around here. Said he knew Clint when I told him what happened. That's why I sent him. I thought maybe you knew him."

Jess shook her head. "He just showed up that day. Said you sent him. He knew his way around ranching though. I'll give him that. He actually seemed to know the ranch itself, so I wondered if he had worked there before we got it."

"I wouldn't know about that. He's pretty tight-lipped around here. He pays his board and the money comes in handy, so we don't ask much from him. I think I have told you everything I know. Sorry. Wish I could give you more information." She shook her head. I can have Cal ask around for recommendations if you aren't comfortable with him."

"No that's okay. He seemed fine, I guess. I just have to be careful. I don't want to get into..." She stopped, shook her head. "I do appreciate you telling me what you know, Mrs. Webster."

"Molly. You can call me Molly, and listen, Jess. You need anything, you call me, okay?" She scribbled her number on a slip of paper and handed it to Jess. "You did get yourself a phone, didn't you? You shouldn't be out here without a phone."

Jess nodded her head, took the pen from Molly, and wrote her own number on the bottom of the slip, ripped it off, and handed it to her. "I can't thank you enough, Molly. Once I get the round-up done, you will have to come over with Cal, and I will make us a nice steak dinner."

"Countin' on it." Molly smiled and gave Jess another hug.

Jess smiled back at her and started to get up.

"Don't feel you need to rush off. I have been dying for some woman talk."

Jess hesitated for an instant, then sat back down. "I can stay awhile, sure."

For the next half hour, they chatted randomly. Jess had never felt so comfortable in all her life. She talked about her life in Boston, her meeting Clint and the dude ranch. She talked about ranch life and the loneliness of the life she had known for the past six years. She couldn't talk yet about Clint's treatment of her, the dangers she had faced because of him.

Molly talked about her family, her two grown boys and their families, her life before she moved to this place. Her love for Cal. Jess felt like she had been saving up conversation for six years, and when she was talking, it all came out in a rush. She was torn. She wanted to stay and talk with Molly, but she also wanted to get back and do at least some small amount of work. Finally, she stood up.

"Thank you so much, Molly. I really needed this, needed to talk with somebody. I can't begin to tell you how much it meant to me."

"It really was my pleasure, Jess. I probably needed it as much as you did. You should be able to tell since I about talked your ear off." She chuckled. "You take care of yourself now, and check-in with me every couple of days so I don't worry about you, you hear?"

She hugged Jess again and gave her an extra little squeeze as she guided her to the door.

"Oh, I'll check with Cal to see if he knows anything more about Casey. I'll let you know what I find out."

"Thanks again, Molly. Talk with you soon."

Jess stepped off the porch and walked to her truck. She opened the squeaky door and climbed up into the cab and looked back at the house as she shut the door. Molly was still standing at the door, and she waved at Jess. Jess waved back, and a warm, comforting feeling swept over her. For the first time in six years, she felt like she had somebody in her corner. She enjoyed the comforting feeling of it as she started the engine and pulled away from the house and onto the road back to her place. She couldn't help but smile as she thought about it.

Chapter 6

Molly heard Cal as he drove into the yard and was waiting for him as he came through the door. He stopped momentarily and looked at her quizzically.

"What's up with you, pumpkin? You look like you are about to burst."

Molly smiled at him. "You know me just a bit too well, Cal Webster. Yeah, I had a visitor this afternoon. You'll never guess who."

"Probably right about that." Cal turned to the row of hooks along the wall next to the door, took off his Stetson, and hung it up.

Molly was right in front of him as he turned around. She gave him a hug and kissed him on the cheek. "Jess Oliver."

"Well, what do you know. You got yourself a woman friend around here now?"

"It was good to talk to somebody besides you and the boys, you big lug. I don't know what kind of friends we'll be, but she really needs us right now, I think. She didn't say much, but I got the impression that her husband was a bit of an asshole. She's left with that ranch to run by herself, and she is going to need some help." She turned back to the kitchen. "I got dinner on, and it should be ready in a few minutes. Whyn't you go and wash up and come on out in the kitchen, so we can talk while I get the pot roast out and ready?"

Cal smiled at her.

"What are you smilin' about?"

"Aww, I just like seein' you all in on somethin' again, that's all. After the boys moved out, back in Phoenix, you had your circle of friends and your house cleaning jobs to keep you busy. I worry about you out here by yourself, that's all. I mean, I like my dispatching job, and I'm glad I found it, but I want you to be happy too."

"Hey, I'm fine, but it's a real treat to have another woman around to commiserate with. I'm happy you like your job, and I especially like that you can come home for lunch like this every now and then. Breaks up my day."

Cal pulled out a chair and sat at the table and picked up the stack of mail Molly had set out for him. "No new bills. That's good. That board money we get from Casey for takin' care of his horse sure has flipped our balance sheet nicely."

He set the mail to the side, got up, went to the sink, and washed up. He walked back to the table and sat down again. "So, what did she have to say. How is she doing? This has to have been a tough week for her."

"Yep. I think she's pretty fragile right now."

"So, what did she stop by for? How come she never visited before?"

"The first thing she wanted was to get our read on Casey. He worked with her that one day when we sent him over there, and I guess he did okay, but I think she doesn't want to get herself into something she can't handle. She had enough of that with Clint. She never visited us because Clint wouldn't let her. I got the feeling she was more of a prisoner than anything else."

"Sorry son of a bitch. I hate guys like that. So weak, they got to take it out on a woman. Sorry to hear that. Maybe a good thing he's gone then."

"That would be my feeling too, but she's going to need some help, especially now while she's trying to decide what to do. So, what do you know about Casey besides the fact that he generally pays us on time? You heard anything from folks in town?"

"Not much. I hear he's a drinker and goes down to the Desert Rat to drink and play a little poker sometimes. Seems to me I heard he knew Clint, maybe even was a friend of his. Weird that she never met him before or heard tell anything about him."

Molly had the pot roast cut up and laid out on a green platter. She spooned potatoes and onions and carrots around the meat and poured the juice from the crockpot over everything.
Cal stood up, pulled out a chair for her and motioned for her to sit. He went to the counter and picked up the platter, carrying it to the table and setting it between them. "Man, this smells good. You keep cookin' like we still have the boys here, and I'm going to end up having to be rolled into work every day."

She smiled at him and sat down at the table. "Doesn't surprise me a bit her not knowing Casey. I think if her husband wouldn't let her visit us, he kept a pretty tight leash on her. Probably didn't let her go into town with him most of the time."
Cal loaded his plate with beef and potatoes and onions but avoided the carrots.

"Hey, you need some carrots on that plate, big boy." Molly laughed and grabbed the serving spoon from him and scooped a couple of carrots onto his plate.

"Now after all these years, you want me to start eating healthy? Fat chance of that happening, woman!" He laughed too and slid the carrots to the side of the plate, so they weren't touching anything else.

Molly just shook her head. "You're hopeless." She worked at her meal for a few minutes and then looked up at him again. "Seriously though, would you do what you can to make sure that Casey isn't going to cause her more trouble? I'm worried about her. She's been through enough."

Cal paused, picked up a piece of bread, and swirled it around in the juices on his plate. When he looked up at her, "Sure. I'll ask around. I'm sure a couple of the guys I work with know him from the bar at least. Not the best way to find out about a guy, but it should tell us something."

"Thanks, babe. I know it's not our problem, but she seems to need our help, and I hope we can do something for her."

When Cal finished with lunch, he hugged her. "You're really special, you know that? How did I ever get so lucky?"

"Well, I'm glad you recognize that," she laughed and punched him lightly in his full stomach.

"Easy, girl. You don't want me losing that lunch already, do you?" He hugged her again, took his Stetson from the rack and walked to the door. "I'm going to be late tonight. The night guy can't get in until 9:00, so I'm covering for him. See you then."

She shooed him out the door. "Get a move on, buddy. You're going to be late getting back to work."

He blew her a kiss, and then he was gone.

Molly leaned against the door and watched him go. When his truck disappeared around the first curve, she turned back to the kitchen and began to pack up the leftovers.

Chapter 7

The stock truck was earlier than Jess had expected. It had just backed up to the barnyard when she pulled in. She had wanted to stay longer and talk with Molly, but it was lucky that she had left when she did. She had to be there to load the cattle, and right now, that was her number one priority.

She got out of her pickup and walked over to the stock truck. The driver was in the back setting up the chute to run the cattle up into the trailer. He touched his hat brim. "Howdy, Ma'am. Clint around?"

"No, he's not." She felt awkward. She didn't want to tell this guy that she saw only once in a while that Clint was dead. She figured it was best to just say nothing about it for now.

"We taking all these in the pen?"

"Yep. I'll saddle up and help you load them."

He nodded.

Five minutes later, she led Faith into the barnyard. She whistled for Blue, stepped into the stirrup, and up onto her horse. Faith was still pretty green, and every chance Jess had for her to work with the stock was a chance for a training session. She circled the herd, bunching them, and started moving them toward the chute and ramp. The driver took a long whip, and as the cattle got into the chute, he waved and snapped it to keep them moving. Within ten minutes they had them all loaded. Jess rubbed Faith's neck, whispered what a good girl she had been, then stepped down and led her filly over to the fence and tied her. When Jess came back, the driver was writing up a receipt. "Thirty-seven is what I got in that bunch. That what you got?"

"Yep. That's it. I'll have more next week. When you make out that check, could you make sure it's made out to me, Jessica Oliver."

The driver looked up. "Clint don't want it made out to him? Why's that?" He sounded suspicious, and Jess decided it would just be easier to tell the truth.

"Clint died two days ago. He had an accident roping a bull." The last words came out broken and soft. The driver took his hat off and wiped his forehead on his sleeve.

"Well, I'm mighty sorry to hear that, Mrs. Oliver. What are you going to do with the ranch?"

"I'm not sure, but for now I'm going to work it like we had planned. I haven't had time to think beyond that yet." She turned away and walked over to Faith, then turned back toward the driver. "How long will it take before I get my check?"

"Well, let's see. The buyers come in tomorrow, so you should have your money by the end of the week."

"Okay. Thanks. Are you all set?"

"You just need to sign this and print your name so the check will be right." He held out a clipboard with the invoice on it, a pen clipped to the top. She signed quickly. He ripped off the top copy and handed it to her. He touched his hat, offered his condolences again as he climbed up into the truck, started the engine, and pulled out of the yard.

Jess stood next to Faith and watched him go, the roar of the truck gradually fading to a low rumble and then disappearing altogether. All she heard now was the cry of a red-tailed hawk as it swept low along the fence line and then rose on an unseen thermal until it became nothing but a dark speck in the sky. She rubbed Faith's nose and stroked the horse's neck. "What say we go do a little exploring, girl." She led her horse over to the gate, swung it open, and stepped up into the saddle. She and Clint had worked the southwest quadrant of the ranch the day he died. Three more quadrants left, but she wanted to think of them only one at a time.

"One day at a time, eh Faith?" She called Blue, turned Faith toward the Southeast, and rode off. She felt nervous. It surprised her when she realized it. She had been doing this same routine for the past six years and knew it by heart, but somehow, doing it alone, she found her heart racing and felt a bit of dizziness as she rode up the first arroyo, until the ranch house disappeared from view. She didn't plan to move any cattle today. She just wanted to get a feel for where they were and plan how she wanted to move them. The group from this next section would be moved to the ranch corral to be worked. It was a shorter drive than their last drive had been, no more than three miles, and the arroyos would help to funnel the cattle down to the pens.

As she rode, she told herself that she could do this, and if she did it in small herds, she could do the whole ranch over the next month and a half, maybe less.

She felt more confident the further she rode. It was all so familiar now, the smell of horse and leather, the landscape of the dry, rocky washes where streams could form quickly in heavy rain and disappear as fast with the Arizona sun sucking up the moisture, the desert flowers starting to bloom setting shockingly brilliant color against the sand and cactus. The stillness of the day was only disturbed by the rattle of Faith's shoes against the rocky ground. Now, despite the heat, the bunchgrass flats were verdant and the cattle had been fattening nicely over the past two months. Clint would be happy to see that. She caught herself. Clint wasn't a part of this equation anymore. She felt a tear forming again and wiped angrily at her eyes. She felt cried out, and couldn't figure where the tears were even coming from anymore. She felt so cried out.

The wind picked up, a hot breeze gusting off the top of a rise. Faith spooked at a dust devil that rose up in front of them. The white filly danced sideways then stopped, watched as the dust devil spun away and disappeared. Jess stroked her neck. "Good girl. Nothing to be afraid of." Jess smiled. Faith would be a good one. Nothing bothered her much. The spook had been mild, and she had settled quickly once she thought about what she had seen. The next time Jess knew it would go even better.

Jess prided herself on her horse skills, not just her ability to ride almost anything, but her training skills, her ability to figure out a horse and do what the horse needed in order to move on, get better. Faith had been a six-month-old foal when she got her, and Jess had started training her the first day they brought her onto the ranch. She had worked with her several times a day, and when Faith turned two, Jess had saddled her up and taught her the basics of being ridden.

After that, she turned her out with the other horses for a year, and when she started her serious training as a three-year-old, Faith took to it like she had been doing it her whole life. Jess hadn't roped off her yet and didn't plan to until Faith put on more muscle and could withstand the shock of a thousand-pound steer at the other end of the rope. For now, she just planned to make her as cow-savvy as she could, and that meant doing just what she was doing now, hunting and herding cattle.

Another breeze stirred the bunch grass, spun up another dust-devil. This time Faith took it in stride, no spook at all. With the breeze, Jess picked up the distinct cow smell as it wafted down off the ridge to her right. She nudged Faith into a trot and climbed up the ridge slowing her to a quiet walk as she neared the top.

On the other side, a mixed herd of calves and mamas raised their heads as Jess topped the ridge. She brought Faith to a stop and sat quietly watching the herd, signaling Blue to lie down. Slowly, the herd went back to grazing, and Jess made a circuit around the outside, keeping her distance the whole time, but looking closely at the brands and condition of the herd. No bulls with this bunch. They must have split off from the larger group recently. Thirty head. Tomorrow she would get an early start and bring them in to be worked. She thought briefly about getting hold of Casey to help, but decided against it. For now, she wanted to do this on her own. She could feel her stomach beginning to growl, so she took a long drink from her canteen to fill her stomach with something. She slung the canteen strap over the horn and turned Faith toward home. Despite the short ride and the easy day, Jess felt immensely tired. The emotions of the past few days welled up in her again. She felt sick to her stomach and ready to cry again. The dry wind tailed them all the way back to the ranch.

After a very late lunch of eggs and toast, Jess busied herself with putting out hay for the next shipment of calves and then spent an hour currying and brushing Faith and Mickey. Working with the horses always soothed her. The smell of a horse brought back the days from her childhood when the barn had been her protection, provided her a sense of peace. It also had been her place of discovery because it was there she had learned that she had a special talent with horses.

Her dad had pushed her in school, and she had done well enough, but there was never any joy in it for her. She knew instinctively that the barn, the horses, this would be her life. She wondered if that was the reason she had fallen so hard for Clint. In the beginning, Clint and horses had been synonymous. She and Clint had worked side by side for those months from mid-May until she had been supposed to go home to begin school, to start another life far different from the one she wanted to have.

Clint had courted her all that summer, and when he asked her not to go back to Boston, to stay and marry him instead, well, it had seemed like the perfect out. He had fascinated her then. She had hardly dated in her old life, and her dad had made sure that when she did, he questioned the dates thoroughly to see if they had "potential."

It had scared off the few boys who had been interested in her in high school.

She thought back to her senior year of high school. There had been one boy who she had a crush on-- her first really-- Kevin McInerny. He had boarded his horse at the barn, and he and Jess had frequently hung out, talking, making a connection like she had never had before. He had asked her out, and they had decided on a movie date. She had told her dad that she was going out with some girlfriends, and she arranged to meet Kevin at the show. Afterward, they had ridden together in his car and gone to a hamburger place for a bite to eat.

Back at her car afterward, he had kissed her goodnight, and the thrill of it left her breathless. Unfortunately, when she got into her car to go home, she found it wouldn't start, and she had to call her dad to pick her up. Of course, the questioning had been intense, and she had to admit what had happened. As a result, he took away her barn privileges for a month. In the meantime, Kevin started to date someone else. It had been her only kiss until Clint.

Her thoughts drifted back to her memories of the first few months together with Clint after their quickie marriage in Vegas. There had been no honeymoon. They had gone directly from their jobs on the dude ranch to setting up their own place. Clint had been a different guy then. They were so busy that they hardly had time to think. Buying stock and moving herds to various parts of the ranch to balance out the grazing had taken up all their time. They fell into bed exhausted every night, where Clint had been at least somewhat attentive. Clint even had taken her out to dinner a couple of times, and they went to the show once. After they got everything set up, things changed though. There was less to do on a daily basis, and Clint started drinking regularly.

Sometimes he would bring a bottle home, and sometimes he would go off to play poker and drink or just drink with his buddies at a bar until it closed. Those were the worst nights because she never knew when he was coming home. He would come in while she was sleeping, and often as not, start yelling at her to wake up. If she pretended to stay asleep, he would slap and punch her while she curled into a ball to protect herself. Eventually, he would tire and fall into the bed going immediately to sleep

When he drank at home, she could see it coming and slip out to be with the horses. If the weather was good, she would jump on a horse bareback and ride out under the stars, the warmth and rhythm of the horse soothing her. In the early morning hours, she would slip back into the house and make him breakfast. He would drag himself out of bed to eat, and then generally, he would go back to bed and sleep until noon. She became accustomed to the routine. Even today, working in the barn, she found herself listening for him, always on the alert. She wondered if that would ever leave her. Lost in thought, she was startled when she heard a horse ride into the yard. She set down the brush she was using and went to the barn door.

Outside the barnyard, Casey had just gotten down from the roan. She watched him as he tied the horse to the fence and looked up and saw her standing there. "Hey. How you doin'?"

"Doing okay. I don't have your cash for you yet."

"That's fine. Didn't figure you would. I came over to see what you was plannin' to do. You goin' to move in some more cattle this week?"

Jess didn't know what to say. On the one hand she knew it would be easier with his help, but at the same time, she still didn't know anything about him. She decided to be vague. "I'm not really sure. Things have been happening pretty fast, and I think I just need a little time to adjust. I'll let you know if I have any more work for you. Maybe when I get your cash, I'll have a better idea where I'm going from here."

"Now I think you know by now that I can handle cattle. You have to bring them in to get them marked and sorted, and doing that by yourself is goin' to be tough. We oughta make a plan now so you can get 'er done."

"I'll let you know." She heard her voice, timid, unsure. She turned away and started back into the barn.

"Suit yourself, but somethin' else might come up for me, and then you'll be up shits creek without help."

She turned back to him. "I guess I'm going to have to take that chance because I'm not ready to decide that yet. I said I would let you know." Her voice was stronger now, more assured. She turned again and went back into the barn and shut the door behind her. She leaned against the door and realized she was shaking.

For a minute there, she had gotten the same feeling she had when she was living with Clint. Casey had worked out okay when they had worked together, but something about him made her feel unsure, and she didn't like that feeling. She wondered if she would ever be able to trust a man again after what she had been through. She heard the saddle leather creak and the hoof beats as he trotted away.

Tomorrow she would see how working alone was going to be. If she could work with smaller batches of cattle, she decided, she would rather do that herself and not hire anyone. She finished with the horses and went up to the house.

She washed the few dishes she had used, sorted out some laundry that she knew she would have to do soon, swept the rough wood floors, and wished for a rug here and there to soften the harshness of the old house. At one point she again opened the fireproof box where Clint had kept the important papers. She had thrown out all the old receipts the first time she had gone through the box. All that was left was the lease agreement, some tally sheets on cattle bought and sold and their wedding license. She picked that up and held it for a minute, felt the mistake of it all over again and put it back into the box. She sat lost in thought as the late afternoon shadows started to lengthen. Blue came and laid his head on her knee. "Nothing in that box to help us at all, is there Blue?" She stroked his head. "I guess when I get things settled more I'll have to get a lawyer to look things over and see if there is anything I need to do."

Jess shut the box and put it back in the desk drawer. "I think a nice, hot shower is what I need now, Blue." She took some clean clothes from the shelf in her bedroom and went out to the outdoor shower behind the house. A large, black plastic barrel sat on a rough framework of 2x6 lumber where it caught the sun all day long. She stood outside the shower and stripped off the T-shirt and dirty Wranglers she had on and stood there for a moment in her underwear and felt the warm sun on her back. She took off her underwear and stepped into the shower. The water was extremely hot and she jumped to the side to avoid it until she could get it moderated with the cold-water tap. She enjoyed the warmth for a while. She shampooed her hair and soaped herself all over and then stood with the warm water cascading down over her head and over her body, rinsing her clean.

When she turned the water off, she rubbed herself down with a rough towel and then stepped out onto the wooden platform outside to dress. As she dropped the towel and started to slip into her clean underwear, she had a strange feeling of being watched. She looked quickly over her shoulder, and then looked off up the hill behind the house. Nothing. It had to be her imagination she decided. She started to slip into her bra when she thought she saw a flash of reflected light at the top of the hill and then it was gone. A cold chill ran up her spine.

She dressed quickly, put on her boots, and then set out to climb to the top of the hill. At the point where she thought she had seen the flash, there was nothing- - no footprints, no other sign that anyone had been there -- but the ground was hard and dry, and it was possible that someone could have been up here and not have left a trace. She turned and headed back down the hill to the house. She called to Blue, and he came running around the corner of the barn where he had been lying in the shade. She rubbed his head and then took him into the house with her, something she had never done with

Clint. She set out a bowl of water for him, and he lapped it up greedily then lay down on the small carpet by the door.

Inside the old, stone house, she felt safer but still uncomfortable. She decided it had to be her imagination playing tricks on her. She tried to put it out of her mind. She set about trying to figure out what she could put together for dinner. She could hardly face another egg but that and a little Spam was really all she had in the refrigerator. If it weren't for her hens, she thought, she would be starving by now.

She took out the wire basket of eggs and set it on the antique kitchen table, looked through the few kitchen cabinets to see if there was anything left to add to the eggs, and finding nothing, sat down at the table. Suddenly, she heard the sound of a vehicle pulling up to the house. She stood and went to the door. When she opened it, what she saw surprised her. An older, red, Ford pickup had pulled into the shade of the big willow beside the house. The driver seemed to be fumbling with something on the seat and then opened the door, stepped out, and bent over to pick up whatever was on the seat. When the driver stood up again, Jess realized it was Molly Webster.

"Hey, you. I hope you haven't eaten supper yet. I thought you might like a meal somebody else cooked and a little company."

Jess smiled. "You don't have any idea how good that sounds. Do you need some help?"

"Nope. Got it all in this basket." Molly held up a large wicker basket with a curved handle.

"Well, come on in then. I really am glad you came and not just because of the food." She thought about the strange feeling of being watched she had felt earlier and felt the chill of it all over again.

She held the door as Molly came in and then pointed to the kitchen table. Molly carried the basket over and set it down in the middle.

"Looks like you were about to start making supper." She nodded at the egg basket. "Glad I got here when I did."

Jess laughed, and it felt strange. She couldn't remember the last time she had really laughed. "Yep. I was just about to whip up another fancy batch of scrambled eggs. Pretty much all I've eaten for the past few days."

"Well, I just happened to have made a pot roast dinner that will have too many leftovers for Cal and me to eat. I can't seem to stop cooking as if I still had the boys at home." She laughed as she took the red and white checked napkin off the basket and began to set the food on the table. Before she had finished, the table overflowed with leftover pot roast, green bean casserole with dried onions on top, redskin potatoes, carrots, onions, and a Tupperware container of pot roast juices. Homemade bread and another container with a half-pound of butter rounded out the supper fare. Also, Molly had brought a peach cobbler in a nine-by-nine metal pan. Jess felt like she could start crying at any minute, so she set about finding the utensils they would need.

"I'm really sorry, but I can't offer you anything but water to drink."

Molly slapped herself on the head lightly. "I forgot. I left something in the truck." She turned and went out the door. In a couple of minutes, she was back with a bottle of wine in her hand. "I don't know. Does white wine go with pot roast?" She laughed and set the wine on the table.

Tears did well up in Jess's eyes this time, but she was laughing at the same time. "You are a lifesaver, Molly. I can't even begin to tell you what this means to me. I've been really short of cash, and until I get my check for that first batch of two-year-olds I shipped, I figured I would just have to live on eggs until my check got here."

"You just set yourself down, my friend. Let's have ourselves a little party." Molly pulled up a chair and they both sat down.

After an hour of eating and conversation they were still at the table, the remains of a glass of wine in front of them and the wine bottle empty. For the first time since she left home, Jess felt really cared for, and the warmth of it, and the unaccustomed wine, left her suddenly without words.

Molly looked at her across the table and smiled. "You know, as much as you might appreciate this little supper, I really appreciate you. Since we moved out here to the sticks, I haven't had a woman friend to talk to, and even though I had always wanted to stop and say hello like I mentioned before, something about your husband kept me from doing it."

Jess looked up from her wine glass. "You felt that without even knowing him?" She shook her head. "I sure wish I had been able to feel that before I agreed to marry him."

Molly shook her head. "If you ever want to talk, I'll be here to listen."

Jess shook her head. "I can't yet. Maybe after a while, but not yet. Too fresh."

"I understand. When you're ready, or even if you never want to, I'm here for you."

Molly stood and walked around the table and bent down and gave Jess a hug. When she stood up, she looked around the room as if seeing it for the first time. "We've got some work to do here. We need to make this place a little homier for you right away. I have some decorations and a couple of pictures that I didn't have room for in our new place, so when things settle down, let's get together and figure out what we can do to make this place a little more cheerful."

Jess smiled up at her. "I've lived this way for so long, I can hardly imagine what it would be like to brighten this place up. I loved your home though when I was over there. I want that feeling here. This place has never really felt like home."

Molly started to clear the table. "You keep the leftovers, and if you can't do any shopping, you come over to our place and eat any time. I mean that now. Any time"

When they had cleared the table and put the leftovers away, Jess followed Molly over to the door. "Molly, I can't begin to thank you for everything. I'll repay you somehow."

Molly gave her another big hug. "That's what neighbors… no, that's what friends do. It really was my pleasure, Jess." She hugged her again and went out to her truck.

Jess watched as she drove away. Somehow even though nothing had really changed, this stone house felt a little more like a home than it ever had before.

Chapter 8

When Jess woke the next morning, her phone was ringing on the nightstand beside her bed. A cool breeze stirred the blinds, brushed her cheek. She reached over and picked up the phone. "Hello. Yes, this is Jessica Oliver. Oh, hi, Officer Contreras. Yes, I can come in today. Probably be about a couple hours. Okay, see you then."

She sat up, rubbing her face. This hadn't been her plan exactly. She had wanted to round up the next batch of cattle, and with the cooler air it would have been an especially good day to do it, but she also wanted to get the details all taken care of concerning Clint. She bent down and petted Blue, who had spent the night on the rug beside her bed. He stood up and licked her hand.

"You probably want breakfast too, don't you?" She hurried into the kitchen and filled his bowl with the dog food that she had brought in from the barn the night before, then turned to the refrigerator to get something for herself. She decided it would have to be eggs again. She wanted to save the leftovers for tonight. She treated herself to a slice of pot roast though while she fried up some eggs, cut two, thick slices from the bread, toasted and buttered them. She felt full and satisfied when she finished. She pushed back from the table and cleaned everything up before going to wash her face and comb her hair.

When she finished, she looked at herself in the mirror. Her face was deeply tanned. She tanned easily, a product of her Italian heritage. Her hazel eyes looked tired. She splashed some cold water on them to try to clear them. She noticed how broken and dirty they were so she spent an extra fifteen minutes trying to clean and at least even them up. She wondered why this all mattered to her all of a sudden. For the past six years, she had been pretty careless about her appearance. It hadn't really mattered because she rarely went to town or saw anybody else, and Clint seemed to have no interest in her anyway except when he wanted sex, and that was frequently when he was drunk.

She shook her head and stepped away from the sink. She decided she couldn't spend any more time on her appearance right now. She had to get on the road and get everything taken care of in town, and then she could concentrate on the cattle operation. She dressed quickly and put Blue outside to keep an eye on the ranch for her, climbed into the pickup, and headed out to the highway. Because the traffic was light, she made good time. She arrived at the sheriff's office by 9:15, went in, and up to the front desk. The same lady sat behind the glass.

The lady looked up as she approached. "You're here to see Officer Contreras?"

"Yes. I'm Jessica Oliver. He called me this morning."

"Just a minute. I'll call him up here." She dialed in a number and said into the phone, "Mrs. Oliver here to see you." She turned back to Jessica. "He'll be right up."

Jess, felt a nervousness she couldn't understand. Had they found something? Were there more questions for her? She also felt a nervousness about meeting with Officer Contreras. He had made her feel so comfortable last time. It had been an experience unlike her experiences with first her dad and then Clint. She hardly knew what to make of it. The door opened, and he was standing inside the room, smiling. "Come in, Mrs. Oliver. This will only take a couple of minutes."

He led the way to his desk and pulled a chair out for her to sit down. "How are you doing?" he asked quietly, a look of true concern crossing his face.

She looked down at her hands where they were folded together on the desk. Embarrassed at her rude attempt at a manicure, she put them in her lap. "I'm trying to figure a lot of things out right now, things that I never had to deal with before. I try not to think about anything but what I have to do that day. That's how I get by." She felt a tear form and run down her cheek. Officer Contreras took a tissue from the box on the corner of his desk and handed it to her.

"I'm sorry. I didn't mean to upset you. I know something about how hard this is." He looked uncomfortable for a second then looked down at the paper in front of him. There was a catch in his voice when he spoke. "After the coroner finished the autopsy, we realized we hadn't given you back your husband's personal effects." He pointed to a manila envelope on the desk. "Why don't you open it to make sure everything is there, then I'll have you sign a release for them. After that, you are free to go."

Jess stared at the envelope and then looked up at Officer Contreras. "No, you didn't upset me. You've been very kind. It's just that this whole thing has been overwhelming, and I'm just trying to cope the best I can." Her hands were folded on the desk in front of her again, and he reached out and laid his hand over hers. She felt comfort in it that surprised her. He squeezed her hands lightly then took his hand away.

"Do you know what you are going to do now? Are you going to stay in the area or do you have somewhere else to go?"

"For now, I'm going to stay here. I still have the ranch to run, so I want to stay for a while and see how that shapes up."

He nodded. She gave him a half-smile and then reached for the envelope. Inside was Clint's wallet that contained his ID and over $200. She took a deep breath. Enough to get her through until the stock check came. Besides that, there was his knife and a small amount of change. She shook her head. This was all his life had amounted to.

The officer pushed a paper across the desk and handed her a pen. She signed where he indicated and stood up. Officer Contreras stood and came around the desk. "If there is anything, I can do for you, please let me know. You have my card?"

"Yes, I do. Thank you so much. You've been more than kind." She turned and he escorted her to the door. He opened it for her, and she stepped outside.

"You take care, Mrs. Oliver." And then the door closed and he was gone.

Outside, the day still was cool and the breeze ruffled her hair, washed across her face, and then seemed to disappear. She got back into the truck and headed to the funeral home. The parking lot was full when she pulled in, but she found a spot at the far side and parked the truck. She walked to the front door and made her way through a group of mourners who were standing outside having a smoke. A greeter met her at the door, glanced at her jeans, denim shirt, and dirty boots, and asked, "Can I help you?"

Jess, nodded. "I'm here to see about my husband's cremation. I didn't get the financial details worked out when I was here before, so I need to do that."

"Mrs. Oliver?"

Jess nodded. "Right this way." The young woman led the way to a side room where a black, plastic box sat on a shelf. "We are sorry for your loss. I don't know if you have any interest in having a nicer container for your husband's ashes, but if you are, we can go into the office and look at the choices."

Jess felt a certain accusation in the question. She looked at the lady's nametag- Julia Samson. "Julia, even if I wanted another container, I would have no way of affording it right now. As it is, I'm only going to be able to give you a deposit. I can have the rest by the end of the week. I'll give you $100 today and the balance by Friday. Will that be OK?"

"I understand," in her most professional, funeral consultant voice. "No need to leave a deposit right now. I hope you understand that we will have to keep your husband's ashes until we have the final payment though."

Jess shook her head. "Honestly, I didn't think you were even going to cremate him until I paid for it, so I'm surprised that it's done"

"We always immediately cremate the remains of someone who comes to us from the county morgue. That is our policy."

Jess felt the condescension in the woman's tone, her look, and just wanted to disappear. She felt like the high school girl she had been when she married Clint, unsure and easily embarrassed. Jess asked for the total and then turned to leave.

"We'll see you on Friday then?"

Jess turned back to face her. "If my check comes in, yes. I'll be in just as soon as I can."

The drive back to the ranch felt longer than usual. All she really wanted to do now was get home and saddle up and get to work. If nothing else, she could get the cattle into the barnyard and could start working them there. Whatever she didn't finish, she could get in the morning. At least there, the cattle would have water, and she could throw them a little hay to keep them busy until she was done. As she pulled into the ranch yard, she was surprised to see Casey's blue roan tied up outside the barn. She pulled the truck into the shade and got out. The horse was lathered up. In this cool weather, it surprised her to see that. It must have been ridden hard.

"Hey there, boss lady." Casey appeared around the corner of the barn.

"What are you doing here? I told you I couldn't use any help right now."

"Now, just listen to me. I ain't askin' for no pay right now. I just need to keep myself busy, and when you get your money, I'll take my cut then. Don't be so damned high and mighty that you don't want any help. You hear."

"Look, Casey. You seem like a nice enough guy and all, but I kind of wanted to do this myself for a while." She felt uncomfortable even saying that. She felt, what exactly? Exposed. That was it. She didn't want him to know how lost she felt right now.

"Nope. Ain't goin' to let you do that. I'll make sure you get this done, and that's all I'm goin' to say about that, so you just go get your horse and let's get movin'. We're burnin' daylight." He turned and busied himself tightening up the cinch on the roan. "You let me handle all the details. You can just be along for the ride."

Jess shook her head, looked up to the sky. She couldn't get out of this, it seemed. She was both irritated, and a little bit frightened. Too much of what he said and how he said it, brought back the painful memories of Clint. There was also a small sense of relief to have the extra help.   Finally, she nodded her head. "Okay. Let's get at it then." She went into the barn and pulled Mickey's saddle and pad off the rack and put them on a saddle stand just inside the door. Then she took her lariat and set out to catch Mickey in the pen. He made a little show of it, circling her at a fast trot at first and then cantering in a circle around the pen. She built a loop and then swung it three times and released as Mickey flew by her. The loop dropped neatly over his head and settled around his neck. She gave a little tug to set it and then drew him to her. The familiar routine of it felt good, and she stroked the soft, velvet of Mickey's nose before she led him over to the hitching rail where she had hung his rope halter and a lead. She haltered him, slipped the lariat off, slid the halter on and tied it, attached the lead, and tied him to the hitching rail. He stood quietly now as she brushed the saddle area, then she threw the wool pad on his back and then the heavy ranch saddle.

When she had first come out here it had been all she could do to swing the forty-pound roping saddles up and into place. Now it felt like second nature to her, and she never really noticed the weight. She was lean and slender, but what remained of her after six years of ranch work was pure muscle, and she took some pride in that.

Back home…she paused in her thought. Back home. What did that even mean anymore? She hardly thought of Boston as home now. Too long ago and too far away. She wondered if that would change when her mom came out to visit. Her mom had always been "home" for her. The house, the neighborhood, none of that had ever felt like a place she belonged.

She reached under Mickey and grabbed the girth and pulled it to her. She ran the latigo through its ring and then through the front rigging dee and pulled it snug. She repeated the process, snugged it further, and then tied it off at the dee. Next, she pulled the rear cinch up into place and buckled it loosely to the rear billet strap. She wrapped her lariat in the leather rope keeper and pushed its large loop around the saddle horn. She pulled a pair of roping gloves out of the bin inside the barn door, tucked them in her belt and then buckled on a pair of worn, leather chinks. When she finished, she bridled Mickey and led him to the door..

"I'm ready when you are."

Casey swung up into the saddle and turned his horse to face her. "Where are we goin' to work today?"

"I think it would be best if you just follow me. We're going to do a small section today. That way, late as it is, we should finish by tonight."

"Lead on, Missy." There it was again. That hint of Clint. She felt that familiar chill. Mickey headed out at an easy lope, and she whistled for Blue to come along.

The cattle were still in the same area where she had seen them yesterday. She pulled her horse to a halt at the top of a rise just above the herd and then sat quietly while Casey came up beside her. "I want you to move slowly around to the other side over there," she pointed to a small rise on the far side of the herd. "I'll take point and you can take drag. Don't let them get away up that little ravine to the east. We'll never get them out of there."

"Ay, Captain. I'll do my best." His sarcastic tone didn't sit well with Jess.

They moved the herd slowly back to the ranch. By three-thirty they had them penned and ready for branding. Two of the cattle belonged to a neighboring ranch and the first thing she had Casey do was sort them out and pen them separately. Casey said he knew the rancher and would let him know to come and get them or would drive them over there himself.

The branding and all that went with it, took them until nearly eight o'clock, and when they were finished, Jess waved Casey over to where she was throwing out hay. "You might as well go. No use riding home in anything darker than this. I can handle the rest of it. Thanks for your help."

"What? You ain't goin' to invite me for supper?"

Jess smiled at him. "Nope. You wouldn't want what I have to put together for supper anyway. I won't be working the next batch for a couple more days, so you don't need to come back anytime soon." She turned away and heard him as he spurred the roan into a canter and disappeared into the growing darkness.

Chapter 9

Morning broke with a hot wind pouring into the bedroom. The cool day yesterday had been a welcome respite. The reality of things here in the high desert was that the nights would stay cool, but the days would most likely be hot until fall made its first appearance. She dressed in the half-light just before sunrise.

A flight of starlings swooped low across the yard then rose in a single mass and disappeared over the barn as she went out to check on the cattle and throw them some more hay. Seventeen more ready to be shipped today. She felt anxious and at first, wasn't sure why. She realized that she was worried about the check from the first batch she had shipped. It hadn't shown up yet. She wasn't sure whether the shipper delivered it, or did they mail it? Clint had kept her completely in the dark about the finances. She felt like a child fumbling around now. Maybe when she had that first check in her hands it would be different, but for now, she felt vulnerable and nervous.

In the house, she picked up her cell phone and called the shipper's number. He picked up after a dozen rings. He said he was swamped right then and wanted to call her back. She made breakfast and ate while she waited. When the phone rang, she picked it up off the table next to her. "Hello? Yes, this is Jessica Oliver. I want to schedule a pick-up. Today if possible." Pause. "I understand. I'll try to call ahead of time from now on. Okay. Tomorrow morning then? Alright. Thank you."

She flipped the phone shut, set it back on the table, rubbed her face, and decided she had better open a bank account. She wondered if Clint had one someplace. He always had cash. She had never seen a checkbook or savings account book lying around anywhere. She decided to thoroughly search the house to see if there was anything she had missed the first time through.

After more than an hour of searching, finding nothing, she decided it was time to go into town and open an account. She still had the two hundred dollars from Clint's wallet. She decided she could deposit half of that to get her started, and then she would grocery shop with the rest. She fed Blue and left him lying in the sun on the front porch. She headed out in the pickup. On the way, she stopped at the Webster's place and waded through the barking dogs as she went up to the door. Before she could knock, Molly opened it.

"Hey, you. What's up?" Molly wore her graying hair loose. She had on an oversized yellow T-shirt, too-long jeans that hung down over and partly hid her bare feet.

Jess smiled. "I'm headed into Kingman and wondered if you need anything I could pick up for you."

"Are you kidding? How about some company? I would love to just ride along. I'm about stir crazy here. Cal is out of town for a couple days, and I would love to go in and do a little shopping." She paused, "I mean if that's okay with you."

"I would love to have you along."

"Great. Let me get changed and get something for my feet."
She came back a few minutes later with brown leather sandals in one
hand and in the other one of the biggest purses Jess had ever seen.
"Let's roll, girl."

In Kingman, they split up to go their separate ways, Jess to
the bank and Molly to the boutique just across the street. The
Mojave State Bank was a single-story, desert-tan structure with a
vaguely southwestern adobe look to it and a large MSB over the
entryway. She stood in the lobby area for a moment to get her
bearings then walked up to a teller who sat waiting for her with a
practiced smile.

"Can I help you with something, Ma'am?"

Jess smiled back. "Yes. I would like to open a checking and
savings account."

"Let me call someone who can help you with that."

The woman, Martha, according to her name tag, dialed a
number and spoke quietly into the receiver. She turned back to Jess

"Someone will be with you in a moment. Please have a seat
over there and help yourself to coffee if you'd like." She pointed to a
cluster of chairs near a bank of glass-fronted cubicles.
Jess poured a cup of coffee, added a generous amount of cream and a
little sugar, and sat sipping it as she waited. Soon a tall, older woman
came out of one of the cubicles and walked over and offered Jess her
hand.

"I'm Darlene Richards. I understand you want to open an
account with us? Come right this way." She led Jess back to her
office.

"So, what kind of an account were you planning to open?"

"I guess I need checking and probably a savings account. I don't know exactly. My husband died suddenly this past week, and I have to have a place to cash checks and write checks for bills, I guess."

"You didn't have a joint account somewhere?"

"No. At least I don't think so. He handled all the financial matters and never let me know anything about it."

The lady glanced at Jess, a look of concern passing across her face. Quickly, she turned away and started gathering paperwork from various racks on her desk. "You can either fill this out now or do it at home and bring it back in later." Her tone was business-like, but her look as she turned to Jess spoke volumes about what she felt, and that was compassion.

Jess studied her and then reached out to take the paperwork. The thought that flashed through her mind, You've been here, haven't you? A kindred spirit.

"I would like to fill these out now if that's OK. I want to get this started because I'm expecting a check for some cattle I sold recently."

"That's fine. You're welcome to sit right there if you're comfortable. So, you're a rancher?"

Jess hesitated for a beat. She had never really considered herself that. Clint had been the rancher. She had just been hired help. No, scratch that. Hired help would be paid. She had literally gotten nothing out of it. "I guess I am, though I hadn't really thought of myself that way until now."

"You may want to open a business account then. We can set that up for you."

"Right now, I just want a personal account. Clint never really ran it as a business, I don't think, so there are things I would have to do, I imagine, to form a business."

The lady looked at her kindly. "That's fine. If you need any help with that, you come and see me. I'll be glad to walk you through the process." She took the paperwork from Jess and looked it over. This looks fine. How much do you want to put in each account?"

"Fifty dollars in each. That's all I have until the check comes in. Will that be a problem?"

"No, that's fine." Darlene took the cash from Jess. "We will have to hold the check for a couple of days until it clears. I hope that won't be a problem for you."

The stressed look on Jess' face told her everything. "Listen, this isn't the bank talking here. If you need a small, short-term loan to tide you over, you come and see me, you understand. I don't want you to be caught in a financial bind. I know something about what you are going through. So, you come see me." She said it emphatically. "This will be a personal loan from me to you. Got it?"

Jess felt the tears well up again and Darlene reached for a tissue from a box on her desk and handed it to her. "You take care of yourself, young lady. I'm going to go deposit this and get you a receipt. Just stay here, or if you want, there is a restroom around the corner to the right where you can wash your face." She stood up and left, and Jessica stood and made her way to the restroom.

She stood in front of the mirror and wiped at her eyes with the tissue then washed her face and dried it with the paper towels stacked neatly on the countertop. You have got to get hold of yourself, she thought. Can't be crying at the drop of a hat every day. She straightened her shoulders and walked back out into the hall and back to Darlene's office. Darlene sat at her desk writing on a pad of paper. She looked up as Jess walked back in.

"Sit for a minute," she said. Jess sat down and looked across the desk. Darlene was looking at her intently.

"Do you feel all right? You're welcome to stay here as long as you want. I'm just working on some paperwork, so no one will disturb you if you just want to sit here."

Jess shook her head. "No. I'm okay now. I just get a little overwhelmed sometimes. I really appreciate your kindness though." She paused and then, "I think I hardly know how to respond appropriately to kindness anymore. It's been so long since I experienced any."

Darlene nodded her head. "I think I know exactly how you feel. I came from a marriage that had no kindness in it. It takes time, but you will recover."

"How long did it take you?" Jess leaned forward in her chair.

"Well, I think I am still in the process, but it has been four years now since I got out of it. I think it was probably two years before I began to feel somewhat normal, to start to trust again. You don't realize it at first because it is so gradual, but one day you will wake up and you will realize a weight has been lifted off your shoulders. For me, that day of awakening was such a relief that I cried my eyes out for the whole morning. Funny thinking about it now. I haven't thought about it for a long time and your coming in here brought it all back to me. It made me realize how far I had come." She tilted back in her chair, her hands together, fingers tented under her chin.

"Look, Jess. I know this is none of my business, and you can tell me that if I have crossed a line, but I want you to know that I am here for you if you need an ear. Recovery from an abusive relationship is tough, and it is even tougher if you have to do it alone." She paused again. Jess sat with her head bowed. Softly now, "You have my card, Jess. I put my cell number on the back. Please feel free to call me any time. I mean that. Here are your receipts, a starting checkbook, and a savings passbook. Stop in when you get your check, and I'll make some arrangement for you to get your money as quickly as possible." She stood up and offered Jessica her hand. Jess shook hands with her, then gathered up her things and put them into her purse.

"Thank you so much, Darlene. I can't tell you how much what you said today means to me. I'll see you soon." She smiled and turned to go.

"Keep your chin up, Jessica. Good things are just around the corner."

"I sure hope so."

Out on the street again, she wondered at herself. She had revealed so much of herself to a perfect stranger. Maybe it had been because she thought she wouldn't see her again, or maybe it was because she had found a kindred spirit. She didn't exactly know, but somehow, she felt better for it. She crossed the street to the boutique to look for Molly.

The store was quiet and smelled of potpourri and lilacs. As soon as she came in, she could hear Molly near the back talking with the owner. Jess walked back to find her, and as soon as Molly saw her, her eyes lit up. "Hey, you. This is Sandra," waving her hand at the tiny little older lady in a sundress with a shawl thrown dramatically over her shoulders. "Sandra, this is my friend, Jess."

Jess felt the tears rise up again. Friend. For the first time in a long time, she had a friend, maybe two. She fought off the tears and smiled at Sandra. "So nice to meet you. What a beautiful shop you have here." She looked around as she said this and realized that it really was quite beautiful with decorative pieces that in another time or place, she would have taken for granted, but after living without any decorations for so long, it felt almost like a magical place. Molly held up a wire sculpture of a girl standing on a rock and holding a wire string attached to a blue, glass balloon. "I got this for you. This is the start of our decorating project. Do you like it?" Jess couldn't take her eyes off it. It really was delicate and beautiful, and, she searched for the word, hopeful. That was it. Her hand instinctively went to her heart. "Oh, Molly. It is so beautiful. But I can't take that. It is too much."

"You can and you will, my dear. I want you to start off right, and this little piece is perfect, don't you think?"

"It absolutely is. How am I ever going to re-pay you?"

"There is no need. This is my gift to you as you start your new life."

Afterward, when Jess got back to the ranch, she drifted through the rest of the day lost in their own thoughts but feeling a warmth that she had lacked for a very long time.

Chapter 10

When Jess got home, she stopped at the mailbox out by the road. She realized that she hadn't checked the mail since Clint died, had rarely checked it before since it was another one of those things that he had not let her do. To her surprise, the box was overflowing with mail. Most of it was catalogs and advertisements, but more importantly, the check from the stock company sat beautifully on top of the pile. She opened the envelope. $25,550. Thirty two-year-old steers that must have averaged around a thousand pounds. She clutched the check to her chest. She felt like crying again. She knew some bills had to be paid off, the lease payment ad to be made, but this was a start and with the calves she had yet to bring in and send, she felt that she could at last breath easier.

She stacked the mail on the pickup seat beside her and continued on up to the house. Blue came running to greet her. She got out of the truck, and he jumped up, paws on her shoulders, and licked her squarely in the face.

"You rascal. What are you so happy about? You figure there might be some food for you in this deal?" She lifted his paws off her and set him back on the ground. "Come on. Let's go get you some food." She reached into the truck and picked up the mail in one arm, then the small package with the girl and the balloon in the other, and made her way to the house. Inside, she filled Blue's water bowl and scooped out a large portion of dog food from the bag under the sink.

She had been stingy with it at first since she didn't know how long she would have to go before she got her money. Now she felt both rich and generous, and she had nobody else to share it with except Blue.

She sorted through the pile of mail. Not much of interest, but there was an electric bill to be paid, and she set that aside to take care of as soon as her money was freed up. The rest went into the trash burner outside. While she was out, she checked on her calves, fed them more hay, and grained the horses. After they ate their grain, she turned them out on their pasture with a couple of piles of hay.

Back in the house, she opened the little box and carefully unwrapped the gift from Molly. She held it up to the afternoon light, and the glass balloon caught the rays and bent them in new directions sending splashes of color across the dirty, stone walls.

"I have to find a place where you will really pick up the light, don't I, little girl? How about on the window sill?" She carried the piece into her bedroom and set it carefully on the window sill beside her bed. "Perfect. I can wake up to your hopefulness, every day now."

Hopefulness. She had thought about it before when she first saw the piece, but somehow now she decided, that was surely what the little piece of art represented for her. Hopefulness. She wanted that to be her focus from now on. She smiled as she stood there looking at it, light playing off the balloon, reflecting on her wall. Molly. Somehow, she had known the exact right thing to get her as a gift.

Jess made a supper of the leftover pot roast and vegetables. Just as she finished with the cleanup, she heard a knock at the door. It surprised and frightened her. She hadn't heard anyone pull up, hadn't heard a horse. She had no way of knowing who was out there without opening the door. Built during the Apache Wars, the house had once had gun ports on the front side. At some point, someone had filled them in with stone and mortar. She had tried to get Clint to put in a window, but that had never happened. She felt some trepidation. No visitors had come at night before. Blue was raising a ruckus with his barking.

"Who is it?" she called, trying to keep her voice steady.

"It's Casey."

She grabbed Blue by the collar before she opened the door. Casey stood there with that big grin of his, dressed in a blue plaid western snap-button shirt and clean Wranglers. Jess could hardly hold Blue back. He had stopped barking but growled threateningly. "What are you doing here now? There's nothing for you to do around here until I get this next batch shipped and sold," she said, her voice, tense and angry.

"Just thought you might like a little company tonight. Has to be lonesome bein' out here by yourself all the time now." He produced a bottle of wine from behind his back.

"Uh, no. I'm perfectly fine on my own. How did you get here anyway? No car. I didn't hear you ride up."

"Oh, came in from the back side. I put my horse in the barn. Didn't figure you'd mind!"

"Listen, Casey. I'm not looking for a friend or anything else right now, so I'd appreciate it if you'd ride out of here. I'll let the Websters know when I need help again, and they can tell you."

Casey's eyes flashed a wave of brief anger, and then he seemed to get it under control. He tipped his hat. "Sorry, ma'am. Just tryin' to be friendly is all. Maybe some other time."

He backed off the porch and Jess watched him go, kept the door open, holding onto Blue until she saw him leaving the barn and riding off up the hill behind the house. When she shut the door and let Blue go, she realized she was shaking. She felt all the tension and fear that came with a guy trying to push himself into her life. She felt too much of Clint in it. Still, he hadn't made a fuss when she asked him to leave. She sat down on the couch and Blue laid his head on her lap. She rubbed behind his ears.

"You're a good boy, Blue. I'm glad I have you here with me."

She decided to call her mom. Since they had talked, she really missed her more than ever. She had hardly had time to miss her when she was with Clint. He had taken up all her time in one way or another, sucked the life out of her really. Now she wanted more than anything to reconnect with her mom.

The phone rang five times. Jess had been just about to give up when her mom picked up. "Hello? Is that you Jess?"

"Me, Mom."

"Oh, Jess. I'm so glad you called. I want to come out and see you. I know this must be a difficult time for you, but I'll just stay out of your way when you have work to do, I promise!"

"You can come any time, Mom. I really would love to see you. I'm in the middle of the spring round-up, but I can make time for you whenever you want to come out."

"I'm ready now. I've missed you so much. I'll get that plane ticket changed and get out there as soon as I can. I'll call you and let you know when I'm coming?"

"That would be perfect." Jess looked around at the bare walls of the house and lack of any real furniture and hesitated a moment. "Why don't you try to set it up for a couple weeks from now. That will give me the chance to get ready for you to visit. Mom, I can't tell you how anxious I am to see you. I've missed you too."

When Jess got off the phone, she looked around again at the house and the bareness of the existence she had lived for the past six years, and decided that one of her priorities as soon as she had her cash in hand would be to fix the place up.

That night as she lay in bed, she looked through her window and up at the sky. High, thin clouds scudded across the moon, but the stars were brilliant in the clear patches of sky. The encounter with Casey had been upsetting, kind of frightening really, but as she lay there, she realized that for the first time in a long time, she felt at peace.

...

She heard the semi pull into the yard as she was finishing her breakfast. Blue reinforced the arrival with his usual greeting until she called him to her, and they walked out to the stock pen to meet the hauler. The same driver climbed down out of the cab.

"Good morning, Mrs. Oliver."

"Good morning, but it's Jess. I didn't catch your name last time."

"Pete, ma'am. I'll get set up here like last time."

"Ok, Pete. I'll go saddle up. Blue and I will move them to the chute."

Ten minutes later she rode Faith into the pen and started to move the cattle to the loading chute. Faith had developed into a great cutting horse, spinning automatically to cut off escaping cattle and circling them back into the herd. Jess felt really proud of her. Faith represented Jess's skills, her training. Jess rubbed her horse's neck as she watched the last of the steers head up the ramp and into the truck. She dismounted and ground-tied Faith while she signed the shipping contract.

Pete eyed, Faith. "You got a real nice little filly there, Jess. Who trained her?"

"I raised her from a foal. Trained her myself."

"Well, looks like you really have the knack, Ma'am. I seen plenty of cutting horses doing this job, but that little filly could compare with the best of them. You train for anybody else? I know some folks that would pay a pretty penny for that kind of training."

"I haven't done that for anybody else for a long time." She paused for a moment, looked off across the yard and out across the open pasture to where the hills rose in a jagged line along the horizon.

"If you hear about somebody wanting some training done, you can send them my way, if you want."

As the truck pulled out, she rubbed Faith's nose. "Well, girl, I guess you get a day off because I have to get to town and deposit the check. You enjoy your rest day. We will have plenty to do tomorrow." She led Faith into the barn, untacked and brushed her, fed Faith and Mickey, and turned them out on the pasture behind the barn.

The drive to Kingman, seemed easier. At first, she thought that it had to be that the traffic was lighter than it had been, but she realized that actually, she had just gotten used to driving again. Like much of her life, her driving had been put on pause with Clint. He had barely let her ride with him and then only to go to the grocery store to pick up the supplies they needed. It felt like she had been in a time warp for the past six years. She had come west in the Spring of 2002. Since then, she had rarely seen a newspaper, watched television, heard the radio. She felt frozen in time, and she ached to know more of the world, the events that had shaped people into who they were. She wanted to know everything at once and decided that as soon as she finished the roundup, she was going to see if she could get a television for her place. She smiled at the thought of such a simple thing that she had taken for granted all those years ago.

She pulled into the bank, parked, and went in and up to a teller. "Could you tell me if Darlene is in?"

"Sure. Could I tell her who is here to see her?"

"Yes, Jessica Oliver."

"Just a moment, please." She picked up a phone and a minute later Darlene walked into the lobby, a big smile on her face.

"So good to see you, Jessica. Come right in. I take it you got your check."

"Yes, I did." Darlene ushered Jess into her office. "Do you have any idea how long it will take to clear?" Jess took a seat across from Darlene.

"Let me see the check." Jess handed it to her. "Oh, it's a local company. Let me see if they bank with us. I'll be just a minute." She stood up and went out to the lobby area. When she returned, she was smiling.

"Good news. They do bank with us, and I checked their account. The check is good and we'll cash it today. How would you like it?"

Jess could hardly believe it. She had expected to have to wait days to get her money. She really hadn't thought about how she should apportion it. "How about seven hundred dollars in cash, five thousand in the checking account, and the rest in savings?" She sounded unsure and   Darlene looked at her and smiled. "First big decision. It will get easier."

Jess blushed. "I'm so inexperienced at all of this. I'm just kind of feeling my way along right now."

"I understand. Remember, I've been there. I'm happy you at least have a little nest egg to get you going. That was more than I had when it happened to me. You go ahead and sign the back of the check. I'll get it deposited and get your cash for you."

"Thank you so much, Darlene. I really appreciate this."

"No need to thank me. I'm happy that I can be of some help to you. Remember, if you need an ear at some point, I might be able to give you a little perspective and guidance. Although you'll want to plot your own path for your future. I'll be right back." She picked up the check and left.

When she returned, she had the deposit slip and seven hundred dollars in crisp one-hundred-dollar bills. She handed both to Jessica. "I hope your new chapter brings you great happiness, Jessica Oliver. It's been a pleasure to meet you." She reached out and shook Jess's hand, and Jess felt so overwhelmed, she gave Darlene a big hug. Tears started to well up in her eyes again, and she turned quickly and left so she didn't end up in another crying fit.

Next, Jess drove over to the funeral home and quickly paid for the cremation, picked up the black plastic box, and carried it out to the truck where she set it on the passenger seat next to her. Writing the check had been a nerve-wracking experience. She hadn't written a check for years, and now she sat in the truck and found herself shaking again.

She wondered if every new event was going to be this traumatic for her. She shook her head to clear it and then sat for a few minutes to compose herself before she went to the grocery store to get a supply of food for the week. She closed her eyes and let the smells and sounds of the street waft in through the open window. There was the constant roar of traffic, the smell of diesel fumes, but also the warm, enticing smells of tacos at a street vendor's cart just down the block. She realized then that she felt really hungry and decided to splurge a little and buy a taco and a coke.

The street vendor had a cart full of Mexican food with a hot grill where he did all his cooking, but the vendor himself appeared to have not one drop of Mexican blood in him. He was an overweight, very white guy with a wild head of greying hair. He smiled at her. "What can I get for you, little lady?"

She ordered her taco which she topped with cheese and tomatoes. The coke she had ordered came in an aluminum can, still beaded with the moisture from the cooler at the vendor's feet. She paid, thanked him, and then went to sit on a bench in the shade of the building across from the stand.

As she was finishing up the last of the taco and wiping her hands on the napkin she had picked up at the stand, out of the corner of her eye, she caught someone staring at her. She turned to see Casey walking toward her.

"Well, well, well. Fancy meetin' you here. What are you up to today? No ranchin' gettin' done?"

She glanced up at him, drank the last of the coke, and stood up to place it in the bin next to the stand. "I needed some lunch, and this happened to be in the right place at the right time.   What are you doing here? No ranchin' getting' done?" she mocked him.

"Nope. Seems my boss is takin' a town day for herself. Ready to get at it though as soon as she sees fit to start up again." He gave her that smile that threw her off each time.

"Tomorrow. We'll get after it again tomorrow."

"Well now, that would be just fine."

"And I'll have your money for you tomorrow." Jess had enough on her now to pay him, but pulling out a wad of bills on the street in Kingman didn't somehow seem like the wisest idea.

"I'll be riding out at eight tomorrow. If you want to work, I'll see you then." She turned and headed for her truck.

"Yes ma'am. You will see me then," he called after her.

She watched him go. She couldn't figure him out. Sometimes he seemed nice, safe, but after their encounter the night before, she wasn't sure how to take him or what he wanted from her. All she knew for sure was that she needed his help, but he made her incredibly nervous.

Before she went to the grocery store, she stopped to pick up some paint and equipment at the home store. She had decided that starting by brightening all the house's walls with a pale yellow would be a good beginning point. She could always add other colors later.

When she finished there, she did her grocery shopping and started the drive home. Only then did she begin to feel the strangeness of having Clint there on the seat beside her, all his nasty being contained in a small black box. She had never been superstitious, but somehow the black box seemed to have a life of its own there inside the truck. It made her uncomfortable in a way she never would have expected. As she pulled through the ranch gate and drove up to the house, she felt a sense of relief that she would be able to get away from it.

The question for her now was, what was she going to do with the box. She sure as heck didn't want it in the house with her like a lot of people did with their loved ones. She wasn't sure about burying it either, but she felt that probably would be the best option. But where? She didn't want to have to pass the spot all the time. It would have to be someplace distant, someplace where she preferably would never have to come across again.

She carried it out to the barn and set it in an empty stall. She decided to put off her decision until later. At least she wouldn't have to look at it there. When she shut the stall door, she had another sense of relief even though she knew it was temporary. On the way to the house, she realized that she had the whole afternoon ahead of her, plenty of time to put a coat of paint on the walls of her tiny house.

After sweeping everything down and moving what little furniture she had away from the walls, she went at the walls with roller and brush until by sunset the interior of the house shone a pale shade of yellow. Her living space had suddenly taken on a completely different personality. It felt as if she had brought the sunlight inside. She sat down in one of the two slat-backed chairs that served as dining room seating and just took in the difference. The brightness of it all, lifted her spirits. She sat there until darkness engulfed the room, thinking again about how much her life had changed already. As the light finally faded, she rose and went out to feed the horses.

As she walked back to the house from the barn, she once again felt that odd feeling of being watched. She called to Blue, and he ran up to her and walked beside her to the house. She stood in the doorway looking out across the fields again. Nothing moved out there. Then from the hills, she heard a coyote howl followed by another one and then another. She smiled. "That's what I must have been feeling," she said out loud, although it seemed more to assure herself than something she actually believed.

She turned and went into the house. She called Blue in with her. Once inside, she bolted the door shut and leaned her forehead against it. She didn't like the feeling that came over her now. She had felt vulnerable before with Clint, but she had known the threat and where it came from. Now the vulnerability descended on her differently, as a general foreboding that she had never felt before. A chill passed over her as she turned from the door and back into the house's new brightness.

Chapter 11

Molly rose early and put together a big breakfast for Cal. He had worked late last night, had eaten cold leftovers for supper, and she knew he was facing another long day again today. They were shorthanded at the warehouse, so he had been working long shifts to fill in. She wanted him to at least have a solid breakfast to start the day. She fried bacon and then added eggs to the grease, scrambled them, and set them on low to cook. She had already heated the cast iron griddle and greased it with some of the bacon grease. Now she poured pancake batter out in six-inch puddles to cook. Meanwhile, the eggs were done, so she took them off the stove, put them on a platter, covering it with a dish towel to keep it warm.

Cal came through the door from the bedroom rubbing his freshly shaved face and broke into a smile when he saw what she was up to.

"Why you little housewife, you. Look at all this food. Are we having company?" He laughed.

"You sit yourself down here, Cal Webster. I know you can do this spread justice."

Cal sat and poured himself some orange juice from the pitcher on the table. Molly busied herself with the pancakes, and once she had flipped the batch on the griddle, grabbed the platter of eggs and bacon and put it in front of Cal.

"You might as well get started on these while I finish up the pancakes. No use in them getting cold."

Cal took the platter and forked large quantities of eggs and bacon onto his plate. "Looks mighty good, Molly. I sure can use a hot meal right about now. Yesterday was brutal. Non-stop all day. I didn't even really get a chance to eat my lunch." He dug into the pile on his plate and stopped talking for a while. Molly finished the pancakes, piled them on a plate, and set it next to the platter of eggs and bacon along with a pitcher of syrup and some butter. She sat down across from him and watched him eat.

Cal looked up. "Aren't you going to eat anything?"

"I will when you're done. I got all day. You don't." She paused a minute, and he could see she wanted to say something.

"What is it, Hon? I can see you got something on your mind."

"I know you've been real busy, so you probably haven't had time to ask around about Casey, have you?"

Cal set down his fork, picked up three of the pancakes, and flopped them onto his now empty plate. "Well, as a matter of fact, I have. I don't have a lot to tell you, but I did pick one or two interesting little tidbits. Molly leaned forward, elbows on the table. "Turns out he and Clint was friends. They hung out at the bar. I heard they did one or two side jobs together although I don't know what that means. Ranch jobs maybe? I don't know. He's a drinker, that much I do know for sure. Had more than one person tell me that Casey goes on a rip-roaring drunk at least three or four times a month. Raises some serious hell in town when he does. Beyond that,

I can't say I know much. Most say he works hard and knows his way around horses and cattle."

"Well, the drinking part doesn't sound any too good, but if Jess just hires him for her cattle work, I guess it should work out alright for her. She needs help. I'm going over there today to see how she's doing. I'll let her know what you told me." Molly stood up. "You want any more pancakes, Cal?"

"Nope. I'm about stuffed right now. This should hold me until tonight I'd say. Thanks, hon." He stuffed the last of his pancakes into his mouth, stood up, and started to clear the table while he finished eating. "I'd better get a move on. Another long, busy day ahead today too."

"Ok. I'll see you when I see you, I guess. I wish they'd hire on some more help so you didn't have to work so many hours."

"It's all good, babe. All this extra money is going to get us caught up on those bills we been tryin' to whittle down." He washed his hands and face at the sink, dried them, then wrapped his arms around Molly, kissed her on the cheek. "You behave yourself now while I'm at work. No wild parties or nothin'." He laughed and gave her a quick squeeze. "I ever tell you how much I love you, Molly Webster?"

She leaned back and smiled. "Once or twice, Cal Webster, but you know I never get tired of hearing it." He smiled back at her and let her go.

"I'll see you later, little lady," and he grabbed his Stetson off the hook by the door and left.

Molly stood at the window and watched him go, then turned back to the kitchen and set about cleaning the mess left from the cooking and the eating. When she finished, she went outside to feed Casey's horse. She was surprised to find that he was already there, his pickup parked behind the barn. She went into the barn to check if everything was alright.

"Hey, there, Molly." Casey's head appeared above the side of the stall.

"How come you're here so early?"

"Figured to get an early start over at the Oliver place. I figure before long, I'll be movin' this boy over there. Makes more sense than havin' to tack up over here and then ride on over there to work."

Molly took a step back, stunned. They counted on the board cash they got from him each month. Without it, things would get really tight again.

"Mrs. Oliver know this?"

"Oh, sure. I mean she's gotta figure it would be better to have my boy right there, so we can start earlier each day. Just makes sense, don't you see?"

Molly shook her head. "Well, I believe you'd better talk to her about this. Don't just spring it on her." She wanted to add, Like you just did me, but she held her tongue, turned, and headed back to the house. She wanted to drive over to Jess's before Casey got there. She locked up, got in her truck, headed out the driveway and onto the road to the Oliver's place. As she passed the end of her fence line, she saw Casey loping his horse up the hills behind the barn. It would take him a good while to go the five miles even going cross country. She accelerated to what she thought the road and the truck could handle.

Ten minutes later she pulled into Jess' drive and parked next to the house. She got out and knocked on the door. "Jess? You in there."

"Out here." Molly heard the faint call from the direction of the barn and walked quickly down there.

"Hey, Molly. What are you doing here so early?"

"Hi, Jess. I wanted to catch you before Casey got here."

Jess set down the brush she had been using on Faith. "Come on sit down with me here." She patted the large bale of hay and sat down on it herself.

Molly sat down and turned so that she could face Jess. "Did you know he is planning to bring his horse over here, and by here, I mean to board here?"

"Casey? No, he never said anything about that. You mean he's going to leave your place?"

"Yes."

"That's not fair. I'll nip that in the bud. You said that money was important to your budget, didn't you?"

"Yes, it is, but if it will help you, we can get by without it." Molly turned away, didn't want to look Jess in the eye after saying that.

"No, that's not going to happen, Molly. He won't be keeping his horse here." She reached out, touched Molly on the shoulder. "I'm not going to let him take away income from you. I'm set now. I got my first check, and I'm comfortable for quite a while. You can stop worrying about me."

Molly hugged her. "Oh, Jess. I'm really glad for you, and I'm not going to worry about you, but I am always around if you need to talk or need somebody to come along on an adventure." She winked and stood up. "He'll be here any minute now so I want to get out of here. I don't want him to know I talked to you. Thanks, Jess. I'll catch up with you later."

Only after she had driven away, did Molly realize she hadn't told Jess what Cal had found out. She had been so upset about losing the board money, it had been all she could think about right then. She stopped the truck and considered turning around, but she knew by the time she got there, Casey would be at the ranch and there would be no way to talk with Jess then anyway. She decided she would just have to wait until she could get her alone. She put the truck in gear and continued down the road.

Jess had just tacked up Mickey when Casey rode up. "Good mornin'. You ready to hit it, Boss Lady?"

Jess tightened the girth one more time before she answered. "I am. I want to bring in the two closest sections today. The other sections will have to go into the two holding pens further out on the ranch, so we will have to do them in smaller batches. That way we can get each section done in a day. More new calves out that way, so more work but less to drive in for shipment."

"Got it. Let's go then. We're burnin' daylight." He turned his horse away from the barn and waited for her to mount up. She walked over to his horse and handed him a roll of bills.

"Here's what I owe you so far. I'll pay you again in a couple days. That okay?"

Casey smiled down at her, took the bills and tucked them into his jeans pocket. "That'll be fine."

Jess loaded water bottles into her saddlebags, stepped up into the stirrup, and swung her leg over.   "I'll lead up to where I think they are."

They rode nose to tail for a while with Jess in the front. After twenty minutes Casey rode up beside her. "So, have you thought about what you're goin' to do about the ranch yet?"

Jess looked straight ahead. The dry, rugged landscape ahead had always seemed an unlikely place to raise any kind of livestock, but she had come to love this, rough, forbidding country with its thorns and hoof-ripping rocks, its dust devils and immense sunsets. She didn't know what she would do, but whatever it was, she didn't see how she could leave this land that had become so much a part of who she was now.

"I can't say that I know right now, Casey. I'm just trying to put one foot in front of the other until I get the branding, sorting, and shipping done for this year. I guess then I'll have to decide. For now, though, let's just concentrate on getting the work done."

Casey nodded. "Yeah. I see where you're comin' from. I just been thinkin' a little bit on this too, and from what I seen, this seems like a pretty nice little spread. Hate to see it get eaten up by developers."

She shook her head. "I know. I feel the same way. I don't know that I'm going to have a choice though. It doesn't look like I can run this by myself, and I don't know that hiring help is going to be the answer for me."

Casey shook his head again. "No need to hire help. You got me right here. Why not partner up with me. We can make a go of this place. I know we can. You seen that I know my way around ranchin'. We'll just split the profits. Keep the ranch in one piece and keep the developers out of it. What do you say? Would that work for you?"

Jess glance over at him. He had that big smile of his "I hardly know you, Casey. You want me to take you on as a partner after a couple days of ranch work?"

"Well, I'm more than willing to let you get to know me as much as you want." Another big smile.

Jess said nothing. She broke ahead and cantered through the brush up a hill to her right.   Casey followed and rode up alongside her again. She turned in her saddle to look at him.

"I'm not deciding anything right now. We'll see how everything goes through the round-up. After that, I'll have a better idea about you, about what I want to do."

"You'll think about it though?"

"Sure. It's a possible option. I'll let you know when I make a decision no matter what I decide. Can you accept that?"

"I guess I don't really have a choice, do I?"

Jess felt the poutines in his voice. "Look. Just don't push me right now. I just lost my husband. I have most of the roundup still to do. Too much on my plate to think about anything else." She pushed ahead again, rode along the ridge top looking down into the valley on the other side.

She spotted a movement, stopped, held up her hand for him to be quiet, and beckoned him up. He rode up beside her and looked down to where she pointed.

A herd of about fifteen cows and babies was working its way along the far hillside. She motioned for him to go around to the west. She moved along the ridge further to set up the point position. She heard the clatter of Casey's horse's hooves on the rocky route down to the bottom of the valley. She stopped, watched as the cattle stopped, and raised their heads to look up the hill behind them. She could hear Casey stopping and waiting. The herd went back to grazing and he began to move down the hill again, more slowly this time, pausing every few steps.

Jess waited for him to reach the sandy valley, then began to move along the ridge again to where it began to fade away and merge with the valley below. Perfect place to take point, she thought. When Casey began to move them, she would be in a position to lead them out into the main valley and then back to the ranch. As much as she knew horses, she had begun to know cattle as well, knew what to expect them to do, how to best move them without losing the herd in a stampede, how to evaluate their health and fitness for market. Despite everything, she had Clint to thank for that.

The drive went exactly as she expected. By ten o'clock, they had the herd in the pen and had begun the process of branding and sorting. After they had finished with the few newborn calves, they split off the five two-year-olds, put them in a separate pen, then herded the rest out in the direction they had just come from. The whole process took less than an hour.

They worked one smaller herd before lunch, and since they were nearby, they rode to the ranch house. Jess invited Casey into the house for lunch since, once again, he hadn't brought any of his own. They sat in the relative cool of the kitchen to eat their sandwiches.

"So, tell me about yourself, Jess. Where are you from originally?"

"What? You don't think I'm from here?"

"Not hardly. Not with that accent you got. I would guess someplace out east. New York maybe?"

"Close but more north. Want to try again?"

"Boston then."

"Bingo. Well, half a bingo anyway. Weston. That's a suburb of Boston. I lived there until I was eighteen. What about you? I would guess from around here."

"How'd you know that, smarty-pants?"

"The accent." She laughed as she said it, and started to choke on her sandwich which threw her into a coughing, and sneezing fit while Casey laughed at her. She got it under control, sat wiping the tears from her eyes, and cleaning up the sandwich she had spit out.

Casey leaned back in his chair smiling at her. "Well, look at you all laughin' and jokin' around. You been so serious since I met you, I thought you was never goin' to crack a smile. I have to say, I like this side of you better."

He pushed back his chair, stood up, and began to wander around the room, picked up whatever was lying around, examined it, and put it back down. He ran his hands along the newly painted wall, then turned back to her. "You done some brightenin' up here, didn't you? Makes the place more cheerful, I'd imagine."

Jess nodded. She wasn't sure what to make of it. Clint had never done anything but complain if she made any changes. To get a compliment, even if it was implied more than stated, made her feel good. She felt a flush move up her face. To hide it, she stood and began to clear the table and take the plates and silverware to the sink. When she turned back to the room, she found Casey standing by the door, his hat in his hand.

"What say we get one more batch in here this afternoon, so we can get them finished before dark. That suit you ma'am?"

"Sounds good to me. You go ahead on out. I am going to use the outhouse before we go." He nodded, put on his Stetson, and stepped out into the midday sun.

Jess took her time in the outhouse, then came back in to wash at the sink. When she had finished, she stood in front of the mirror hanging over the kitchen sink. "Who are you, Jess Oliver?" she asked herself quietly. For the first part of her life, she had been Arthur Russo's daughter and for the past six years, she had been Clint Oliver's wife. So, who was she now? She studied her reflection. When she had married Clint, she had been a child really with features more teenlike than adult. The person looking back at her from the mirror now clearly was not a teen. The six years had changed her. She still carried no spare weight on her five-foot-ten frame, but now there were curves where there had not been before. Her olive, Mediterranean complexion had tanned to a clear, nut brown, and dark eyes dominated a face that she hesitated to call pretty and certainly not beautiful, but the word that came to mind was striking. It sounded about right. Not too vain, but descriptive of the person who now surprised her in the mirror. Her shoulder-length, dark hair, a little greasy from sweat and dirt, hung straight down, framed her face. She hardly knew what to think. All she knew was that she needed to find out who she was now that she wasn't connected to a man. She took her flat-brimmed Stetson and carefully set it on her head, the headband resting just above her eyebrows, turned away, and walked out to where Casey held her horse.

The rest of the day went quickly. They hunted out another small herd of twenty-five and worked them and added the seven more two-year-old steers to the nine they already had in the pen from the morning work. Together, they watered and fed them, then Jess set about untacking Mickey.

"I think you might as well head on back to the Websters now. We have everything under control here. I'd like to get one more group in tomorrow before I call in a shipment. You available tomorrow?"

"Sorry, but I already agreed to work a couple days at another ranch. I told you though, I'm ready to be a partner here. If we did that, I'd always be available. You keep my proposal in front of that pretty little head of yours, now. We'll make a great team."

Jess turned away from him. "I'll keep that in mind, Casey. I'll let you know what day we will get back at it then."

Casey tipped his hat to her, rode off back behind the barn and up the ridge behind the house. The sun flashed off his belt buckle as he turned and waved to her, then he disappeared over the ridge top.

Jess finished the chores and went into the house to wash up and make supper for herself and for Blue. By the time she finished and cleaned up, the sun had fully set along the western horizon, the lingering rays spreading yellow, orange, and red across the sky. She took her cup of coffee and sat on the porch and watched night creep up out of the earth like a phantom. A coyote's cry echoed across the flatlands and surrounded her and then rose up the hills behind the house. She felt a familiar thrill at the wildness of the cry.

Chapter 12

After morning chores and a call to the shipper, Jess decided that she wouldn't start another gather until the day after tomorrow when Casey was available again. Even working small groups of cattle could be difficult for one person, and the effort probably wasn't worth it for what she would be able to accomplish on her own. It surprised her how much she had come to depend on Casey despite her misgivings about him. As she came back from the barn, she started to think about what she wanted to do about decorating her home. As if Jess had sent out telepathic signals, Molly showed up shortly after ten with boxes of pictures, a Navajo rug and a variety of knickknacks she had salvaged from her storage room.

"Molly, I was wondering what I should do about decorating this place. How did you know?"

Molly laughed. "I was just planning to drop this stuff off, but if you're game for some help, I'm your woman."

For the next two hours, they chatted and struggled to find a way to hang pictures on the rough stone walls. The Navajo rug went into Jess's bedroom, and with some old barn wood, they cobbled together a small set of shelves that held the knickknacks. They hung some curtains in Jess's room and over the one other window in the back of the house.

Jess looked around and smiled. "Thank you so much, Molly. This is so much nicer already. When the roundup is done, I'm going to get a sofa and a chair and a television. I am also going to get a bathroom put in."

"Hey, it sounds to me like you're planning to stay around here. Have you made a decision yet?"

Jess smiled. "I'm not sure really. I guess I just got carried away in the moment." She looked around the room again. "I sure like the way this all looks though. Hey, how about something to eat? I actually have some food in the house this time to feed you lunch." Jess laughed as she went into the kitchen to put something together.

It always surprised her now when she laughed because she had gone so long without laughter that she thought her laughter was like seeing a glimpse of herself BC, before Clint. Still a feeling of strangeness hung over her as if somehow it would all disappear soon. She shuddered slightly as she opened the refrigerator. She just needed to adjust to living alone, she told herself. She looked into the frig and called to Molly. "How about a grilled cheese sandwich and some chicken noodle soup? Not homemade, but pretty tasty anyway."

"That would be great, Jess. I hardly ate any breakfast. I'm really glad you were home so I didn't have to just drop off the stuff. It was fun working with you, if you weren't home, I might have had to start on it myself." She laughed, her loud, unrestricted laugh, filling the whole of the little house.

Jess smiled at the sound of it. "I would have been happy with whatever you did. I love your place, and if mine were to look half as good, I would be ecstatic."

After lunch, Jess brewed up some tea. While they sat sipping it, Molly started." So, I know about the dude ranch and all, but tell me why you wanted to come out to Arizona in the first place, Jess?

Jessica felt uncomfortable. She had hardly ever talked to anybody about herself. She had gotten that from her dad, she thought. Never too personal. Never anything someone could use against you. Still, she wanted to be friends with Molly. Wanted to know about Molly's life. She decided she would have to open up a little. She sat quietly for a while, searching for words.

"It's okay if you don't want to talk about yourself. I understand."

"No, it's not that. I just never have talked about myself, my history. I never thought anybody would be really interested."

Molly reached across the table and gripped Jess's hand. "I am interested, but tell me only what you want. We have plenty of time to get to know each other, so we can take it as slowly as you feel comfortable with."

Jess smiled at her. "I guess I need to tell you a little about my history first. My name before I was married was Jessica Angelina Russo." The sound of it rolling off her tongue seemed so foreign to her now, so from the distant past.

"My dad definitely didn't want me to come out here. He had other plans for me. He never let me out of his sight unless it was to go to school or to work with the horses at the barn where I rode.

Never had a good thing to say to me either that I remember. Always put me down, talked to me like I didn't have a brain in my head. All I wanted to do was get away from him."

Jess suddenly felt the need to stand up, to do something. She took her teacup to the sink, then turned to face Molly. "Coming out here for the summer to work as a wrangler on a dude ranch? Well, I still don't know how I talked my dad into that. I think my mom probably put some pressure on him. Must have cost her something too, because he treated her the same way. I don't know that Arizona mattered at all at the time. I just wanted to get away is all. As I said before, Clint was the head wrangler. He kind of put me 'under his spell', I guess because by the end of the summer we were married and had moved here."

She paused, rubbing her face with both hands as if to clear her thoughts then continued. "I was just eighteen. I didn't know anything about *anything*. "All I wanted to do when I came out here was to work with horses. It seemed like Clint was offering just that. I don't know that I even loved him. I was fascinated by him, I'm sure. He was good looking and a cowboy through and through. Somehow, I guess, I thought that would be enough." She sat down now across from Molly again, her face once again in her hands, but now to hide the tears that had started to flow.
Molly reached across the table again and took Jess' hand. "You don't have to say anymore, sweetie. I understand."

Jess looked up. "No, there's much more to it, but the most painful part for me was it cut me off from my mother. I'm hoping she'll come out here in the next couple of weeks so we can reconnect. You'll like her. You helping me with the decorating, Molly, means the world to me. I didn't want her to see how I'd been living before."

"You poor kid. I'm so glad we've been able to connect with each other. As I said before, I really needed you as much as you needed me, I think. I am really glad to help you whatever way I can."

Molly gave her one last squeeze and then sat back in her chair. "Anytime you feel like talking or just want someone to sit with you, I'm a phone call away. Don't hesitate. I don't know squat about ranching, but if there is anything I can do here to help with that, I'm more than willing. I'm just happy to be able to call you friend."

"So, enough about me. How did you and Cal end up out here? "

"We were from Phoenix originally. We went to high school together and then got together a couple years later. I guess you could say we fell in love then. Been together twenty-five years now and two grown kids off on their own."

"Why did you leave Phoenix?"

"Cal's job dried up, and my little part-time gig cleaning houses wasn't enough to keep us going. A friend told Cal about this job working as a dispatcher. It meant more money, but it was an expensive move for us. Just beginning to recover from that after three years here. The hard part for me was leaving our friends. I'm really glad that you're here now." She smiled and stood up. "I think I better head on home. I want to make a good supper for Cal. He's been working a lot of hours lately."

Jess stood up with her. "I'm so glad you came over. I'm really happy with everything we did today. Thank you so much, Molly."

"Oh, stop it. I had so much fun doing it, I should be thanking you." She laughed again.

After Molly left, Jess sat for a while at the kitchen table. As she looked around, she felt that for once the house looked more like home. Everything about the place felt brighter. The words, more hopeful, came to mind again as she surveyed their work. Finally, Jess went out to check on the steers. A few were working away at the piles of hay she had set out earlier, but most were standing, tails to the sun, asleep. Blue lay in the barn's shade and watched her as she refilled the water trough and threw some more hay to the horses.

Suddenly, he stood up, alert, and facing the hill behind the house. The hair along his back stood up and he started to bark. Jess looked up the hill. On a boulder near the top, a flash of color, then she saw it. A large cougar stood up, casually stepped down, made its way along the ridge top, and disappeared over the other side. Jess wasn't sure what to do. They had never had a cougar there before. Oh, they had some bobcats occasionally, plenty of coyotes, but nothing that had presented such a big threat as this. She didn't even own a gun, and Clint had sold the 9mm revolver that he had carried. He had intended to pick up a 45 automatic he had said. Instead, he had died first.

Now she felt vulnerable. Blue might be able to fend the cougar off, but he would surely get badly hurt in the process. She couldn't stand the thought of that. Blue was her one true companion. She decided she needed to get a gun, but she also didn't feel like she could leave the ranch right now with the cougar so nearby. She didn't know what she could do if it tried to get after her steers, but she knew she would have to try something.

She went up to the house, found the ax buried in the block they used to split firewood and pulled it loose, and carried it down to the barn. If Blue let her know the cat was near at least, she would have some kind of weapon. She spent the rest of the day cleaning the barn, brushing the horses, so she would be near the pens. By evening she had seen no more sign of the cat and went up to the house to make some supper. By the time she had eaten and cleaned up, full darkness had descended. She sat for a while on the porch listening to the night sounds and petting Blue.

As the moon rose above the cliff to the south, she went into the house, turned off the lights in the main room, and got ready for bed. She lay on top of the quilt once again, the window open, a soft, desert breeze fluttering the curtains that Molly had brought to replace the old Venetian blinds. Cool air drifted across her as she lay listening, straining to hear anything unusual in the night. Sleep came over her without warning, and she slept undisturbed until the cool, morning breeze rustled the curtains and washed gently over her.

Before she made breakfast, she went to the barn and checked the steers. Everything seemed okay. Hopefully, the cougar had moved on. At least this batch should be alright, she thought. The stock hauler should be there shortly, then she would just have to deal with the possibility of an attack on the stock out on the range. She decided she would have to get a gun today and learn to shoot it.

The stock hauler, Pete, got there at ten, and they followed the same procedures as the last two times. He was more friendly now. When they had loaded everything, he stopped just as he was getting into his truck. "Say, you know how I said that I would pass the word around about your horse training skills?" Jess nodded.

"Well, I did pass that around, and one of the horse breeders at one of the ranches I pick up at is looking for a good trainer. If you're interested, I'll tell him to call you."
Jess felt the excitement of the possible rise up in her. This was really what she was meant to do. In her heart, she knew that. If she could only get enough clients, she could get out of the cattle-ranching business. She hardly dared to hope. She nodded her head at him. "Sure, Pete. Pass along my number. I would appreciate that."

He nodded, climbed up into the cab. "I'll see him later in the week, and I'll pass it along."

"Thanks, Pete. I really appreciate that. See you next week."
After the truck pulled out of the yard, Jess turned the horses out in the paddock and headed to the house. She knew nothing about guns, had no idea what she should get or how she would learn to use one when she did get one. She felt at a loss. At the house, she sat down at the kitchen table to try to evaluate what she should do next. She moved a cup of pencils and pens off to the side and found the card the deputy had given her. Michael Contreras. She had forgotten that she put it there. She flipped the card over and looked at the cell

number he had printed on the back. He had said that if she needed any help with anything, to call him. If anybody would know guns, it would be him. Maybe he could at least give her a tip on what to get, but she felt conflicted. She had rarely asked for help with anything in her life, and to ask someone who was really a total stranger to help her out, went against everything she had done her whole life.

She got up and paced back and forth across the kitchen. He had seemed so kind. Maybe he wouldn't mind if she at least got some information from him. She walked back to the table and picked up the card. He had written his cell number on the back. Surely, that meant that it would be okay to call him. Being unable to think of an alternative, she picked up her phone and tapped out his number. The phone rang five times. She was about to hang up when he picked up.

"Hello."

"Hi, Officer Contreras? I don't know if you remember me. This is Jessica Oliver."

"Sure, Mrs. Oliver. What can I do for you?"

"Just call me Jess, please. I'm sorry to bother you, but I have a cougar on my ranch, and I think I need to get a gun of some kind to protect my livestock. I don't know the first thing about guns or anyone who does and wondered if you could give me some advice."

"Of course, Jess. I'd be happy to. When's the next time you're coming into town? I have the day off tomorrow, and I could help you pick something out and at least take you out and show you the basics. Would tomorrow work?"

Jess felt a wave of relief wash over her. "That would be perfect. Where would you like me to meet you?"

"You know where the station is, so why don't you come by there at let's say ten o'clock and we'll leave from there. Will that be all right?"

"That would work. Thank you so much, Officer." She heard a laugh on the other end of the line.

"Why don't you just call me Mike."

"Okay, Mike." It sounded foreign rolling off her tongue. "I'll see you then."

After she hung up, Jess sat down in the kitchen chair again. She realized she was shaking again, and couldn't understand why. She was nervous about the whole thing. Too much like a date, she thought. That was something she had really done only once in her life. She stood up again. "This isn't an actual date, date, Jess. Get hold of yourself." She shook her head as if that would clear it, then headed back out to the barn. She took a bridle from the hook just inside the door, walked out to the paddock, and whistled for Faith.

Faith trotted up to her, and Jess rubbed her forehead, the velvet softness of her muzzle, then slipped the bridle on her, and led her over to a tractor tire used as a feeder. She stepped up on the tire and hopped up on Faith's back. She guided her to the gate, opened and shut it, then rode out into the open land behind the barn. She turned Faith to the flat field to the west and squeezed her legs to send her into a gallop. They raced across the field, Jess's legs clinging to her pony's sides, the wind whipping Faith's mane and Jess's dark hair until they almost seemed to be one creature, flight animals caught in motion. After a half-mile, Jess pulled Faith back. They settled into an easy canter, then a trot, then, a flowing walk.

When they returned to the barn, Jess rode past it and up the hill behind the house. At the top, she saw the cougar scat, fresh and soft in the dirt behind a small boulder. It scared her. That scat somehow made it all real for her now, and she knew that she was up against something that wasn't going to go away on its own. She slid off Faith and walked her back down the hill. She had used her ride to calm herself, but the reality of the cougar had set her nerves on edge again. She looked forward to tomorrow and the chance to get a weapon to defend her stock. She hardly admitted to herself that she was equally excited to see Mike Contreras again.

Chapter 13

Jess pulled out of her driveway at nine-thirty the next morning. She had woken with the sunrise, but what with the chores and the need to get cleaned up and to dig through her clothes to find something she considered suitable, she found herself running late. The traffic on I-40 was heavy and the truck traffic particularly so. She felt overwhelmed by the density of it and wanted more than anything to get off the freeway onto a side road to avoid the traffic, but as late as she was, she knew there would be no way to do that and get to the sheriffs' office in time. She gripped the wheel tighter and wove in and out of the line of trucks until she pulled into Kingman, and followed the now-familiar route to the office.

When she pulled into a parking spot in front of the building, she saw Officer Contreras standing in the lobby talking with the receptionist. Before she could get out, he looked up, saw her, waved, then held up a finger for her to wait for a minute, He finished his conversation, came out the glass entry doors, and into the sunlight. As he walked toward her truck, she realized he was taller and even better looking than she remembered. His hair was a dark brown, almost black, and he was deeply tanned. His brown eyes seemed to bore right through whatever he looked at. He wore a western-style snap-pocket shirt, jeans, and a worn pair of cowboy boots Suddenly, she felt plain, uncomfortable. What had she been thinking to ask him to help her with this? She wanted to just pull away, disappear, but then he smiled at her and leaned down to her open window.

"Why don't you put your truck in the parking lot behind the building. We'll take my truck. It's parked back there, so I'll walk around and meet you." He turned and walked away.

Jess started the truck and drove around the building. She looked for a spot and saw him getting into a newer model, red, Ford pickup. She found an open space two down from him pulled into it, shut the truck off, gathered up her small purse, and got out.

Mike backed out of the parking space and pulled up to where Jess stood. "Hop in. I know a shop where we can pick out something that will work for you. They have a range there too where I can teach you the basics anyway."

Jess opened the door and pulled herself up into the passenger's seat. She felt breathless with anxiety. Here she was, sitting two feet away from this guy she hardly knew and feeling as uncomfortable as she could possibly imagine. She realized she would have to say something. "I really hate to put you to this much trouble, Officer..." She stopped. "Mike." He laughed, and she felt embarrassed but more relaxed.

"Really, it's my pleasure, Jess. I know you're going through a hard time right now, and if I can do anything to ease that, I'm happy to do it. Besides, I had nothing planned for today anyway. It gives me a chance to get in some range time myself. Just relax. We'll find you something you can use to keep your cattle safe."

"Well, thank you. This really means a lot to me. I know nothing about guns, and I've always been afraid of them. Clint had a gun, but he had just sold it before he died and hadn't replaced it yet. Besides, even if I had it, I'd have no idea what to do with it."

Mike smiled again. "By the end of the day, we'll have you ready to shoot a cougar. You'll see. Nothing to worry about. Once you know how to handle the weapon, it will be safe for you to use it. The main thing to remember is never point it at anything you don't intend to shoot. A simple rule that a lot of people forget. That's where most of the accidents happen. I want to make sure to teach you that if nothing else."

Ten minutes later they pulled into the parking lot of a large storefront. Across the front window, Mojave Guns was written in white. In smaller letters underneath, Indoor Range, Expert Gunsmithing, and the hours of operation.

Mike parked alongside the store and shut off the engine. He picked up a small, canvas bag from the floor, looked at Jess, and smiled at her again. "You ready?"

"I guess. We'll see, won't we?" She managed a half-smile of her own, opened her door, and climbed down out of the truck.

The store was pretty non-descript. The walls were grooved plywood with various long guns displayed there. The rest of the store consisted of a horseshoe of glass cases with every kind of pistol that Jess could even imagine. There were no other customers at the moment. The man behind the counter, a tall, potbellied, balding fellow with a massive gray beard, looked up as they came through the door.

"Well, look who we have here. Long time, no see, Mike. Who do you have with you today?" He smiled at Jess.

"Hey, Bill. This is, Jessica Oliver. She needs to buy a gun and learn to shoot today. You think we can arrange that?"

"You bet, buddy. What kind of a weapon do you need?" He addressed the question to Mike.

"Well, we haven't exactly talked about that yet. She has a cougar that is hanging around her place. I don't figure she aims to kill it, just scare it off for the most part, and since I assume she'll be riding out to check on things… that is what you do, isn't it, Jess?"

"Yes. I'll need something I can carry when I'm riding out to check on the cattle."

"I'm thinking a handgun might be the best bet for her then. Easy to carry when she's in the saddle and effective enough with the right caliber, at close range if need be."

"Sounds about right to me. We can get her a holster so she can carry it with her easily when she's out riding the range, eh? What caliber you thinking, Mike?"

"I'm thinking a 9-millimeter, but I want her to try a .45 too to see which one suits her best. The .45 would have more stopping power if she needs it, but I think the 9-millimeter would be easier for her to handle."

"Alright. How about the Glock 17, 9-millimeter, and maybe the Kahr CW 45? That's the lightest 45 that I have. The price of each is close to the same."

"That sounds like it should give her a good comparison. How about fifty rounds for each one and enough time on the range for her to make a decision, get the feel for each of them?"

"Anything for you, boss." Bill started to pick boxes of shells out of one of the glass cases behind him, then took two pistols from the case in front of them. Jess watched with growing trepidation. This anxiety she felt was so different from anything else she had known. New experiences before had been anxiety-inducing, but there had generally been a sense of knowing something about the thing she had faced. This was entirely different. She had never shot a gun, never even held one, and here she was about to invest in one, carry it on her person. She knew that if she had been alone, she would have walked out by now, given up on the whole idea. She felt really grateful that Mike had agreed to help her with this.

"You ready to try this, Jess?" Jess nodded her head even though she didn't feel ready at all. "Bill, you have some glasses and a set of ear protectors we can borrow?" Bill nodded, reached under the glass case, and came up with a set of safety glasses and a headset with two large ear covers, handed them to Mike, then led the way to the range.

After some instruction from Mike and a few practice rounds, they spent the next hour with Jess getting the feel of both guns, then concentrating on the Glock. Mike watched her and coached her for the first half-hour then did some shooting of his own as he kept an eye on her target and saw it gradually being eaten away in the center of the man shape that made up the target area. He was impressed. He had never seen a beginner pick up shooting so quickly, and when the ammo ran out and the echoes died, he told her so.

Jess smiled and felt the color rise in her face. "I'm sure you say that to all the girls you teach to shoot." She turned away to hide her embarrassment, both at his compliment and her response. She grabbed a broom and a dustpan and started to sweep up the shell casings that were scattered over the floor.

"I'm serious, Jess. You're a natural. Let's get you a holster for that thing. I'll teach you something about how to draw safely." He paused for a moment. "Any time you want to do a little practicing, give me a call. I can always use the practice, and it really has been a pleasure watching you learn so quickly."

After she paid for the Glock, the holster, and two boxes of ammunition, she thanked Bill for his help. "My pleasure, ma'am. You be careful out there now. That isn't a toy you are going to be carrying. I don't want to hear about you getting hurt."

Mike glanced at Jess then turned back to Bill. "You don't have to worry about that. She's more careful than most guys I know, and she shoots better than half the guys on the force."

Jessica felt grateful for Mike's support. Bill's remarks had felt like those she had heard from men all her life. Part of a condescending attitude that said, you're not good enough or you don't match up to a man. Funny, it had never really occurred to her before that those comments could be so hurtful, demeaning really. She had taken it for granted that she maybe was less in some way. Mike's defending her had been like an awakening. She picked up her purchases and turned away to hide the smile that she couldn't stop from creeping across her face.

After riding back to the station and getting into her own truck, Jess felt a special sense of accomplishment. She couldn't remember when anybody had validated her the way Mike had today, not her dad, and sure as hell not Clint. Her mom had done her best to make up for it, but she was her mom after all. She had to do that, so it hadn't held that much significance for her. She made the drive home as if in a dream and felt a sense of surprise when she pulled into the drive and saw a strange pickup at the house.

She pulled up alongside it and got out to see Casey coming out of the house. "Just checkin' to see if you was home." He looked uncomfortable as he said it.

"You couldn't just knock on the door?"

"I did knock, but thought maybe you didn't hear me."

Jess shook her head. "Okay. Next time, knock. If there's no answer, don't go in, please. That is my home, and I don't appreciate somebody just walking in with or without me there. Do you understand that?"

Defensive now, "Yes, ma'am," his tone dripping with sarcasm.

"What are you doing here anyway? I told you I would contact the Websters the next time I needed help."

"I just wanted to see where you stood. I could be takin' on other work right now, you know. I can't just wait around for you to decide whether you're goin' to work every day or not."

"Okay. I get that. I have had a few things I have had to do to get organized here, so I'm sorry I didn't let you know what was going on." More cordial now. "I figure to start up again tomorrow, do another gather on another quadrant. Are you available?"

"Well, as a matter of fact, I am. I'll be here by eight. That work for you?"

"That would be fine. I'll see you then." Jess watched him go, then got the Glock, ammo, and holster out of the truck. She had some work to do with the horses before she would be able to shoot off of them. If she was going to have to take on the cougar, it would most likely be when she was out riding.

For the next hour, she set up a series of targets just outside the paddock where Mickey and Faith were eating hay. She took her time, shooting once every few minutes until they both settled and didn't stop eating when she fired. Eventually, she moved closer, fired more frequently. After a half-hour, she walked into the paddock, stood close to each of them, and fired a shot. She didn't tether or hold them so that they didn't feel trapped, unable to escape, and soon, they began to stand still when she fired, simply raising their heads from the hay they were eating. She tacked up Mickey first and rode him around the paddock, stopped, and fired. Nothing. He stood for her as if nothing had happened. She repeated the process three more times until she felt confident that he knew it would be okay when he heard a shot. Another half-hour with Faith and when she reacted the same way, Jess felt she had two horses ready to be shot off of. She felt happy with the results. She dug some apple-flavored treats out of the metal box in the barn and gave each of them a handful, then took the horses inside the barn and grained and brushed them before turning them out for the night. She rigged the holster to her belt and practiced drawing for another half hour before darkness started to descend on the ranch, and she called it a day. She went inside, fed Blue, and then made dinner for herself.

That night she slept with the Glock beside her bed and the feeling that she now stood a fighting chance against the cougar if it came to that.

Chapter 14

True to his word, Casey rode into the yard at eight the next morning. Jess had already been up for two hours, had fed the horses, collected the eggs, watered and fed the chickens and made herself some breakfast. Mickey stood tied to the willow already tacked and ready to go. Jess had loaded and holstered the Glock and pulled her shirt down over it. She didn't know why, but she thought it might be a good idea not to let Casey know she had it just now. If worse came to worst and they encountered the cougar, she would use it.

"Good mornin', Miss Jess. How're we feelin' this mornin'?"

Jessica looked up from under the brim of her hat. Casey had that big smile of his wrapped halfway across his face. "Well, Mr. Casey, I am doing just fine. Are you ready for some work today?"

"Always ready for anything." He touched his hat, flicking his fingers against the brim, then pointed at her and laughed. Jess stepped up into the stirrup and settled into the saddle.

"Let's get at it then, buddy. We're 'burnin' daylight' as you like to say." She spurred her horse into a fast trot and headed out of the yard to the northeast.

The sky rested gray and heavy over the desert. Jess could feel the possibility of a rare spring rain in the air. They needed the rain, that was for sure. The wildflowers had just started to show and their leaves were stubby and wilted already. She loved the Pelotazo and its yellow flowers especially and didn't want to see the spring bloom hurt by the drought, but she wanted more than anything to get the next bunch rounded up and at least back to the ranch where they could do the branding and sorting tomorrow if they had to.

A wind kicked up, and the clouds began to build into great masses hovering ominously above them as they headed into the hills a mile out from the ranch and the holding pens. By nine they had located the herd and begun to move them slowly toward home when the first clap of thunder crashed down around them. Jess's horse, newly accustomed to the sudden explosion of gunfire, didn't flinch, but Casey's roan bolted across the back of the herd and began to buck and twist. The cattle now, without Casey directly behind them, started to break away, and Jess found herself racing after the largest bunch to turn them back into the valley she had used to funnel them to the holding pens. Mickey headed off that batch, and she began to work them as slowly as she dared back to the center of the valley and the remnants of the herd. Casey got the roan under enough control to chase down the outliers that had been making a break for it.

By the time they had the herd completely gathered again, the storm rolled in with a vengeance, the wind whipping the rain against them, instantly soaking them to the skin. The water trickled down her pants and filled her boots. Warm as it was, she felt chilled, and by the time they got the small herd to the ranch, her teeth were chattering, and her hands didn't want to properly grip the reins anymore. They drove the soaked cattle through the gate, and the cattle immediately settled into eating the hay Jess had put out before they left. Both she and Casey rode their horses into the barn and dropped down off them.

Jess started to untack Mickey. She looked over at Casey. He stood looking out at the rain, and she could see he had begun to shiver. "Untack your boy, and set your tack out to dry off. You might as well stay here until the rain stops."

Casey turned toward her and despite the shivering, he had that big grin on his face again. "You invitin' me to stay for lunch, Missy?"

Jess grinned back at him. "Nobody said anything about food, did they? Why? You hungry?"

"Well, you just don't know me well enough yet, do you? I can eat just about any time. So how about it."

Jess shook her head. "I guess I could find something for you to eat. You can come in, and I probably have a dry shirt of Clint's you can put on."

Casey laughed and started to tug at the soaked latigo on his saddle He got it loose enough to undo the cinch and he untacked his horse and propped the saddle up on a bale of hay. Jess waited at the door for him to finish. He put the horse in a stall, then they both made a mad dash across the yard into the house.

They both were laughing when they got inside, the water puddling on the plank floors underneath them. Casey took off his Stetson and hung it on a hook behind the door, then swept, Jess's hat off her and hung it next to his. The only thing dry on either of them was their hair. "Well, that was fun, wasn't it?"

Jess couldn't help but laugh at that. It set off something in her. She had the giggles now and just couldn't stop herself. The giggles unexpectedly turned into tears, and she stood there in front of him crying. Casey put his arms around her, gave her a hug. "Hey, you. Stop that now. You're goin' to dry off and be just fine."

Jess pushed away, turned to go to her room. "I… I'll get you a shirt, and you look like you might be able to wear his jeans too. Wait here."

She disappeared into the bedroom and a couple minutes later came out barefooted with a towel, a plaid, snap-button shirt, and a pair of worn-out Wranglers. "I'm going into my room to dry off and change. You're welcome to change where you are. Just let me know when you're finished." He took the clothes and the towel but said nothing. She turned and headed back into the bedroom, shut the door behind her, and locked it. It felt so odd right now. Here another man stood in her front room about to put on Clint's old clothes. Somehow the whole thing, innocent as it might be, felt uncomfortable, too intimate. She stepped over to the window, stripped away the soaked clothing, removed the holster and pistol from her belt then dried herself and the Glock off with a towel from the dresser. She slipped the gun under the corner of the mattress. She put on a dry set of underwear, a clean shirt, and jeans, and she was ready.
Jess walked over to the door. "Are you decent?"

"About as decent as I get, I guess."

Jess opened the door and walked into the front room. Casey wore the jeans but he held the shirt in his hand. He stood like that, bare-chested, smiling, seemingly in no hurry to put on the shirt. Jess couldn't help but notice the definition of muscle across his chest, the abs clearly defined. She also couldn't miss the scar across his belly, old, but still red and angry. She turned away and began to busy herself with getting lunch together for them. She could hear him slipping on the shirt, snapping the snap closures, unzipping his pants to tuck in the shirt, then the sound of the zipper going back up, something familiar and erotic about it somehow. A recollection of those first few months with Clint flashed across her memory.

She had been just a child then, and everything had been new, romantic. She had known none of that before Clint. Oh, she had heard the talk in school. Some of the girls had done this or that, but it had never seemed real to her then. The reality of her first experience with sex had been painful at first, then pleasurable, and then, when the real Clint began to show himself, painful again, both physically and emotionally. Now she wondered if she could ever again feel what she had felt in that first rush of romance when their marriage had been brand new. She also wondered if she could overcome the frozen period of no growth during these past six years when she had essentially remained an inexperienced eighteen-year-old. She stood at the sink, fingers pressed to her temples. She stood that way for a moment then she began to busy herself taking things from the refrigerator.

"What do you want for lunch? I have a little bit of roast beef or Spam that I could fry up or peanut butter and jelly. Take your pick." Suddenly, she realized he was pressing up against her from behind, looking over her shoulder. She moved away quickly. "Look for yourself then. She stepped back, arms crossed, Casey facing her now, smiling that smile of his.

"I guess I'll take the roast beef then."

Jess, uncomfortable now, stepped away, pulled a loaf of bread from the cupboard. "Why don't you sit down at the table. I'll get it for you."

Still smiling, he walked around her, brushing against her as he pulled out a chair and sat down. "So, you met Clint at a dude ranch, eh?"

The comment startled, Jess. "Where did you hear that?"

"Oh, I don't know. A friend of a friend of Clint's I think." He smiled at her again. "How were those dudes anyway? I bet they was just full of themselves, thinkin' they was cowboys out there ridin' the range, chasin' those dogies." He laughed.

Jess, put his sandwich in front of him. "All I have is water to drink. That okay?"

"Now I guess it has to be, don't it? Yeah, that's fine."

Jess poured water from a pitcher in the refrigerator into two glasses and set them on the table. She made herself a peanut butter and jelly sandwich and sat down across from Casey to eat. "So how did you get into ranch work? "she asked.

"Oh, I grew up on a ranch. Been doin' it since I was a kid. My pa never would let me do nothin' else really. I wanted to play football. Thought I'd be pretty good at it, but he wouldn't hear nothin' of it. He was a mean son of a bitch. Beat me whenever he got the chance, and that was regular. You see that scar on my belly"

Jess nodded.

"He cut me with a knife one day when he was blazin' drunk. My ma got me out of there and took me to the hospital. Saved me I believe 'cause I was bleedin' pretty good. She never could protect me, but she saved me that time. I'll always appreciate that. I left home right after that. Never been back since."

Jess felt a wave of compassion sweep over her. She had lived some of his story. Not the violence, but just as controlling. "I'm sorry, Casey. That must have been hard."

"Well, the one thing my old man gave me was an education in ranchin', so I've never gone hungry since I left there. Somebody's always lookin' for a cowboy."

Jess wanted to say something to ease the pain that she figured that revelation must have brought him. "Well, you have been a godsend for me here, Casey. I'm not sure how I would have handled it all by myself. This is the first year we've been seriously shipping stock, and we have 350 head to sort through to separate out the two-year-olds. Your help has really been appreciated; I'll tell you that."

Casey smiled at her again. "Are you finally warmin' up to me, girl? Well, ain't that fine?"

Embarrassed now, Jess started to clear the table. As she reached for Casey's plate, he put his hand on hers, looked up at her, and said, "Thanks for takin' me on. I needed the work right about then. I really appreciated you takin' a chance on me too." He squeezed her hand, stood up, and stretched. I could really use a nap right about now, but it looks like the rain has stopped, so I guess we are probably goin' to go back at it."

Jess glanced out the window. Sunlight had partially broken through the cloud cover and now streamed down like spotlights here and there across the open fields. "I guess we better do that. Let me get you a pair of dry socks for your boots, and we'll head out again."

The rest of the day they worked hard together in the mud and renewed heat, but at the end of the day, nine more steers were ready for shipping. After they sorted out the steers and released the rest of the herd, they looked at each other and started laughing again. They were both covered in mud and manure from head to toe.

"Well, look at you. I'm not sure you can go home that way. You'll mess up that pretty saddle of yours for sure." Jess hesitated for a minute and then said, "Maybe you should take a shower. I can probably find you one more outfit to wear for your ride back to the Websters."

Casey smiled back at her in a way that made her wish she hadn't offered that. "Well, now, that would be mighty fine, Jess. I'll just step around behind the house and get cleaned up. If you want to bring me an outfit, I'd appreciate it. You sure you don't want to join me? You're lookin' pretty muddy yourself, girl." That smile again.

"You can take yours now. I'll take care of myself after you're gone." Jess blushed, backed away, and turned to go to the house. Out of the corner of her eye she saw, Casey heading toward the shower. Casey seemed like the other two men in her life, and that scared her. She had fallen under Clint's spell and somehow ended up with a worse version of her dad. She couldn't let that happen again with Casey. Right now, all she wanted to do was get him cleaned up and, on his way so she could take care of cleaning herself up.

When she had put together another outfit, she carried it to the corner of the house and called out to him, "I have your clothes and a towel here. I'll set them outside the shower."

There was no response, so she peeked around the corner. The shower was still running, so she quickly walked down to the chair that sat outside the enclosure. As she put the clothes down, the shower curtain opened and Casey stood there in front of her in all his nakedness. Jess dropped the clothes and towel on the chair and backed away, blushing.

"Well, now you see what you were missin' by not showerin' with me, eh?" Casey laughed and stepped out to get the towel.

"I'm sorry. I called to you, but you seemed to be…" Jess turned and walked quickly back around the corner. All she could think about was getting into the house and away from her embarrassment. Inside, she shut and locked the door then sat at the table, her head down on her crossed arms, a mix of feelings washing over her.

Casey was Clint in so many ways. The pain of her last six years cut deep as she sat there. Feelings that she had buried, came to the surface, and the memories of those years flashed back in painful scenes one after another. When they first married, the sex had been a binding force. The unaccustomed intimacy, quickly became something she had craved, and for a while, that intimacy had been enough to cover up all of the other deficiencies in their marriage. When Clint's drinking became the rule rather than the exception, Jess found ways to avoid going to bed with him. She would disappear into the night, riding one of the horses through the dark desert until she felt sure he had fallen asleep. There were times when she had longed for that intimacy, they had shared in those first few months, but eventually, even that hunger died. She wondered if she would ever feel such desire again.

A knock at the door. "I rinsed off the dirty clothes, left them on the chair. You okay? You want me to come in?"

"No. I'm fine." Her voice sounded hoarse, ragged. "Thanks for that. I'll get them later. See you in a couple days."

"Alrighty then. You get cleaned up and get yourself some rest, little missy. I'll see you then." And he was gone. She heard his horse as Casey rode up the hill and away toward the Webster's place. She waited another half hour before she could bring herself to go out to the shower. After she had cleaned herself, she took her clothes into the shower with her and rinsed them off too. As she dried off, she once again had the feeling of being watched. She looked up, searched the hill for any sign of the cougar. Nothing. She dressed hurriedly and carried the wet clothes around to the clothesline running from the corner of the house to the willow and hung them all loosely over the line. As she went about her evening chores, the feeling of someone, something, watching her stayed with her. That night, once again she slept with the Glock next to her bed.

Chapter 15

Officer Mike Contreras sat in his usual seat near the back of the room for roll call. Next to him, as usual, his best friend Jason Fancher sat drinking from a large paper cup of black coffee while they waited for the Sergeant to go over the day's assignments. Jason turned to Mike, a big grin on his face.

"So, somebody had a date the other day I hear."

"Where'd you hear that?"

"Oh, it's all over the department." Imitating an on-air reporter, he continued. "News flash. Officer Mike Contreras of the Mojave County Sheriff's Office had a date with a tall, model-level, good-looking lady. He came back smiling." Some chuckles from everyone in earshot.

"It was nothing. I just helped out that lady who lost her husband in that accident out there on their ranch is all."

"Oh, come on. I see that look in your eye. You're sweet on her. I can tell."

"She's a nice lady. She needed some help getting a weapon and learning to use it. I felt sorry for her and wanted to help her out. That's it. Nothing more to tell. End of story. Since when are you into office gossip anyway?"

"Since it involves my best buddy, who hasn't had a date in the four years since his wife died. I'm glad to see you getting out there again, big boy. I was beginning to worry about you." Big smile.

"Look, I'm fine. You don't need to worry about me. I haven't been ready to get involved with anybody else. That's all. I guess, if the right someone comes along, I might be interested, but for now, I'm just fine."

"Sounds like somebody protesting a little too much there, Mikey. We will have to discuss this further over supper after our shift. Come on over to our place. Jean is making a turkey dinner tonight. She forgot she had it in the freezer and decided tonight was the night to cook it up. You game?"

"For supper? Sure. To discuss this further? No way. I told you, I'm fine. I don't need you meddling in my love life."

"Oh, now it's love life, eh? Wow, this little romance is progressing fast." Jason ducked to the side as Mike took a playful swing at him.

"Okay, okay. Just supper then. Can't guarantee that Jean isn't going to do some interrogating though."

Mike gave him a dirty look. "Let it go, man. Nothing going on there. I promise you will be the second to know if ever there is."

"The second? What? Have I been demoted from best friend? Who's going to be the first?"

"The woman, of course, you numbskull."

"You boys in the back finished playing?" The sergeant looked meaningfully at Mike and Jason. "We have some actual work for you today, so listen up."

For Mike Contreras, the day crawled by. He hadn't been able to stop thinking about Jessica since he met her. He wasn't sure what it was about her that had attracted him so. Maybe it was that she seemed so fragile, and he wanted to protect her. The sheepdog instinct in him was strong; he knew that about himself. At the same time, she had a toughness about her that he admired. He had grown up on his family's ranch. He knew how tough and dangerous ranch life could be, yet, she was tackling it by herself. That took some guts. He respected that.

He felt confused and a little like he had as the teenager he was when he had met Christine. High school sweethearts, they had carried their passion into adult life, and then it had all been snuffed out in a single moment when a drunk driver had crossed the center line and hit her little Ford Fiesta head-on with his pickup. The drunk walked away. She didn't. Mike had been the first on the scene, and it nearly destroyed him. He had wanted to tear the guy apart. Luckily, Jason had showed up right behind him, restrained him and talked him down. It had been four years since that happened but the result had been that he wasn't sure he ever wanted to risk loving and possibly losing someone ever again. So, his sudden interest in this young widow had been a shock to him. Maybe it was because she had lost someone too. Or maybe something about her reminded him of Christine. He felt unsettled, confused. The feelings were so unexpected and complicated, he didn't know what to do with them. He had decided once she had left after their date, not date, that he would just let it go, but he had just not been able to get her off his mind.

When he pulled into the station lot at the end of his shift, Jason was waiting for him. "Hey, buddy. You ready for some turkey?"

Mike smiled at him as he unloaded his gear and carried it in to be checked in. "You know I'm always ready to eat. I really appreciate Jean inviting me. I know it couldn't have been your idea."

Jason laughed. "Hey, you've known me too long, I guess. Get that stuff checked in, and let's get out of here."

The smell of turkey cooking almost overwhelmed Mike as he walked in the door. It brought back so many memories of Christine and even further back to his parents' place on Thanksgiving and Christmas. From the kitchen came Jean's greeting, "Hi, Mike. So glad you could join us. Jason would have just hogged all the good parts. Now he has to be on his best behavior and share like a good boy." Jean came into the living room drying her hands on a dishtowel. She gave Mike a hug. "Can I get you something to drink? Wine? a beer?"

"No thanks, Jean. Just some water for me with dinner. Not a drinker anymore. I've seen too much of what it can do." Then embarrassed, "I don't mean that I have anything against somebody having a glass of wine or a beer or two. It's just not for me anymore."

Jean smiled a sad smile at him. "Come on into the kitchen and give me a hand. You can carve the turkey. Jason always makes a mess of it." She stuck out her tongue at Jason and took Mike by the arm. "I think we have something to talk about anyway." She gave him a sly smile.

"Oh, no. Not you too. I already explained to Jason. There is nothing going on. I just helped a lady who needed some help. End of story."

"Oh, I don't think so, my friend. I sense something different from you. Call it woman's intuition or a sixth sense or whatever, you look happier than I have seen you in a long time."

"Okay, I give up. What do you want to know? Is she pretty? Yes, quite. Is she smart? Yes. What else?"

"Did she show any interest in you, you big goof?"

"I guess you'd have to ask her. I don't know. She seemed to have a good time, under the circumstances. I just don't know. I can't read those kinds of things. How does anybody know?"

"You like her, don't you? I can tell. So, why don't you ask her out? Take a chance. Find out what she thinks, feels. You have been hiding from life for too long now. It's time for you to get back out into the world."

"Look, Jean. She just lost her husband. I know how losing someone feels. I'm sure that, even if I was interested-- and that's a big if-- she is not ready for anything new. I had a nice time with her. Let's leave it at that."

"Okay, okay. I won't say any more. Just keep an open mind about it. You don't know what she's thinking or feeling. Things might have been different from your situation. You never know."

Mike looked sideways at her. "Let's just enjoy this delicious-smelling turkey dinner that you made for us. Thanks, by the way. I know it had to have been you who thought to invite me." Jean laughed.

"Oh, I'm sure Jason would have thought about it halfway through the meal. You're welcome. We always like having you visit. You're welcome anytime."

After supper, they sat around the table and the men swapped the day's stories while Jean sat back with a glass of wine and asked a question here and there to keep the conversation going.

"Hey, I ran into Cal Webster yesterday," Jason said. "You know him? He's the dispatcher down at the truck depot. He tends to eat lunch at about the same time and place I do every day. He's neighbors with that girlfriend, oh, I mean that lady you know." Jason chuckled. Mike gave him a dirty look. Jason ignored it and went on. "He wanted to know if I knew anything about a guy named Casey Parker. You know anything about him?"

"No, can't say as I do. The name seems to ring a bell. What about him?"

"Well, he boards his horse at the Websters, but he's been helping with the ranching over at your girlfriend's spread. They wanted to know if there was anything that Jess- that's her name, isn't it? - should know about this guy. He and his wife are kind of protective of her, I guess. She had a rough time of it with the husband who died. He was an asshole, and they don't want her getting involved with somebody else who is going to cause her any harm. They wanted to know if I knew anything about this Casey dude?"

"Like I said, the name's a little familiar. That's not a good thing. I'll do a little checking tomorrow and let you know."

"Well. You might just want to pass that information along to her directly, don't you think?" Another laugh.

"Will you stop with that? I'll check him out and get back with you. You can pass it along to Webster."

By ten o'clock the conversation wound down, and Mike helped clear the table and said his goodbyes. On the way home, his mind couldn't get away from Jessica Oliver. How did he remember this Casey Parker? He knew he would be going in early in the morning to check it out.

Chapter 16

Once again, the shipper came early, and after loading the steers, Jess took off Faith's tack and turned her out with Mickey. She loaded all of her dirty clothes into a basket and put it in the truck. She wanted to make good use of the day and had already decided to go into town and do her laundry and a little grocery shopping while she had the time. She gave Molly a call to see if she needed anything or wanted to ride along, but Molly said she had a migraine and just needed to take it easy and try to get rid of it. Jess set out a bowl of food and water for Blue and headed into Kingman.

The day had clouded over and the overcast skies left her feeling a little gloomy. She wondered if it was the weather or what had happened yesterday with Casey. The whole thing had left her feeling uncomfortable and a little concerned about continuing to have him work with her. After thinking about the situation all the way into Kingman though, she began to feel silly about it. They were, after all, both adults. It wasn't like she was a teenager who hadn't ever seen a man before. Just a coincidence that he had opened that shower curtain when he did. She decided to shake it off and just move ahead. She had too much to do right now to let him go, and besides, what was she going to say? "I'm sorry, but since I saw you naked, you can't work here anymore." The whole thing just felt foolish on her part.

The laundromat bustled with activity, and she had to wait for a machine. While she did, she read one of the dog-eared magazines on the folding table. It had been a long time since she had read a magazine, and she felt like she had been in some kind of time warp as she read the articles about celebrities she had never even heard of. The more she thought about it, the more she realized that she had literally been a prisoner in solitary confinement for most of the past six years. She felt sadness for her lost time but felt a sense of elation to be out of that situation.

While her clothes went through the wash cycle, she realized it was noon, and, even though she always felt uncomfortable in restaurants, she decided to go to the restaurant next door and grab a sandwich. When she walked in, she saw Cal Webster sitting at a table talking to a sheriff's deputy. They both looked up as the bell on the door rang. She waved before shutting the door behind her.

Cal waved her over. "Just the person I want to see. Thanks to Jason here, I have some info for you. Why don't you grab a bite and sit down with us?"

Jess smiled at the men before walking over to the counter to check the menu board posted on the wall over the pass-through from the kitchen. The waitress was behind the counter wiping up a spilled drink. She looked up and asked, "What can I get for you?"

Jess ordered a Pepsi and a tuna sandwich then sat down next to Cal. "What information did you have for me, Cal?"

"Listen, this is Officer Jason Fancher. He's friends with Officer Contreras." Jason waved his hand in greeting. "Jason, this is Jessica Oliver. It seems that Officer Contreras…"

"Just call him Mike, Cal," Jason interjected and winked at Jess.

"Well, it seems that Mike took Casey's name from Jason the other day after I asked him about Casey's history, and Mike did a little research. Seems Casey has gotten into trouble a few times, generally small stuff, drunk and disorderly mostly, but he had one fairly serious arrest for assault. It went to court but was dismissed when the other guy didn't want to press charges."

"Mike is worried about you," Jason said. "He says to be careful with this guy. It probably will never amount to anything, but just be careful, Jess. Mike wouldn't want to see anything happen to you."

Jess felt the flush creeping up her neck, spreading across her face. Mike had taken the time to do some checking and now had passed the word along to Jason to warn Cal for her to be careful. She didn't know if that meant anything. Probably just standard police procedure, but somehow it made her feel really good. Cared for and protected. That wasn't what she had ever looked for. Other than her mom, she couldn't ever remember anyone doing that for her before, not her dad, certainly not Clint. She held the feeling for a moment, let it warm her heart briefly, then stored it away in her memory bank.

"Officer Fancher..."

"Jason, please. No need for formalities here. I think Mike had planned to call you, but since Cal had asked, I figured I should let him know what Jason found out." He paused for a moment. "Well,

Mike is probably going to be pissed that he didn't get to tell you. My bad."

There was the embarrassment again. She couldn't believe Mike would be that concerned that he would have wanted to call her and tell her himself? Well, as little as she knew about men, that seemed like a possible sign that he had more than a passing interest in her. She didn't know what to do with that information, or maybe it was just a feeling. Whatever it was, it added to the protected feeling she had felt before.

Jason had gone back to eating the burger he'd been working on when she first came in. Cal patted her hand. "Molly and I'll keep an eye out for you. Casey keeping his horse at our place keeps us in touch with what he's doing. We'll be watching him more closely now to see what he's like. Molly especially. She's concerned about you. You let us know if there's anything we can do for you."

Both Jason and Cal got up at the same time, left tips, and went to pay their bills. When Jason finished, he walked over to Jess and touched her on the shoulder. "It was really nice to meet you. I want you to know, Mike is a good guy. He'll look out for you." He turned and walked out of the restaurant. Cal waved at her and followed Jason out. Jess sat and sipped at the Pepsi the waitress had brought for her.

A few minutes later the waitress brought the tuna sandwich and a plate of fries. She smiled as she set them down in front of her. "Always good to know some lawmen, ain't it? You enjoy your lunch. If you need anything else, you give me a shout."

Jess ate slowly enjoying the fries, a rare treat in the past six years. It occurred to her that she felt a little like a newborn, or to be more precise a newly reborn. So much of what she had taken for granted growing up, now had come back to her as a completely new experience, and she wanted to enjoy it fully this time around.

After lunch, she went back to the laundromat, put her clothes in the dryer, and headed to the grocery store for a few essentials and a new bag of dog food for Blue. She had only been in the store a few times over the years, so it took longer to shop than she anticipated as she hunted the aisles for the things she needed. The nice thing about it, she decided, was that she didn't feel rushed or uncomfortable. The absence of Clint made it more like a holiday than a chore, and she took whatever time she needed to find everything she wanted. When she finished at the grocery store, she loaded the groceries and her clean laundry in the truck.

On the drive back to the ranch, she felt the most relaxed and satisfied she had felt in ages. She stopped briefly at the Webster's' and dropped off some chicken noodle soup for Molly. Molly held an ice pack to her head and thanked Jess profusely.

Jess laughed it off. "I don't know if chicken noodle helps migraines, but it is good for one thing and that is not having to cook dinner."

When she got home, Jess called Blue to her, rubbed behind his ears, and gave him a hug. She carried the groceries inside then took the laundry in and put it away. When her phone rang, she thought about letting it go to voicemail and allowing the peace and happiness of the day to flow on unabated, but on the fifth ring, she picked it up. "Hello"

"Is this Jessica?"

"Yes, it is. Who's this?"

"This is Logan Miller. I got your name from the shipper, Pete. He says you have quite a hand with the horses. Would you be willing to take on a couple of my geldings?"

"What kind of training are you looking for?"

"Well, I need some more all-around good cow horses trained, but I especially need at least two good cutting horses ready for market as soon as possible. I don't need it to be a rush job though. I want it done right, no short cuts. This would be a kind of trial. If I like your work, I have more horses that I would like you to work with, and I can send more work your way from other breeders, if you want it. I'm a breeder, but my trainer took off on me, and these horses don't sell unless they're well trained. Most of them will end up in competition. Most of my horses are out of the old Two Eyed Jack bloodlines. They make good ranch horses with the right training. Is this something you might be interested in?"

Jess covered the phone and took a deep breath. This would be her ideal job, no question about that. It seemed overwhelming right now. She would be adding to her already heavy workload. That would be temporary though. The roundup would be finished soon, and then she would have plenty of time to devote to it.

"Hello, are you there?"

"Yes, I'm sorry. I just had to think about my schedule for a minute." Jess decided on the spot. "Yes, I would be happy to take them on. Will you deliver them to me or do you need for me to pick them up? I'm finishing up branding and shipping. Would next week work for you?"

"Sure, I can deliver them to you. That would be fine. How about Tuesday? That gives you a week to get all your stock work finished. Is that enough time?"

"I'll make it work. I guess I will have to ask you what you have been paying for training. I haven't trained for pay before, just the horses we use here."

"You provide the feed and the training. I'll pay fifteen hundred a month per horse. Does that sound fair?"

Jess didn't want to sound too eager, but that figure was far greater than she had expected. "That would be fine. I have good hay, and you'll have to get me a list ahead of time for any feeds and supplements you use so that I can have them on hand when they arrive."

"I'll do that. I have your address here from Pete. I'll have one of my hands drop the feed and supplement list off in your mailbox today. See you next week, Ms. Jessica."

Jess disconnected the call and then collapsed into a chair. Three thousand or so a month to do what she loved doing more than anything? A dream come true. She would have to keep enough cattle to train the horses, but she could ship the rest of them if the training turned out to be satisfactory for this Mr. Logan Miller.

Jess hesitated to call Molly, worried about disturbing her, but she needed for them to let Casey know she was going to need his help for a week of heavy work. When Molly picked up, she sounded like her old self. "You sound a lot better. Is that headache gone finally?"

"You better believe it. I only get those things once in a great while, but when I do, they lay me right down. No doing anything until they're gone. What's up? Did you just call to check on me or did you want to chat?"

"Well, both I guess. I got an interesting call today, and I'm going to need Casey to get over here early tomorrow and plan to work every day for a week."

"What kind of interesting call?"

Jess spent the next half hour filling her in on the horse training job and sharing her excitement. It felt strange to be talking to someone she could be herself with. No worrying about what she said, always protecting herself.

"Hey, you're going to be working long hours for the next week, and I know you aren't going to feel much like cooking. You have your food stocked up?"

"I just went to the grocery store today."

"Ok then, let me do some cooking for you, at least the suppers. I have nothing to do most days and it's driving me bonkers. I can get over there in the late afternoons and get everything ready for you so all you have to do is heat it up when you come in. How's that sound?"

"Oh, Molly. I can't ask you to do that. That's way too much work."

"Look, I'm happy to do it. Cal is getting home late working a lot of overtime, so I have a lot of time on my hands in the afternoons. Just let me do this for you. I know you'd do the same for me if the situation was reversed."

"You probably will have to make enough for Casey too. He isn't going to want to go home and cook as late as we will be working."

"Not a problem. You just get everything done that you need to get done, and I'll be your back-up person. You okay with that?"

Jess laughed. For the first time in maybe forever, she had people who had her back. Molly laughed with her on the other end of the line. Eventually, they both regained control. "Yes, a thousand times yes, Molly. I can't tell you how much I appreciate you."

"Jess, I feel the same way. I can't wait for you to start your horse-training business. That sounds perfect for you. Casey will be by later to check on his horse. I'll tell him then. Good luck this week. I hope you get everything done, so you can just concentrate on the horses."

"Me too, and thanks again."

That night, Jess could hardly sleep with all the plans that were rushing through her mind. The morning seemed miles away.

Chapter 17

Up at four the next morning, Jess fed the horses and Blue then came back into the house to eat breakfast and make a lunch for herself and Casey. Casey rode in at 6:45 looking like the night had treated him roughly. Jess had already mounted up. She waved him along with her as she headed out. She whistled for Blue, who was busy chasing a rabbit. Casey grumped about everything as they started off. No coffee for him. How was he supposed to work on an empty stomach? Jess ignored him. He settled into a sullen silence, slouching in his saddle as they rode the seven miles to where she thought the herd might be.

She wanted to start the drive at the farthest point on the ranch and work their way back in. That way each day would be a little shorter and they could breathe a little easier. They had approximately one hundred seventy-five more head to work in the next week. It wouldn't break down into nice neat numbers, but it meant at an average of twenty-five a day. They would be finished by Monday. Today she wanted to go where she figured the biggest concentration of cattle would be. That would mean a drive of between thirty-five and fifty head, a big move for two of them and Blue.

They found the cattle grazing in a grove of pinon pine and scrub oak on the backside of a high, rocky outcrop. As they crested the ridge, the cattle, spooked by the sudden appearance of the riders, scattered across the valley, up the other side and over the top of the next hill.

"Shit." The first word out of Casey in the past half hour. "Now it's goin' to take us forever to gather 'em. Why the fuck didn't you come around the hill, so we could get in behind them? At least that way they'd be movin' in the right direction if they was goin' to spook. I thought you knew what you was doin'."

Jess felt the old "Clint feelings" creep up on her. She went into the mode she had used so often over the past six years and said nothing. Fighting back had never worked for her, only gotten her more beaten up each time, once so badly she had really wanted to go to the hospital, but afterward, Clint had sworn he'd get her patched up, had bent over backward trying to make her comfortable, feeding her and plying her with aspirin. The black eye healed. The busted-up rib or ribs eased enough to get back in the saddle, and the routine started all over again. After that, she didn't respond unless he goaded her into it, and then only to apologize for her supposed screw up.

They made a wide, slow circle of the area and gradually started to bunch the loose herd and get them moving toward the holding pen where Clint had died, the closest spot to do the cutting and branding. As they moved them along the valleys where they could and over hills where they couldn't, Jess thought about what the past six years had been like. The first two were very rough. They had been buying cattle with whatever spare money they could come up with. Clint had taken every job he could find, and by year three, they had put together a decent size herd, but it wasn't until year four that they had much of anything to start shipping. When they did start to have money coming in, Jess had no idea how much it was or what happened to it except on the nights Clint went to town to drink with his buddies. She knew a large chunk of it got spent at the bar in Seligman or one in Kingman. It had actually been worth it though because those nights she knew he would come home drunk. Knowing ahead of time helped because she would take her horse and a blanket and go out and ride in the darkness, find a place to tie up, roll up in her blanket and sleep until she was sure he had passed out at home. In the morning she would return and deal with who he was when he woke up.

The freedom she felt now felt temporary to her. All her life a man had directed her, controlled her either directly or indirectly. Men had defined what she could do, what she could say, where she could go. Now, when she went into town or made a decision, she felt like she should be looking over her shoulder to see what some man would say. Somehow, she knew she had to get over the incredible insecurity and nervousness that she felt, but there were times when she worried that those feelings would never leave her.

Casey's shouting broke her out of her reverie. "Look up there." He pointed at a rock outcropping that hung out over the trail about one hundred yards ahead. Jess looked closely at it. At first, she saw nothing except the tan of sandstone, and then she realized that what she was seeing was the cougar, its only movement, a casual flick of its tail. She instinctively reached under her shirt where the Glock rested in its holster, gripped it, and then decided, not yet. The cat wasn't a threat up there, and a shot would do more damage than help. The cattle would surely spook, and they would have to go through the whole process again. And, this time it would be much harder because the cattle would definitely not stop soon once they were spooked.

She saw the cat rise and quietly move away, its tawny body rippling with muscle. Jess had never seen anything like it. She admired the pure, wild beauty of it. Jess felt the big cat's wildness and suddenly realized the experience had touched a wildness in her that she had hardly known existed. She breathed a sigh of relief, released the pistol grip, and settled into a watchful mode as they neared the catch pen.

At the end of the day, they had rounded up and worked two separate herds and separated out twenty more two-year-old steers for shipping. Jess felt tired but extremely satisfied with the day's work. Casey had been quiet and sullen for most of the day, but he had worked hard and at the end, he managed to crack a joke or two and get her laughing. As they ushered the last of the two-year-olds into the pen at the ranch, he rode up beside her, reached his arm around her shoulders, and gave her a light hug. "Congratulations, little lady. We got a lot done today. You're goin' to be rollin' in cash before long. You happy?"

Jess looked over at him. He had that smile on his face that had won her over at the beginning, and she couldn't help but smile back at him. "Yep. We got more done today than I had hoped. A couple more days like this and we'll have it pretty well whipped, I'd say."

"Then what? You just goin' to sit around the ranch drinkin' coffee or you got other plans? You think about my partnership offer?"

"Right now, I don't know. I have some projects I do want to get done, fences to mend, and I'd like to build a round pen out to the west of the main paddock. I might need some help with that." She didn't want to say anything about the partnership. In reality, she didn't believe there was enough to support two separate people. It had hardly supported her and Clint living together, but she didn't really feel comfortable saying anything to Casey. The self-protective mechanisms she had built up over the years with her dad and then Clint kicked in again now with Casey.

Casey, waited for her to say more, and when she didn't, rode ahead of her and shut the gate behind the last of the steers. Jess could tell he was irritated with her, but she wasn't about to say any more about any business deals just yet. When they had the cattle settled in, she invited him up to the house. "I think, Molly made us some supper if you want to stay."

Casey gave her a look like he was checking for a double meaning, and immediately, Jess felt uncomfortable. She hurried on. "I think she made up some potatoes and steaks. I told her to make enough for you since I knew we would be working late. You okay with that?"

"Sure thing. I can always eat."

"Okay then. Why don't you go wash up, and I'll get things set up?" She pointed to the shower area and then slipped into the house to wash up herself before setting up for supper. When Casey came in, Jess studied him. He looked tired, and Jess could see that the bags under his eyes were clearly defined.

"You look like you could use a good night's sleep. Were you out late last night?"

"Yeah. I didn't get to bed until around two. Even then I didn't get much sleep."

Jess didn't want to guess why. She busied herself with heating up the steaks and potatoes in the cheap microwave she and Clint had bought that first year. She set two plates on the table with a fork and a knife beside each one and looked up at Casey standing there watching her. "What can I get you to drink? I have water or a couple of Pepsis I think."

"How about a beer?"

"That I don't have. Sorry." Not sorry really. The drinking had caused her no end of pain over her short marriage.

"Okay, then. I guess I'll take one of them Pepsis." He sat down at the table and waited for her to finish getting everything ready.

After supper, Casey stood up, walked around the table, and gave her a hug just as she stood up to clear the table. He held her and then took hold of her shoulders, holding her out at arm's length.

"I really appreciate this, little Missy. I'd of had to go home and try to scrounge up somethin' from an about-bare frig."

Jess, nodded, twisted slightly to get out of his grip, and started to clear the table. "You're welcome, Casey, but you need to thank Molly. She's the one who suggested this and got it all ready for us. I didn't do anything more than you did, and that's eat what she cooked."

Casey looked disappointed like he had wanted to say or do something more. He turned away and started for the door. "Yeah, I'll be sure to do that." And he took his hat and was gone.

Jess put the dishes in the sink and then sat down again. The little sequence had once again made her uncomfortable, and she could hardly pinpoint why. It hadn't been anything more than a friendly gesture, really. She didn't want to put up barriers where she didn't have to. She wanted to break the old habits which she had just begun to recognize. They didn't have to be a life sentence. She stood up, went to the sink and cleaned everything up, then seeing that it was just nine o'clock, she decided to call Molly.

The phone rang five times. She was about to hang up when Molly picked up. "Jess? How did the day go?"

"Great day and great ending with you prepping that meal for us. Thank you so much, my dear friend. I don't know what I would have done without you these past couple of weeks. You have been a godsend."

"Really, my pleasure, Jess. You didn't have to thank me, but I am glad you called. I know you heard what Cal and that Deputy had to say, but I have some other things to tell you about Casey that I think you should know."

Jess, sat down at the table. "Like what kinds of things?"

"Well, none of this is for sure, but Cal asked around a little bit more about him. It seems he moved to Kingman about two years ago. He came from some little town in New Mexico. When Cal started asking about him, very few people seemed to know much, but there apparently was a rumor going around that he beat up his last girlfriend pretty bad, put her in the hospital. She wouldn't press charges, and he left town just after that. It's just a rumor of course, and there may be zero truth to it, so I don't want you to worry too much about it. He has always been polite and responsible around us. I just wanted you to know that so that you are careful. I've found it best to not take anything for granted until you really get to know someone, and then, still, keep an eye open."

Jess stood up again and began to pace back and forth. "So, what's your take on it? Should I just let him go and look for some other help? I mean I'm kind of in a bind here right now. I have a lot of cow work to get done in a short period of time, and I don't have anybody else lined up to help me."

"No, no. I think it will be fine. You don't have that many days to work with him, and it has been working out okay so far, hasn't it? I didn't mean to upset you or make you worry. I just want you to be careful. That's all. I'll get your supper prepared for you tomorrow too. How'd that work today?"

"Just right. Thanks again, Molly. It was a wonderful thing to be able to come home to an already cooked meal after a hard day. You're the best."

After Molly hung up, Jess went out to the barn to check on the calves and the horses. The night air had settled like an ice cloud over the ranch. Six years and she still felt surprised at how much temperature difference could occur in a few hours in the high desert. Sweating during the day and seeing your breath at night. Hard to believe that could happen on the same day, but it did regularly here, and she realized it was one of the things she treasured about living on this land.

The rich, animal smells and the cold air filled her with an unfamiliar sense of peace. This was who she was. This life, this connection to the land and the animals, she had been drawn to this all her life. She threw out hay for the stock and stood in the moonlight and watched her breath drift out before her, catch the moonlight for an instant then disappear. She turned and headed for the house. Blue stood in the yard facing the hill, back fur standing on end, a low growl resonating in the back of his throat. Suddenly, he started to bark, fierce and loud in the silence. Between barks, Jess thought she heard the sound of rock on rock or hoof on rock and then Blue stopped and a palpable silence settled once again over the ranch, but now the silence felt less peaceful.

As she lay in bed that night, she began to think maybe she should talk with Officer Contreras. She still didn't quite dare think of him as Mike. She didn't want to be overly paranoid about it, but Blue's reaction tonight had been a kind of confirmation for her that her uneasy feelings were not just in her head. She decided she would try to work up the nerve to call him in the morning. She called Blue to her and stroked his fur as she lay there. She fell asleep with her hand resting on his head.

Chapter 18

At six-thirty the phone vibrated on the sink next to where Mike Contreras stood shaving. He took one last swipe with the razor, grabbed a towel, wiped away the remaining shaving foam, and picked up the phone. The caller ID showed, "Jess." He had never put a work client's name in his phone before, and seeing it come up like this for the first time, stirred something in him. He hit the answer button. "Mike here."

"I'm so sorry to call so early, but this is the only chance I'll have today. I feel kind of silly even mentioning this, but I think I need your advice about something. Oh, this is Jessica by the way. Jessica Oliver." A pause then, "I'm sorry. I'm rambling. Do you remember me?"

Mike had to smile at that. He had hardly been able to get her off his mind since he met her. "Sure, Jess. What's up?"

"Well, this is all going to sound really vague and maybe paranoid. I don't know, but several times lately I have had the sensation of being watched when I am around home here. I passed it off for the most part as just being me being alone and having too much imagination, but last night, Blue, that's my dog, by the way, really reacted strongly to something up on the ridge behind the house. Is there anything I should be doing about this? It kind of is creeping me out." She paused. "I feel like now I am really rambling here. Does this make any sense to you?"

"I can come out and check it out for you. Is there a time when you would most likely to be home?"

"Well, I'm in the middle of roundup right now so I won't be back until about seven tonight." A pause and then, "I'm sorry. That probably is too late for you."

"I get off at five. I'll just stop out unofficially if that's ok with you."

"Oh, I hate to put you to the trouble on your time off. It's probably nothing. It could wait until I'm home regularly which should be in about a week."

"No. It's no trouble really." He felt embarrassed at how strongly that came out. "I mean, I like to drive out in the desert in the evening sometimes anyway. It relaxes me somehow. If it's okay, I'll stop out tonight. I don't want you to have to worry." He felt like someone else had taken control of his mouth. Everything he said sounded to him like it had another meaning.

"If you really don't mind, that would be great. It would help to ease my mind if nothing else. I'm sure it's nothing, but I would love for you to have a look."

Once again, a pause, and now he could feel her embarrassment through the connection. "Okay, looking forward to seeing you then. I mean, I'll see you at seven." Mike disconnected and then sat down on the edge of the tub. "What the hell, Mike? You sounded like a hormonal teenage boy. Get a grip, man."

The rest of the day seemed like a blur to him even though it moved painfully slow. Every ticket he wrote had at least one mistake on it and had to be redone. At one point he sat alongside the road in his cruiser and just stared into space for five minutes. All he really wanted was for the day to be over. And, then it was. He checked out and headed home to make himself supper and get cleaned up before driving out to her place. He kept talking to himself, trying desperately to calm himself down. On the job, coolness had always been his trademark no matter how intense the situation, and here he found himself in new territory, a place where his emotions were not completely in control. "She has just gone through a trauma, Mike. What in the hell are you thinking? She isn't ready for any kind of relationship and especially not with you, you big jerk."

No matter how much he talked to himself though, the feelings wouldn't go away. He headed out early, drove deep into the desert before swinging back onto the main highway and heading to Jess's ranch.

...

Casey had been sullen and out of sorts all day. His attitude had made Jess uncomfortable so she had decided to do less and finish early. By five they had another segment of the herd separated and the breeding stock on its way back to where they had picked them up. She fed herself and Casey and hurried him on his way. She didn't want Casey here when Mike came.

She felt funny thinking that. It wasn't like there was anything between her and Mike or her and Casey for that matter. It just felt awkward somehow. She decided not to overthink it. She hurried to get cleaned up a bit. She didn't feel she had enough time to take a shower. It was too much of a hassle with the outdoor shower. As she washed up in the kitchen sink, she decided that one thing she would do with some of the money would be to get a septic tank and an indoor bathroom and shower put in. She did the best she could, washing her face, combing her hair, and putting on a clean T-shirt. Before she could think twice about it, she dabbed on a tiny amount of perfume she had been hoarding.

She had just finished washing the dishes when she heard a vehicle pull into the yard. She dried her hands on the dishtowel as she walked to the door. Mike had just gotten out of his Jeep and was standing looking up the ridge behind the house. "Hi, Mike. You see something up there?"

"Not exactly. There was a brief flash of something as I pulled in. Nothing obvious. Might have just been the way the sunset is hitting the rocks is all. I'll go up and check it out though. How are you doing? Everything going okay?"

"Good as can be expected, I guess." She really wanted to tell him about the horse training. She was trying to keep her enthusiasm in check, but finishing the cattle work and starting the horse training excited her beyond words.

"That's good. Okay. Let's go up there and have a look. Have you seen anything at all that makes you think this is a problem?"

"Just little things, really. A flash like what you saw for just a second once. Blue's reaction the other day was the most definite. He knew something was up there and told me about it. Otherwise, it is just a gut feeling, a feeling of being watched mostly. "

"Any time frame?"

"Generally, in the evening. Although the one time, I was taking a shower that was in the midafternoon. I suppose this is all pretty silly. I'm embarrassed that I got you all the way out here for it."

Mike stood close to her, looked into her eyes. She turned away somewhat unnerved by it. "Okay. Let me get Blue. He might be able to tell us if there was anything just up there."

She turned to the house and whistled. Blue pushed open the screened door and came running to her, tail wagging. Jess rubbed his ears then turned back to Mike. "Let's walk up starting along the lower part of the ridgeline and not go straight up to where Blue was looking yesterday. That way, it will be easier climbing and give him a chance to start to gradually home in on whatever he might have been barking at. If any sign of it is up there still."

"Sounds like a plan, Jess. You have the makings of an investigator." He smiled at her.

Jess felt the warmth creeping up from her neck to her hairline. "I don't know about that. I just tend to know the way animals work. I guess I've been better at that than I have been with people over the years."

"I get that. I have always trusted people who are good with animals before anybody else. Animals read people better than people read people. If my dog doesn't like you, then I am damned sure I won't like you."

Jess looked over at him. He appeared engrossed in the terrain, head down, forehead wrinkled with thought. She studied him for a moment. Tall, maybe a little over six feet, muscular but not in a bulky, weightlifter way. He moved with a simple grace that reminded her more of a dancer than a cop somehow. His face was tanned with a strong jawline and chin covered by the traces of a very slight beard. She had to force herself to look away. There was something about Mike Contreras that fascinated her, something that made her feel safe when he was nearby. The feeling surprised her. She couldn't remember ever feeling that way around a man before. Even in the earliest time with Clint, before he revealed who he really was, she had never felt safe with him. Now as they walked up along the ridge, she found herself wanting to know more about this Mike Contreras.

When they got to the spot where she had seen the flash before, Mike held up his hand to signal for her to stop. "I'd like you to stay back a bit. I want to do a methodical search here and see if there's anything that might give us a clue as to who or what has been up here. Do you mind?"

Jess shook her head. "No. That's why I asked you for your help. I knew you would do a better job of figuring this out than I could. I'll sit on this boulder until you're finished." She rested against a large piece of sandstone, leaning more than sitting while she watched him move in a slow, careful pattern back and forth across the area. Occasionally, he would stop and squat down to look carefully at something then move on. Eventually, he had widened the grid until he had reached the crest of the ridge. He squatted low there where he could see the patterns of light and shadow created by the setting sun along the back side of the ridge. Suddenly, he stood, took a couple of steps to his right and several down the ridge then squatted again and laid his hand lightly on a sandy impression.

"Your horses come up here at all? I mean are they free to roam up here?"

"No. I keep them penned mostly. They have a fenced paddock on the other side of the barn and the only time they are out of it is when they are with me and working."

"Anybody else up here at all?"

"Well, my hired hand, Casey, heads this way on his way back to the Websters' ranch where he keeps his horse, but he doesn't come all the way up here. He crosses farther down along the ridge. I don't think he would have any reason to come up here at all."

"Any other riders possible?"

"This is open range country, as you know, so this ranch has been broken up into a lot of little ranchettes of five or ten acres. A lot of them keep a horse or two and some ride and some aren't real careful with keeping them fenced so we have strays come through every now and then. I can't remember when the last one I saw was through here, but it has been a while. You think it was just a horse I saw?"

"No, I'm not saying that. I can't tell you for sure what you saw, and I sure don't want to discount what you felt. I have always counted on my gut to tell me when something isn't right. It's kept me safe in some pretty dangerous situations." Mike stopped. He regretted saying that first because it kind of sounded like bragging, and second because it might further scare her. "I mean, trust what you feel. We'll figure this out eventually, but when you have that feeling, you get yourself someplace safe, and you can call me any time. You understand? Any time, day or night. I don't live that far from here, and if I can't get to you, I'll get another deputy out here right away. I don't want you to hesitate."

Jess felt a wave of relief wash over her. "I hate to put you to so much trouble, but I can't tell you how much I appreciate that. I hope I don't have to call you again, but it is reassuring to know that you at least know my situation."

Mike smiled back at her. He had a tremendous urge to give her a hug but knew it would be inappropriate. Besides, she was a perfectly capable young woman with a strength he admired. She just had been through a lot. He really wanted to be there for her.

"Would you like to come in for a little dessert? I have some coffee on, and I made up a quick little apple thing that I think is pretty tasty."

"Oh, I don't want to put you to any trouble, Jess. I probably should just go. I'm sure you're tired after a long day in the saddle."

"Don't be silly. You're the one who has gone to the trouble for me coming out here on your time off. Come in and sit for a while. You have to be tired too after a full day of work."

Mike hesitated for a moment and then said, "Okay, sure. I would love a cup of coffee for sure, and I am never one to turn down a dessert." He patted his stomach and laughed.

"Yeah, you look like you have been just shoving down the calories." She rolled her eyes. "Come on, chubby boy." She chuckled and started down the hill to the house.

In the house, Jess set cups and a pot of coffee on the table along with two plates of apple strudel. "Nothing fancy but I wanted to have something to thank you for making a special trip out here. I really appreciate it. I know the whole thing is probably in my imagination, but telling you about it at least has eased my mind a little bit."

"Really, Jess, I'm happy to do it." He poured himself a cup of coffee and took a sip. He picked up a piece of the strudel, took a bite, and set it down on the plate. "That's really good." He ate a little more before continuing. "I don't think you're being paranoid. The gut feeling that I talked about earlier is pretty accurate, I've found. Trust it. Do you carry your gun with you all the time?"

"Not really. I haven't gotten used to it yet. Do you think I should?"

"I know you should. You're by yourself out here. It's probably as safe as anyplace, but I have seen too much in my job to take anything or anybody for granted. I don't want to scare you or anything. I just want you to be careful. I don't want anything to happen to you." He stopped, embarrassed at the emphasis he had put on the last part.

Jess looked up, saw the color rising up his cheeks, and wanted to brush it away, make him feel comfortable. "Thanks, Mike. I will from now on. I guess I've been kind of naive. I don't think of things like that. I appreciate your looking out for me."

"Hey. Let's talk about something else. Enough of this stuff. How are you doing? I know this had to have been a tough adjustment losing your husband so suddenly. How long were you married? And if you don't want to talk about this, I understand. I really just want to know how you're doing." He paused. "Here, now it's me who's rambling, isn't it?" He laughed again.

Jess smiled at him. "It's okay. I don't have a problem with talking about it. We were married for six years. Six pretty miserable years, really." She stopped, stared off into space and then down at her hands wrapped around the coffee cup.

Mike reached across the table and laid his hand on hers. "We can talk about it or not. Your choice. I'm not trying to pry. I'm just not very good at making small talk, I guess. It seems like I do this all the time, hit on somebody's sore point. I don't know. Maybe I'm not very good with people."

"No, not at all. I can tell you care. I don't mind at all. It's just that there's a certain embarrassment now. I stayed in a dangerous situation for way too long, and only pure chance got me out of it. I should have had the courage to leave long ago. I just didn't know what to do." She stopped again. "You don't need to hear my woes. Tell me about yourself. Are you from this area? Did you grow up here?"

"Actually, further east. I grew up on a cattle ranch near Flagstaff. I went to Flagstaff High School and then from there to Glendale Community College for Police Academy. I think I always wanted to be a policeman. Not sure exactly why, and there are days when it's brutal, especially those days where you work a fatal traffic accident." He paused, looked out the window. "All in all, though, I think I have always been attracted to the helping part of it, and that never gets old for me."

"I sensed that in you. You've been most kind to me. When I felt the most vulnerable, you made me feel comfortable, safe really. That's a gift. There haven't been many times in my life when I felt that. It meant a lot to me, Mike."

"Actually, when you came in, and I had heard what happened to you, I could relate better than you know. I lost my wife four years ago in a car accident. A drunk driver killed her. I had a sense for what you were going through, although I know now that your situation wasn't as happy as mine was before the accidents, we each had to deal with."

He stood up and turned away from her. He didn't want her to see his face, see what he felt right now. This all had happened too soon. She wasn't ready, and he sure wasn't. He felt more confused than anything, but he had always felt that being straight with someone was the best policy. He turned to her. "I just want you to know, no matter what, I'll look out for you." He paused and studied her face for a minute then turned and took his hat from the peg by the door. "Well, I think I'll take off. You call me if you see anything or need help in any way. I mean that now. You don't have to handle everything by yourself even though I know you are perfectly capable of doing that." He turned one last time at the door. "Goodbye, Jess. Thank you for the coffee, dessert, and conversation. Can't remember when I felt so much at home with someone." He paused. Looked down. "Seems like an eternity ago instead of four years."

Jess sat at the table and stared at the door after Mike left. She was stunned. She had never met a man like this. She had no idea what to make of it. All her experience had taught her to feel defensive around men. Here was a guy who just came out and said what he felt and didn't do it as a pressure tactic or to control her. It left her confused. She didn't know what to feel about it and really was almost afraid to think about it right now. He had made her feel comfortable from the first time he met her, but somehow, yet she still didn't know how to trust. She did feel glad though that she could call on him if she needed to.

After a few minutes, she stood, cleared the table, washed the few dishes and put them away, then got ready for bed. She felt emotionally and physically exhausted right then, but when she got into bed, it took forever to fall asleep. When she did, restless dreams disturbed her throughout the night.

Chapter 19

Her phone chimed at six, and Jess swung her legs out from under the covers and got out of bed. She looked at the caller ID. Mom. She hit the button to answer. "Hi, Mom. How're you this morning?"

"Not so good, darling. I'm sorry I haven't called. It looks like I'm not going to be able to make it out there for a while."

"Why? What's happened? Are you sick?"

"No, your father has decided that he doesn't want me leaving him, and I have had to go into hiding for a while. I won't say where I am because I don't know if he has a way of tapping into my calls, but I'm safe for now."

"Mom, why don't you come out here and stay with me then? He isn't going to find you here."

"No, baby. I don't want you in the middle of this in any way. He can be a very violent man, and I'm not going to do anything that could get you involved in this."

"Wow. I never saw that side of him. I know he was controlling and nasty, but I never saw him do anything violent."

"We never pushed him. Always did what he wanted, so it never came out. Now he has lost control of you, and here I am getting out of his life. I didn't say this before, but I've quietly been going to therapy the past few years to try to get an understanding of what has put me in this situation and why I haven't been able to walk away sooner. I understand a lot of it now. My own background growing up, plus the fear he created in me, kept me there. When you came along, I felt that I had to protect you. I did what I could, but the damage got done. I think someday after this all settles down, you'll probably have to come to terms with it and seek some help in doing that. It's tough to do on your own."

"Oh, Mom. I didn't know. I am so sorry. You really should come out and stay with me. I want to make sure you're safe."

"No, no I'm fine. And I don't want you to feel sorry for me. I'm sorry I didn't get you out of that situation. If I had only done that sooner, maybe you wouldn't have ended up in the marriage you had to deal with." She paused for a moment, then asked, "How are you? Is everything okay there with you? How are you doing on your own?"

Jess spent the next twenty minutes telling her mom about Molly and Cal and briefly mentioned Casey and Mike. She didn't want to go into too much detail about them just yet. When she had to let her mom go to get ready for the day, she found it really hard to say goodbye. The sound of her mom's voice was comforting in a way that she couldn't explain. Despite the bad news, she felt calmer.

She grabbed a quick breakfast and hurried through the morning chores. At 7:30 Casey came over the crest of the hill, slouched badly in the saddle, obviously another bad night behind him. Jess didn't look forward to dealing with him when he was like this.

She said nothing, just mounted up, whistled for Blue, and headed out. Casey dropped in behind her, and Blue ranged out in front of them. When Casey said something, the words were slurred and thick. "What we got today, little missy?"

Jess half turned in the saddle. "You're drunk, aren't you. Maybe you should just head on back home. You aren't going to be of any use to me today in that condition."

"Not drunk. Just had a little nip to start the day is all. I'm fine. "Besides, I can out-rope you blind drunk, anyway. I ain't goin' home. Don't get your panties in a twist."

Jess stopped Mickey and turned him to face Casey. Blue stopped and looked back to see what Jess wanted him to do. "I'm not dealing with a drunk. You make a mistake and either one of us can get badly hurt out here. Too dangerous. Just turn yourself around and get sober before you come out here again. Blue and I will take care of this today. If you still want to work here, you come sober tomorrow."

She turned Mickey around and continued on with Blue leading the way. She felt that old familiar sense of fear she had whenever she had tried to confront Clint. Things were changing for her, but deep down she somehow felt a need for the approval of the men she dealt with. Casey's roping comment had cut deep, and even though she knew it was a drunken comment, she wondered if that was the way he felt. Did he think she didn't match up somehow?

She worked the small herd with Blue's help and moved them steadily back toward the holding pen where Clint had died. When this one was done, she would have just two more bunches to bring in, one large and one medium, and she would be finished with the herd for a while and could put all her efforts toward the horse training opportunity. Her mind wandered to that pleasant thought as she slowly moved the cattle the last mile down to the pen. Suddenly, Casey was beside her. Startled, she turned to look at him. He sat straight and easy now in the saddle although his eyes were bloodshot. He looked like he had been rode hard and put up wet.

He looked back at her. "This satisfy you, Missy?"

"Well, you look a little better."

"I'm fine. I was fine when I saw you earlier too. You don't have to worry about me fallin' off no horse. I don't care what kind of shape I'm in. I can ride anything, so just relax. We'll get this bunch done in no time."

Jess shook her head. "Yeah. OK. If you say so, cowboy. Just stay alert. We have one bull in there that's pretty aggressive."

"Don't you worry about me. I can handle it."

They moved the herd the rest of the way into the corral and started the sorting right away. It went quickly with the two of them working together and Blue picking up any slack. Jess had to admit that they worked pretty well as a team. Even after such a short time of working, they had developed a sense for what the other one planned to do, then worked from that to get things done efficiently. Better actually than it had gone with Clint. Clint had always tried to take over no matter how well Jess worked. It had only added to the confusion and slowed the process down. Then he would yell at her for screwing things up. She had never felt anything but tension working with, no, make that for him. Casey presented his own problems, but as far as the work went, the only issues they had were related to who should be on the ground, and who should be in the saddle. Casey always thought he should be in the saddle. As far as he was concerned, that was the man's job and no woman could possibly do it as well as he could. Most of the time Jess had deferred to him. Today she felt a need to prove her roping skills, so when it came to the branding, she directed Casey to do the groundwork.

"Oh, come on. You know it will take us twice as long with you doin' the ropin'. That's my job. I been cowboyin' since I was first able to get on a horse. You let me handle that."

Jess stood her ground. "My herd, my rules. Today you do the groundwork unless you want to just head on home and let me do this by myself."

Casey looked for a minute like he was considering it, then, he stepped down off his horse and tied him out of the way. "Alrighty then. Let's see what you got there, cowgirl." The disdain in his voice rang clear.

Jess moved into the herd, her rope loop built and ready. She picked out the first calf she wanted to work, let Mickey do his job of cutting it out, then Jess flipped the rope around the calf's hind legs and dragged it out of the herd to Casey. He said nothing as he dropped the calf on its side, tagged, branded and castrated it. Jess and Mickey kept the rope taut the whole time and when Casey finished, she eased it off and the calf staggered to its feet and hurried back into the herd to its momma.

It went smoothly for the next few calves, but at one point, a momma got very upset and aggressive when her baby was pulled away from her and charged toward Casey. Casey had his back to the herd. and Jess yelled at him. He turned just as the cow hit him and knocked him ten feet back. He landed hard on his back. Jess tried to release the calf to get her rope on the cow, but couldn't get the loop to loosen since the calf kept trying to get to its momma. Casey struggled to get out from underneath the cow, as it pinned him to the ground with its head. At one point he screamed in pain as the cow stepped on his leg.

Jess got her rope free, rebuilt her loop, and dropped it around the cow's horns then backed Mickey away and dragged the cow off of Casey. She flipped her rope free as the cow and calf settled back into the herd. Casey lay still in the dirt and manure of the pen.

Jess called to him, but he didn't respond right away. She jumped off of Mickey, ground tied him and went to Casey. He lay on his back, a pained look on his face. His jeans were bloody where the cow had stepped on him. He tried to move, and he moaned in pain. He looked up at her as she knelt beside him.

"What the hell happened?" he managed to groan out.

"That mama wasn't happy we were messing with her calf. You okay? How's the leg?"

"Oh, it's just peachy. Hurts like a motherfucker."

"Ok. You want me to get an ambulance out here? You think you need to go to the hospital?"

"I can't afford no ambulance. Get me up so I can walk this off." He struggled to sit up.

"Maybe you should just lie there for a while. Let yourself recover a bit before you try to stand up."

He paid no attention and pushed himself up into a sitting position. "Give me a hand here, will you?" He reached a hand up to her, and she helped to steady him as he stood up. He tried to walk a few steps and limped badly.

Jess felt tears start to form again and walked over to the fence. She turned away from him, so he couldn't see her face. Maybe he'd been right. Maybe she couldn't rope as well as he could. She felt like she had caused this, and now she didn't know what she had to do to make up for it.

"Hey, Jess. Come here, will you? Do you have any water out here? I need a drink."

Jess walked over to Mickey, took the canteen from her saddlebag, and helped Casey take a sip. Clearly, he could hardly stand the pain, and she wished she could do something more for him.

"I think you're all done for today. Let's get you back to Molly's, so you can get on home and get some rest."

"Bullshit! You think a cow steppin' on me is going' to hold me down? Then you got another think comin', sister."

"I don't care what you think you can do, tough guy. You're done for today. Now you want me to ride back with you or are you just going to tough it out and ride alone?"

After a struggle to get him up into the saddle, they rode together toward Molly's, but Jess could see how much pain he was in and changed course to head back to the ranch. "I'm taking you into Kingman to the medical center. You need to get that leg checked out and get some x-rays."

"I'm fine, I'm tellin' you. I don't need no hospital visit. I got no insurance, and I sure as hell can't afford no hospital charge."

"Look, I'm going to take care of the bill. You're just going to have to accept that. Let's just make sure you don't have a break in that leg."

By the time they got to Kingman, Jess felt totally stressed. The sun had already started to dip below the horizon, and again she had stock left out in the branding pen with no food or water. She made arrangements at the front the desk to pay whatever bills came along with his treatment then went to check on Casey. She found him on a wheeled stretcher in the hall outside the x-ray lab. He looked unhappy and awkward there. A man so accustomed to being outdoors was now confined to a two by seven cart. He let her know how he felt as soon as he saw her.

"You have got to get me the fuck out of here. I'm goin' nuts. They took the damned x-rays, and then they just left me here."

"Hang on. Wait for the results, and then if everything is good, I'll give you a ride home. I'll get your horse back to Molly's and maybe you can get a friend to get out there and get your truck."

"Okay, okay. I guess I can hang on for a few more minutes. I sure as hell don't like bein' in here though."

It took another half hour for the doctor to get back with them, and by that time, Casey had started to make so much noise, they wanted him out of there as soon as possible. The doctor, a short balding man with a Sam Elliot mustache and a set of wire-rimmed glasses perched on the end of his nose, studied a chart as he walked down the hall toward them.

"So how are you feeling, Mr. Parker?"

"Oh, just wonderful, Doc. I always like layin' around in the hospital like this."

"Well, we can get you out of here right now then. No breaks. Pretty badly bruised and cut up a bit. You'll have to take it easy for a week or so until it starts to heal up. Use ice on it for a couple of days. You can take Tylenol if you need to for the pain, but a week or so of rest should put you back into shape, I'd say. If you have any problems, don't hesitate to call or come back in. Any questions?"

"That ain't likely, Doc. I got no money for medical stuff. I'll heal up just fine on my own. You know what I mean?"

The doctor nodded his head. "I understand, but be sure to call anyway if you have any further problems." He turned and walked away without waiting for an answer.

Casey slid off the gurney and winced as he put weight on the leg. He stood for a minute, getting used to the pain, then, "Okay. Let's get out of here so I can get home and start getting' better. I can't take a lot of time off for this. I wouldn't have this problem if you had been any good at ropin'."

There it was, just what Jess had been thinking. She had blamed herself, and now he had confirmed it for her. A nurse rushed up to them. "You have to wait here. I'll get a wheelchair for you."

"I don't need no fuckin' wheelchair."

"Hospital rules, sir. I have to put you in a wheelchair to get you to the door."

Casey slumped back against the gurney. "Okay then. Hurry up. I can't wait to get out of here,"

Jess said nothing as they all rode down in the elevator. When they got to the lobby, she turned to him. "You wait here. I'll get the truck."

A few minutes later Jess pulled up in front of the entrance and let the truck idle while she got out and helped Casey get in. "Directions?"

"Yeah, that's right. You never been to my place, have you? Okay. Let's go. I'll tell you where to make the turns."

For twenty minutes they zig-zagged through the back streets of Kingman until she pulled up in front of a fifty's-modern style, one-story apartment complex, its yellowish brick exterior tagged with gang graffiti. Jess pulled into a parking place, shut the engine off, and came around to help Casey get out. She let him lean on her as they made their way to the door. Once inside, she felt a little shocked at the general disaster he seemed to be living in. Bottles, some partly full, littered every horizontal surface, beer mostly but with an occasional whiskey bottle, too. The smell of the place overwhelmed her-- stale cigarette smoke, cooking odors that reeked of onions and rancid grease. She helped him down a hall with three closed doors and one open one which turned out to be his room. She helped him into his room and supported him while he sat down on the edge of his bed. It surprised her how neat and clean his room was given the state of the main living area.

"You have roommates here?"

"Yeah, two of them. Sorry about the mess. They ain't the neatest boys in the world."

She nodded her head. "Yeah, I can see that."

"I guess you can go now unless you want to get me undressed and ready for bed." Half joking but with a serious undertone.

"No, I think you can handle that yourself. If you need anything, you can give me a call." She turned and walked to the door, then turned back to him. "Casey, sorry about his." She didn't wait for a response and turned and made her way back out to her truck. Once inside, she locked the doors. It was fully dark now, and the streets around here had started to come alive with groups standing on the corners, loud music pumping from a low-rider Chevy down the street.

She pulled away from the curb and started the ride home. The night stretched clear and starlit before her, and I-40 held very little traffic. She made good time, and when she rolled into the yard, the clock in the dash read 10:00. Blue came running to meet her barking his greeting and then jumping up on her as she got out of the truck.

"Hey, boy. Have you been taking care of things for me around here? Let's get you something to eat."
She turned the lights on in the kitchen and filled Blue's bowl with the dry food from the forty-pound bag under the sink. She looked around the kitchen thinking she might cook something for herself, but then decided she wasn't hungry. She had been worried about the cattle since they left and decided she should take some hay out to them.

A half-hour in the barn loading the pickup and then fifteen minutes filling a water tank on a trailer that they used to fill tanks when the rains didn't come in time, and she was ready. She drove cross country slowly to the branding pen, the headlights first picking up the glow of eyes as she approached the pen then defining the cattle shapes as they stood staring at the approaching truck. She pulled parallel to the fence then made her way along the side of the pen throwing hay out over the fence, the cattle pushing and fighting to get to the feed.

The hay unloaded, she pulled up to the empty stock waterer and uncoiled the hose and started to fill it, the water splashing noisily against the galvanized steel, then flowing more quietly as the water level rose. When she finished, she stood on the trailer and took in the endless sky, filled with stars. She never tired of looking at the night sky out here. Soon though, she felt the evening chill creep over her, and then the piercing, woman-screaming sound of the cougar split the silence. The goosebumps that crawled up her arms were from a combination of the night chill and the chill of the wild call. She shivered and jumped down from the trailer, climbed back into the truck, and headed back to the ranch.

She slept fitfully, and in the morning, rose before dawn, ate a quick breakfast, and rode out as the sun had just started to crack the horizon. She and Blue worked steadily through the morning and by noon, they had finished the branding and worked together to get the two-year-olds back the mile to the ranch. As she pushed the last of the herd through the gate and swung it shut, she felt a sense of pride. She dropped down off Mickey and called Blue to her.

"Blue, we did it, boy." She rubbed his ears, and he squirmed and wagged his tail. "You are such a good boy. I don't know what I would do without you."

She untacked Mickey and put him out with Faith. When she finished, she went in to make some lunch. She made a sandwich and gave Blue some of the hard salami she used for it. Afterward, she called the shipper and arranged for a pick up. As good as she had felt when she brought the herd in, she began to feel a little overwhelmed thinking about all that she had to do before next week. She had at least one more large herd to bring in and doing it by herself, even with Blue's help, would be very tough. She decided she would take the rest of the day off and go into Kingman and cash and deposit the checks she had gotten for the other shipments.

When she finished at the bank, she got into her truck again and just sat there for a while. Things had been moving so fast, she had hardly had enough time to process everything. She had just kept moving, doing what had to be done, one step at a time. She rested her hands on the steering wheel, then leaned her forehead against them, tears beginning to form. Suddenly, she heard a voice beside her.

"Jess? You all right? What are you doing here?"

She looked up, and her tear-stained face gave her away. Mike pulled into a parking place ahead of her, got out of his patrol car, and came back to talk with her. He opened her door. "Come and sit with me in my car, and tell me what's going on, Jess."

She hesitated for a moment then got out and followed him back to the patrol vehicle. He opened the passenger side door for her then got in the driver's seat. "So, what happened? What are the tears about?" He wanted to know everything at once.

Jess felt embarrassment overwhelming her. "No, I…There was an accident. Casey got pinned by a cow that was defending its calf. Hurt his leg, and I think it was partly my fault." The last part came out in a rush like the only way to get rid of the guilt was to put it right out there. She looked up at him now. "I think I did a stupid thing, and now I don't know how to make up for it."

"What are you talking about? Slow down. What stupid thing?"

"Yesterday I insisted on doing the roping while he worked on the ground. I think if I had been a better roper, I could have caught the cow in time to save him. Now he's laid up at least a week, and I really needed his help right now."

"Hey, hey, hey. Don't beat yourself up that way. It's a ranch. Stuff happens, and you can't always prevent it. You sure as hell, excuse me, don't have to feel guilty about it."

She nodded her head. "I really appreciate your support, Mike. Somehow, just talking with you makes me feel better."

He reached across the console and squeezed her hand. "You be careful with this guy. I can't say for sure he's a bad guy, but if he gives you any trouble, you call me, you hear? He smiled at her and gave her hand a reassuring squeeze.

Jess smiled back at him. "Thanks, Mike. I better go. I have a lot to do in the next couple of days." She opened her door.

"You take care of yourself, Jessica Oliver. I'll check in on you when I'm out that way."

She smiled and waved as she shut the door. The drive home carried with it a mixed bag of emotions. On the one hand, she still felt nervous about all she had to do, but on the other, she felt protected and cared for after talking with Mike. She felt grateful that she had him in her corner.

She stopped at Molly's to let her know what happened. The cars were gone from the yard when she got there, so she left a note about where Casey was and that she would be bringing his horse back later.

At the ranch, she saddled the blue roan then saddled Faith too. She would ride the roan over and Faith back. It was getting late and the wind had picked up. Tumbleweeds drifted across the trail as she rode. The roan was skittish and didn't want to cooperate at first, but Jess worked him as she rode, and he settled in and they loped for a mile with Faith trailing behind on a lead rope. They slowed to a steady walk as Jess made her way down through a rocky valley and into the yard at Cal and Molly's place. Molly stood out in the yard waving to her.

"Hey, you. What happened anyway? I got your note but didn't really understand it. I was going to call you, but then I saw that you were going to bring his horse back over."

Jess got down from the roan and, led the two horses up to Molly and gave her a long hug. When she stepped back, tears were running down her cheeks. Molly stepped forward and took the roan's lead rope from Jess and started toward the barn with him. "You tie up your horse, and come in and sit with me for a while. Cal won't be home for a couple of hours, yet and it looks to me like we need to have a little talk."

Jess nodded her head and walked Faith over to a spot of grass and ground tied her by dropping the lead in front of her. She knew Faith would stand there for hours. Jess had trained her that way. Useful, especially in Arizona where there wasn't always a convenient tree or bush to tie a horse to if you needed to get off and do something else. Jess headed out to the barn to help Molly.

Molly had the horse untacked and had already turned him out into the paddock. She had climbed up into the loft and now threw down some hay which Jess picked up and took out to the paddock. When they were finished, they walked up to the house. Molly put her arm around Jess's shoulders as they walked. "Looks like you had another rough day. Let's get a cup of coffee and talk about it."

Jess nodded her head. She couldn't get any words out yet. She couldn't understand why she was so emotional. Since Clint died, she had cried more than she had in her entire life before then, and she couldn't figure out why. It sure couldn't be because she had missed him. The emotions were so raw and just under the surface now, she didn't know how to deal with them. For the first time, she had to make all her own decisions, and they had come one after another and worn her down.

She sat at the kitchen table as Molly busied herself with pouring two big mugs of coffee and heating up a couple of cinnamon rolls in the microwave. She said nothing as she did this. Jess could feel that somehow Molly knew she needed a little time to pull herself together before she could talk about it. Molly sat down and they sipped their coffee for a while. They nibbled at the rolls until Jess looked up.

"I don't know where to start. I think I told you in the note that Casey had an accident in the branding pen this morning. What I didn't say was that I felt responsible for it. I'm both in need of his help and feeling guilty that I caused the problem for him."

Molly shook her head. "Oh, Jess. Don't be so hard on yourself. Stuff happens." Molly reached across the table and took Jess's hand. "We're here for you if you need anything. Just a phone call away. I can be there in five minutes. You remember that."

Jess smiled at her. It felt so much like what Mike had said earlier. If nothing else, she now felt she actually had friends, people who would be there for her if she needed it.

"Thanks, Molly. I can't tell you how much your friendship has meant to me. I'm going to pay Casey's board for him this week. I figure it is the least I can do since he doesn't have any money coming in right now."

"Oh, Jess. Forget about that. We can get by for a week or two without that money. You have enough on your plate right now without worrying about us too. You're something else, girl."

"No, I insist. I'm not going to let you bear any of the burden. Besides, if this horse training works out, I'll be selling most of my cattle, and I'll have plenty of money available while I get that business established. I just have to wait and see how it's going to go, but I'm really hoping that it will be a business that I can do on my own. I never was crazy about the cattle business. That was Clint's thing, and if there is any way for me to get out of it, I'm going to do that."

Molly shook her head. No need to pay us anything. I mean it. Your money is no good here."

"Then, I'll bring you some hay and grain this week so you aren't out anything there."

"You drive a hard bargain, little lady," Molly laughed. "Okay. If you are going to insist. That's fine."

Jess looked out the window and saw a shaft of low sunlight catching the side of the tool shed. "Well, it's about sunset. I'd better get on home. I have a lot to do tomorrow. I really feel better now."

"Probably the cinnamon rolls and coffee, but anytime, Jess." Jess laughed, stood up, helped clear the table, then walked to the door. Molly held the door open. "You take care of yourself now. Be careful riding home. It'll be dark before you get there."

Jess thought about all the late-night rides she had taken to get away from Clint and felt the relief this ride would be by comparison. She smiled at Molly.

"You don't know how many of these I took over the past six years. I frequently would ride out and sleep in the desert when Clint was on one of his drunken rampages. It kept me safe, and I got to like the night's, I don't know, softness is the word that comes to mind. There is something gentle and beautiful about moonlight, and whenever possible, I like to spend time outside at night."

"You sure made something good out of all the bad you dealt with. You're pretty remarkable, Jess Oliver. Glad I've gotten to know you."

"The feeling's mutual, my friend." Jess stepped into the stirrup and swung up onto Faith. "I'm going to be pretty busy for the next couple of days. I'll talk with you soon and let you know how it's going." She reined Faith around and headed into the growing darkness.

Chapter 20

Jess rose before dawn and fed the horses and cattle in their pens. The still air carried with it all the rich, earthy smells of animals. By the time she had finished breakfast, the sun had just begun to color the horizon. She took her coffee out onto the porch to enjoy the display. Streaks of red, gold, and a hint of purple pierced a thin layer of stratus clouds resting along the horizon. She never tired of this technicolor wonder that most days played out twice, at dawn and dusk. She felt the rhythm of nature in it and watched the seasons flow by marked by the positions of sunrise and sunset along the eastern and western horizons.

She tossed the last of her coffee out of her cup onto the ground, set the cup on the bench, and went to the barn to saddle Mickey. She thought back on yesterday and all that had gone on, both the good and the bad, and she smiled at the thought of the new friendships she had formed in just the short time since Clint had passed.

Her thoughts were interrupted by the sound of a pickup truck coming down the road then pulling into her drive. When it pulled up to the house, Jess realized it was Mike Contreras, a pleasant surprise.

She stood on the porch and watched him as he got out of his truck. He wore jeans, well-worn boots with a pair of handmade spurs with custom rowels, a snap-button western denim shirt, and a black

Stetson hat that had seen better days. He had a pair of well worn, leather chinks slung over his shoulder.

Jess smiled up at him. "What are you doing out so early in the morning?"

"Well, it appeared that you were short a hand when I talked with you yesterday, and today is my day off. I assume you have a spare horse around here?"

"Well, I do have that, but are you sure you want to do this? It's hard work and this is your day off."

"Apparently, you don't remember that I told you I grew up ranching. I still go home on vacation and work with my folks and younger brother who's taking over the ranch. I know exactly what I'm getting into here ma'am." He laughed.

"Well okay then." She smiled. "I sure can use the help, and experienced help is hard to find." She couldn't stop smiling.

"What's on the agenda today?"

"I have one last big gather to do, and then we bring them back here for branding, cutting, and sorting. You up for that?"

"You bet I am." He looked to her like he really was up for it and even enthusiastic about it. She felt like a weight had been lifted off her shoulders.

"Okay, let's get you saddled up. How is your roping?"

"Still have the skill. Maybe a little rusty, but I will get up to speed pretty quickly. Takes me a few throws to get it back when I work for my dad."

"That's good because I have just one roping horse. The other one is in training, so I would rather ride her. Meet Mickey. He's your ride today. His tack is right on the top rack there. I'll go get Faith and tack her up."

By 7:30, they were headed back into the hill country and starting to work the last quadrant on the ranch. They said little as they rode along, but a couple of times she caught Mike looking over at her. They found their first herd by eight but left them alone while they made a wider sweep to gather the other parts of the herd together. It was tough to find the herds in the mesquite and scrub oak, but when they came upon a bunch, Mike surprised her with how well he moved around the cattle, never too quickly, just a nice slow steady pace that made the cattle feel confident there was no threat.

They moved the herds steadily forward until they had gathered all of the bunches and had them headed back toward the ranch. Mike motioned for Jess to take the point position while he worked the dusty drag. No discussion. He just took the dirtier job. Jess marveled at what she saw in this guy, not like any man she had ever met before. It actually made her nervous for a man to be so thoughtful around her.

The herd numbered over forty head now as they made the final push to the stock pens at the ranch. This would finally be the last drive of the spring, and Jess had already started to drift off into thinking about telling Mike about her new job training the horses. As a result, she didn't see the Hereford bull that had worked its way to the front of the herd. The bull pawed at the ground, head lowered. Mike yelled to her to watch out, but as she turned, the bull charged her. Faith danced out of the way, but the bull wasn't finished. It turned and prepared to charge again. Suddenly, Mike rode in front of the bull, his rope circling overhead. He dropped a loop over the bull's horns, and Mickey dragged it away toward the back of the herd. The herd began to scatter, and Jess set out after the runaways. Mike loosened the rope, flipped it off the bull's horns, and drew the rope back to him as he joined Jess. Together they brought the herd back into a tight mass again.

They moved the cattle into the long chute that led to the pen. Jess rode ahead to open the gate. The bull trailed along at the back of the herd, and Mike kept moving him to the back whenever he tried to move into the herd. As the last of the herd moved through the gate, Mike cut the bull off and separated it from the herd. Mike slipped through the gate that Jess held open for him and left the bull outside bellowing loudly.

Mike rode up to Jess. "No need to have him in here to screw things up, I figured unless you are going to sell him."

"Thanks for cutting him off for me. Things looked a little bad for me there for a minute."

"Ah, no problem. Mickey did all the work. He's a keeper. Where did you get him?"

"We got him as a green three-year-old. I trained him. Yes, he is a keeper."

"You trained him? I'm impressed there, ma'am. I've ridden a lot of horses, and it's rare to find one so willing and responsive. You have a talent."

Jess laughed. "Funny you should say that. I never thought much about it. I've been working with horses most of my life and always thought I would like to make a living at it, but...."

He grinned at her. "But what?"

"My dad would never approve. When I married Clint, my dad disowned me. He said he never wanted to see me again. It would have been the same if I had become a horse trainer as far as he was concerned. But that's all in the distant past now. As it turns out, some horse breeder, a guy by the name of Logan Miller, heard about me and wants me to train a couple of his horses. You ever hear of him?"

"Sure. Everybody around here knows Miller. He produces some really good horses. That's really great, Jess. If these two horses here are an example of your training, you are going to do great."

"I didn't want to actually talk about it yet. I don't want to jinx it or anything. I'd appreciate it if you didn't say anything to anybody. I want to see how it goes."

He made a motion like a key locking his lips. "Will you stay in the cattle business too, or are you just going to concentrate on the horses?"

"I haven't really decided on that yet. Too soon until I see how I'm doing. I'll always have to keep a few head for the training. He expects me to train ropers and cutting horses so…"

Mike laughed. "So, you will need enough cattle to rope and cut."

"Exactly. I really would like to get out of the cattle business though. I can't say I ever liked it. There is a brutal quality to it that I always had trouble with. No offense. I know you were a cattle rancher."

"None taken. I understand what you mean. It definitely isn't for everybody. I hope the horse training works out for you. Seems like a perfect fit to me."

Jess shrugged her shoulders, "I don't know. I sure hope so. Thanks for the encouragement, Mike. I'm feeling pretty nervous about the whole thing. So many changes in my life, and so sudden. I feel like half the time I'm lost."

"Hang in there, Jess. I've learned that things have a way of sorting themselves out, and if you pay attention to the feelings in your heart, you'll make the right choices." He rode up next to her, wrapped his arm around her shoulders, and gave her a slight hug.

The rest of the morning they worked together with Mike doing the roping, and Jess doing all of the groundwork. By noon, they were nearly half done, and Jess called a halt to things so that they could go in and have lunch. She managed to whip up a hearty ranch lunch of potatoes, eggs, and a steak apiece along with coffee. When they finished, he picked up the plates and made her sit while he washed and dried them, then cleaned and wiped out the cast iron fry pan. As Jess sat there watching him, she noticed the economy of motion that he used to do each task. He had an athletic grace to him that she had noticed before and that made his everyday movements beautiful. She couldn't hold her question any longer. "Did you play a sport?"

He turned, smiled, and threw the dishtowel over his shoulder. "Why do you ask?"

She suddenly felt embarrassed. "Uh, I don't know. Just something about you, I guess. A way of moving. Oh, I don't know. It's not important, really. Just curious, I guess."

He laughed, a full, unchecked laugh that seemed to fill the little kitchen, echo off the stone walls.

Jess felt the warmth creeping up her face. "Are you laughing at me?"

He stopped, although he still smiled. "No, no, not at all. I just thought it was funny the way you got embarrassed asking something about me. You don't ever have to feel embarrassed about asking anything about me. From the little I know about you, you should have asked a lot more about your husband before you married him." He turned back to the sink now and picked up the last plate to dry. It appeared to be his turn to be embarrassed.

"I'm sorry. I shouldn't have said that. Way too judgmental and personal. I apologize, Jess."

Jess felt the tears forming again, running down her cheeks. When Mike turned away from the sink and saw her crying, he sat down across the table from Jess and took her hands in his.

"I say what's on my mind sometimes without really thinking. I didn't mean to hurt you."

"No, that's not it at all. You're right. I sure should have asked more. I was so naïve. I thought what I was feeling right then was love. I know now that it was nothing like that." She stopped. "I can't believe I'm telling you this. I hardly know you either." She paused again and then said, "It's just that I somehow feel comfortable talking with you. You have a way of making me feel safe. I'm not used to that. I've had very few friends that have made me feel that way. My dad kind of taught me to always be guarded, and I've let my guard down with Molly and now with you. It's a little overwhelming. Do you understand?"

"I do, but I'm not sure about the tears. Would you rather not talk about what you're feeling? I don't want to intrude on your privacy."

"No, that's not it at all. When you said that, I just realized that with Casey, I'm doing the same thing, letting a man into my life and not really knowing anything about him. I feel like I haven't really learned a thing."

Mike stood up, went to the sink again, wiping at the sink with the washcloth. "All right. Let's change the subject. I'll tell you my sports story. Wasn't that the original question?"

Jess, wiped away the tears with the back of her hand and smiled at his back. "Yes, it was. Tell me a little about yourself, Officer Contreras."

He laughed that room-filling laugh again. "Not much to tell really. Yes, I played both football and basketball in high school, but my love was really basketball. Pretty good at it too. I had a full ride to the University of Arizona, but in the summer before I was to start my freshman year, an accident on the ranch tore up my left knee pretty bad. Bad enough that I wouldn't be playing college ball, so I decided to get a law enforcement degree. I attended the Academy. Short athletic career, but I still stay in shape. Have to in this job. You never know when you're going to have a foot chase or have to fight a bad guy. I also study Hapkido, a martial art used to control your opponent." He paused and looked down at her. "So, yeah, I guess I am still an athlete in a way. I don't know if that mindset ever leaves you once you have seriously played a sport."

"Thanks for that, Mike. I think I just needed to know some personal thing about you. I've shared more than I probably should have with you, and I needed to know more about you, to know who you are."

"There's plenty for us to share I'm sure, Jess. Like I said, you can ask me anything you want. I don't want to hide anything from you."

Jess smiled at him, stood up, and started for the door. "Enough of the emotional stuff. Time to get back to work. We're burnin' daylight." She took his Stetson off the rack and tossed it at him like a Frisbee.

"Hey, you! Take it easy on that hat. Took me years to get it in that shape. He fake chased her out the door. She ran, laughing, to the barn.

They worked steadily through the afternoon with more laughter than Jess remembered ever sharing with anyone. They had just finished up and were heading up to the house when a pickup pulled into the yard. Casey sat in the passenger seat, and two bearded men, one the driver and the other seated in the middle seat, were with him. Blue ran barking to meet them.

Jess felt the familiar chill run along her spine, but she called Blue to her and waved to Casey.

Mike looked at her. "What are they doing here?"

She shook her head. "Darned if I know. He's supposed to be resting that leg to get it healed up again."

Casey opened the door and stepped out on one leg, wobbling precariously. He started to limp toward Jess. "One day and you already replaced me, eh? Didn't think I was that disposable." The words slurred; his face flushed. He stopped a few feet away and stood there trying to keep his balance.

Jess looked over at Mike, his face a mask. One of the beards, the driver, climbed out of the truck. stood to the side watching and smoking a roll-your-own cigarette.

"What the fuck, Jess? You had to go hire some cowboy to do the little bit you had left to do? You might not be the best roper, but you sure as hell could've handled that little bit. Or better yet, you could've waited for me to heal up. Wouldn't have killed you."

There it was again, the roper comment. The guilt and shame of it poured over her like a pitcher of cold water. She turned away, shook her head.

"I didn't hire anybody. Mike just showed up to help out. Why would it matter to you anyway?" She turned away before he could answer and headed toward the house. Over her shoulder, "What exactly are you doing here anyway? Aren't you supposed to be resting?

"Well, me and the boys, Bear here and Hank over there, we picked up somethin' to drink and a bucket of wings and thought you might want to party with us."

Jess didn't even know how to respond to that. "You're drunk, Casey. You and your friends need to go back where you came from."

Casey started to make a move toward her, and Mike stepped in front of him. The beard from the truck stepped quickly up beside Casey.

"You heard what she said. Get back in your truck and get out of here."

"Who the fuck you think you are? You can't tell me what to do, cowboy." Casey, swayed back and forth as he talked.

"You don't want to know who I am. Get back in the truck, or I'll help you if that's the way you want it."

The beard moved away from Casey, stepped in chest to chest with Mike now. He smelled of whiskey, but he was big and he reached for Mike's shirt. As he gripped it, Mike covered the beard's hand with his, pinning it in place, stepped back and to the side locking the man's elbow and putting him on the ground.

Casey turned back to the truck. "Let him go. We're gettin' out of here. We got better things to do than party with this bitch."

Mike let loose of the beard who was struggling to get up and grabbed the back of Casey's collar and half pushed, half carried him to the truck. Casey struggled and protested, but in his drunken state, his struggles were ineffective, and Mike threw him up against the door of the pickup.

"Now, you and your friends get out of here, and don't come back, you hear? Any time you come on this property again, it will be trespassing, and you'll go to jail for it. Do I make myself clear enough for you?"

"What are you talkin' about? I work here. Ask Jess if she wants me here or not. This ain't none of your business. Jess, tell him."

Jess stood tensely in the middle of the yard where she'd stood through all of it. "Mike, it's alright. Let him go. Casey, I'll settle up with you when you get better. You should go now though."

Mike stepped back. "You heard the lady. Get in the truck and get out of here."

The look on Casey's face said everything, but he got into the truck. "You and me ain't done with this, you hear? I'll see you again, and when I do, it'll just be me and you. You got that?"

"Looking forward to it."

The driver stumbled back to the truck and got in. The truck started up. The driver put it in reverse, floored it and spun it around then roared out of the drive onto the road.

Jess stood there crying again. She thought how much she hated that she cried all the time, but she felt it had been a relief too. Not everything felt pent up inside her like she suspected it had been for so long.

Mike looked at her, tears running down her face then reached out a tentative hand and wiped a tear from her cheek. "Hey, hey, hey. What's this all about? I hope I didn't upset you."

"No, that's not it. I just…" She paused, turned away and looked off across the open fields to the hills beyond. "The ugliness of it, the threats, they all bring back memories I would like to leave behind. I don't want to be that person in that situation anymore. It seems like guys like Casey are always in my life. I have to find a way to change that."

Mike stepped closer, stood in front of her. "Look at me, Jess. You're a strong, smart woman. You've been under a man's thumb too long. You should be able to see it coming now. You know the signs of an abusive guy. Don't let it go anywhere when it shows up. You don't need a guy in your life. You're plenty capable of doing for yourself. The next time you want to have a guy in your life, let it be on your terms, not his."

Jess, head down, nodded. "I'm trying, Mike. I really am. Just not really good at it yet."

"Okay. You take care of yourself, Jess Oliver. I can tell you that guy is trouble, but until you see it for yourself, there's nothing I can do about it. I've seen his type too many times before. I just don't want to hear that he gave you a problem again. Not sure I would be as gentle next time, whether he's drunk or not." He stepped back and took off his Stetson, wiped the sweat off his forehead with his shirtsleeve, and then put the hat back on. "I guess maybe I better go. I'm sure you want to get cleaned up and get some supper. I'll talk with you soon. Let me know if there is anything else I can do for you, you hear?"

Jess smiled at him. "I can't thank you enough for all you did today, Mike. It would have taken me three or four days to get all that done working by myself. I wish you'd stay for supper. I could put something together."

"No, you've had enough to do today. Some other time." He turned and went to his truck and got in. Jess stayed where he'd left her, eyes downcast until she heard the truck start up. She absently stroked Blue's head. As the truck started to pull away, she looked up, and raising her hand, gave a feeble wave. Mike waved back, and then he was gone.

Chapter 21

Jess again brought Blue into her room and put the Glock on the nightstand before she went to bed. Nevertheless, she felt nervous and anxious and slept fitfully, tossing and turning and sitting up for long periods of time. She was up at dawn. She washed up, made a pot of coffee, took her phone, and walked out onto the porch to call the shipper.

"Good morning. Pete here. What can I do for you?"

"Hi, Pete. This is Jess Oliver. I have one more load of steers for you. Do you have any openings when you could pick them up? There's about thirty of them."

"Well, little lady, you are in luck. I had a cancellation today, and if you want, I could be there in about an hour. Would that work for you?"

"Perfect. Thanks, Pete. See you then." Jess disconnected and turned back toward the house.

She ate breakfast and then sat for a few minutes on the old kitchen chair on her porch and drank another cup of coffee. The March air, still a little cool from the night, smelled of the desert flowers that had begun to bloom and brighten the sepia landscape. A rare morning mist still hung over the low areas. She stood up and looked down at Blue sleeping. His feet were twitching like he was chasing something. She smiled. "Sweet dreams, Blue. I'll whistle for you when I need you."

She stepped quietly off the porch and headed out to the barn. She climbed up into the loft and threw down hay for the cattle and horses, then climbed back down and spread it around the cattle pen. She put another half bale in the paddock for the horses. One foot in front of the other. She had heard that expression all her life. Right now, it would be her mantra. The busier she kept herself, the less likely she would be to have to confront the confusion and fear that seemed to underly everything right now.

She grained, groomed, and saddled Faith, and as she was finishing, she heard the shipper's truck pulling into the yard. She went to the barn door and waved to Pete as he started to back up to the loading chute. "Be right out." Blue came running from the house as she tightened Faith's girth one more time and climbed up into the saddle.

The loading went quickly and Faith and Blue worked in tandem to get the steers into the chute and up the ramp. Jess felt a quiet satisfaction as the animals she had trained worked without a hint of direction from her. As the last steer loaded into the truck, she got off of Faith and called Blue to her, rubbed his ears and gave him a light hug. She rubbed Faith's neck and withers, and Faith laid her head on Jess's shoulder. Pete slammed and latched the loading door.

"Well, that's it for you then? This all of them this spring?"

"Yep." Jess smiled now, wanted to laugh out loud actually. "I wanted to thank you, Pete, for putting in a word for me with Logan Miller. I really appreciate it. I hope I can do the job he wants done."

"Oh, I've seen you with your animals. You don't have any worries there. Your horses are as good as any I've seen. You just do the same with his, and I'm sure you will be more than fine."

Jess laughed, turned Faith back toward the barn. "We'll see about that, I guess. Take care, Pete. If this goes well, I'll be selling off most of my herd probably, so I might see you again later this summer."

"Good luck, Jess. I'm sure I'll be getting updates from Logan along the way." With that, he climbed up into the truck cab, started the engine, and drove out of the yard. Faith never flinched at the roar of the big diesel, and Jess felt a sense of pride in that. "Good girl, Faith." She stroked her horse's neck as she walked her to the barn.

By ten she was headed toward Kingman, first stopping at Molly's on the way. Molly was feeling ill, a spring cold, and too miserable to talk. As Jess drove out of their yard, she felt a hole in her day. She couldn't believe how quickly she had come to depend on Molly, to value her friendship. Growing up, most of the girls she knew didn't understand her, and the barn girls tended to be stuck up and standoffish, so she had learned to go it on her own, never really confiding in anyone. She didn't trust easily and wondered why she had trusted Clint so quickly back six years ago. She put it down to her inexperience with men, but deep down she suspected something more had attracted her to him. Maybe her mother was right. Maybe she did need to see a therapist to help her work through this. It just went so against her whole experience to drag someone else into her life to help her figure it out. She always felt she should do that herself.

Right now, though, she didn't want to think about it. She had shopping to do, and then when she got back to the ranch, she wanted to set up a round pen. The horses would be there in three days, and she needed both space to work with them and a plan of how she wanted to go about it. She had always formulated a plan when she got to know the horse. Like people, each horse was different. Each one required a different approach. The problem now became getting this done efficiently and with more than one horse at a time. She didn't know how that would work with her individualized approach. She shook her head. Second-guessing herself. That was a weakness. She needed to trust what she had always done that had worked so well.

She turned into the Safeway on Stockton Hill Road. She found a space at the outer edge of the lot and squeezed the truck in. She had been concentrating so hard on getting the truck into the tight space that she hadn't noticed the truck that had pulled up in front of her until she turned off the engine. The truck was the one that had been in her yard yesterday, and behind the wheel sat the beard. He got out and, Jess locked her door.

He stood at her window and knocked. She lowered it an inch so she could hear him. "You listen to me, you little slut. You tell your cholo boyfriend that I'll be looking for him. Nobody pushes me around that way. You hear me? He needs to watch his back." He punched her door and turned and got into his truck and left.

Jess sat in her truck shaking for a few minutes and then picked up her phone and called Mike. The call went to voicemail, and at first, she didn't know whether to leave a message or not. The call disconnected. She decided that it was too important to not at least give him a heads up. She didn't know how serious the threat might be, but, she decided, Mike should at least be aware of it.

She called again. This time, Mike answered. "Jess? What's up?"

"Oh, Mike. I don't know how important this is, but ..." She hesitated.

"What? Has something happened out at the ranch?"

"No, right here in Kingman, actually. You know that guy that was driving that truck yesterday, the bearded one? Well, he just stopped me in the Safeway parking lot and threatened to get you. He seemed pretty serious. Said you should watch your back."

"Jess, I get that all the time in my job. They are all big talkers when you aren't around. Never amounts to anything. I appreciate you letting me know though. Just don't be worried about it, okay?"

"I am worried about it. I feel like I got you in the middle of my problems. I feel bad about that. You were so nice to help me, and now these guys want to get you. I feel like it's my fault."

"Okay. That's enough. You don't need to worry about me, and if it was anybody's fault, it was mine. I could have let it go and let them leave. It just bothered me how crude they were there in front of you. I wasn't raised that way. Listen, I have to get back to work, but you take care of yourself, you hear? That crew is pretty worthless in my estimation, and if anything isn't right, you let me know right away. I'll talk with you soon." And then he was gone.

The shopping took longer than she expected. The aisles in the store were jammed. When she finished, she realized that she would have a tough time getting anything done on the round pen she intended to build. Instead, on the way back, she stopped at a little lunch shop and picked up some chicken noodle soup and a loaf of French bread to go.

When she pulled into Molly's drive, Molly waved to her from the front porch. "Just sitting here in the sun, trying to bake this cold out of me. I hate these Spring colds almost more than the winter ones."

"I have something here to fix you right up." Jess picked up the bag from the seat next to her and carried it to the porch.

"Don't get too close. I don't want you catching this." Molly held a tissue up to her face to cover her mouth and nose.

"Okay. I'll just leave it here on the porch. You should try some while it is still hot though. It's chicken noodle soup with some bread to dunk in it. Always helps me when I have a cold. I'm sorry you're sick, my friend. Do you want to talk, or should I just leave you be?"

"No. I'll go get a couple of bowls and spoons. I want to hear how it is going with you and that deputy."

"Just the one bowl for you. I already had lunch. I'll stay around for a little while, but I don't want you getting too tired. And how do you know anything about the deputy?"

"Oh, I have my sources." She winked at Jess and turned to go into the house.

While Molly ate, Jess filled her in on what had been happening over the past couple of days. When she told her about Mike helping her, Molly gave her a sly look.

"I would say you have yourself a suitor. What's he look like?"

"It's not like that. I think he just feels sorry for me, that's all." She paused, looked off toward her ranch, and then, smiled. "He's really good looking. Dark hair and eyes, tall with a nice build." Jess stopped, embarrassed.

"So, you have been noticing more than him just being a nice guy helping out a woman in distress then?" She laughed. "I think you kind of like him back."

Jess stood up now. "I think it's time for me to go. I have some things that need to go in the refrigerator. And no, I don't like, like him. He's just a friend. I don't want any complications in my life right now, and that definitely would be a complication."

"Okay, okay. I get it, but he sounds like a keeper to me."

"Yeah, I think I thought that about Clint too. I don't want that again. What I need right now though is a way to get a round pen built before I get those horses in. I'm going to have a busy couple of days and I don't know if that even will be enough time. Plus, I need to pick up the materials tomorrow. Seems a bit overwhelming right now, but I'll just keep plugging away at it. Thanks for being an ear for me, Molly. I hope you feel better soon. Eat up that soup and get healthy!"

By the time Jess got home, it was after two, and she hadn't accomplished much of anything she had set out to do. She put away the groceries and sat down at the kitchen table to make a plan for the next couple of days, but somehow, sitting there brought back sharp memories of her days with Clint sitting at this same table. She remembered clearly an argument they had had the morning that he died. She had been concentrating on getting breakfast ready and had been lost in her own thoughts. She didn't hear Clint ask her a question.

"Not goin' to answer me? What are you, deaf?"

Jess turned around. "What? Did you ask me something?"

Clint came around the table and stood close to her. "Don't you sass me, little missy. I don't take that shit from nobody, you hear, and especially not some skinny-ass bitch like you."

Jess, had slid away from him. "Fix your own breakfast if you're going to talk to me like that. You should be able to handle that."

She walked quickly out the door and headed for the barn. When she got there, she had to stop and sit on a bale of hay so she could stop shaking. It was the last thing she clearly remembered about that day now. The death, all the time with the police, all that seemed faintly unreal. What now was most real was Clint's quick anger, the bitter insults. She was all too familiar with that. In a way she had felt comfortable with it. At least then she knew what she was dealing with. After all, hadn't she experienced much of that with her dad even before Clint. What she felt now, though, as she sat at the kitchen table could only be described as a nagging fear that she had let it start all over again with Casey.

She stood up, went into her bedroom. She lifted the corner of her mattress. There on the box springs lay the Glock. She picked it up and put it in its holster and then fastened the holster behind her. At least now she didn't feel helpless. If things went further with

Casey, she didn't need to take the beatings she had endured so many times before. A small sense of empowerment, but also a sadness settled over her. It had come to this once again, her pitted against some controlling man, someone who made her feel less than him. She shook her head and then decided she had too much to do to worry about it now. She needed to at least lay out the round pen so she could figure out what materials she would need. She went back through the living room and out the front door.

Outside, she once again felt that freedom that she had found so elusive most of her life. The sun, low on the horizon now, had taken the heat of the day with it. The cool evening breeze was beginning to wash over the ranch. It brushed her face, played with her hair. She headed out behind the barn to the level area she had chosen for the round pen. She didn't have any kind of measuring device, but she knew she wanted it to be about sixty feet in diameter. She had heard that the distance from your nose to your extended arm was approximately three feet. She took the used baling twine that she had saved and started to measure out enough for thirty feet of it. She took a shovel and a stake she had found in the barn and used the shovel to drive the stake in the middle of the area for the round pen. Then she took another piece of wood and sharpened a point on it. She attached the twine loosely to the two stakes and then drew a circle in the dirt.

When she finished the circle, she paced off and marked where the poles would go. They would be roughly eight feet apart. When she finished, she counted up the number she would need to buy tomorrow. She figured four boards between each post to build the fence and memorized the quantities. The biggest part of the job would be hand digging a large number of post holes in the hard desert soil. She couldn't see how she could finish it any sooner than a week. That would mean she would have to approach the initial training differently than she would like. She knew she could do it. After all, she had done it with Faith and Mickey, and they had come out fine. She had just thought it would be easier with the round pen for her to establish dominance, an important part of the training.

Little she could do about it now though. She would get the poles tomorrow and get started. She would just plug away at it until she had it finished. Right now, she didn't want to go back into the house. She decided to do what she had done so many times before and saddled Faith and rode out into the coming darkness. The night sky seemed huge, brilliant, with stars filling every inch from horizon to horizon. The only sounds were the occasional yap of a coyote, answered by another and then followed with howling that seemed to fill the air all around her. She loved that sound. It spoke to her of wildness in a world that had tried to tame it. Coyotes were survivors. The native Americans had spirit animals. She pictured the coyote as hers, a survivor in a harsh world. It gave her a sense of connection that felt right.

At the top of a hill, she pulled up and sat looking at the landscape below. Barrel cactus, prickly pear and jumping cholla, sagebrush, and bare rock covered much of it, a forbidding landscape for sure. She often wondered how the cattle managed to fatten at all in this country, but with the few sections of bunch grass and wheatgrass, and chaparral, they did. The cattle found what they needed.

The moon had risen, full and bright along the horizon now, so much of what she saw before her rose in silhouette from the desert floor. Suddenly, she saw a movement on a distant hilltop and then, directly against the backdrop of the rising moon, the shape of the cougar as it glided along the ridge. The sight of it gave her a thrill. She knew it should make her fearful both for her cattle and herself, but somehow the big cat's appearance was an affirmation of the wildness she felt when she rode out here, a wild freedom she had begun to really feel now in her own heart. As she turned Faith back toward the barn, she realized just how connected she was to this place and the creatures that inhabited it.

Chapter 22

In the morning, there was no wind, and the sun was already heating up her land as Jess rose and began to make breakfast with Blue by her side. She wanted to go into town for a while, to pick up at least all of the poles. The fence boards might have to wait. She could pick those up tomorrow if need be. She ate and hurried out to feed the horses. When she finished, she headed back to the house, washed up, brushed her hair, and put on a clean shirt.

As she was getting into the truck, her phone rang. Mike's number popped up on the screen. "Hello?"

"Hi, Jess. I just wanted to check-in and see how you were doing. Everything okay?"

"Good as can be expected, I guess. A little sore from all my time in the saddle, I think." She laughed.

"What are you up to today?"

"Well, as a matter of fact, I'm headed your way. I'm coming into Kingman to get some posts for the round pen I'm building."

"Round pen? That sounds like a lot of digging. You have some kind of power equipment for that?"

"Nope. Just muscle power is all. I figure it's going to take me a while."

"Listen then, I'm going to take tomorrow off, and Jason has a tractor with an auger. Why don't you get your materials together today, and I'll get him out there tomorrow? We'll get it all put up in one day. How's that sound?"

"Oh, Mike. That sounds wonderful, but I can't ask you to do that. You can't take time off for this, and I don't know what I can pay you and Jason. No, that's just too much."

"Forget it. I have a massive amount of vacation time built up. Tomorrow is Jason's day off, and he owes me a favor anyway. Besides, you're not paying me anything. This is a gift from me to you. I just want to see you get off on the right foot with your new business. Just plan on it. No use in you doing all that by hand when we can bring in machinery and get it all done in a day for you. You take care, and I'll see you tomorrow."

The phone went dead and Jessica sat for a minute holding it in her hand, staring off at the hills in the distance. Mike Contreras. Who did this kind of thing? There had to be something he wanted. Nobody had ever been this considerate and helpful for her before without wanting something in return. She put the phone in her shirt pocket and called Blue. He hopped into the truck and sat beside her. She started the truck, pulled out onto the road, and headed to I-40.

She had already decided that the best place to get fence posts would be the TSC store in Kingman, a general, farm and ranch supply store with a variety of fencing materials. She planned to buy the posts first, take that load home and then go to pick up the rough-cut lumber she would need for the fencing. The problem was that the only rough-cut lumber supplier was located in Flagstaff, more than an hour and a half away from the ranch. If she hurried, she figured she could make it there and back before dark, but it meant that she wouldn't be able to do any other prep work. Nothing she could do about that, she figured, as she pulled into the lot at the TSC.

Within a half-hour she had paid for and loaded the twenty-four posts she needed. It was a big load for the pickup, and she decided she would have to haul the horse trailer over to Flagstaff for the lumber because she would never be able to fit all of it in the truck. She thought about that all the way home and was in fact thinking about how she was going to hook up the gooseneck trailer when she pulled into the yard. There in the drive, in front of the house, sat the pickup from the other day. She saw no one as she pulled up, but when she shut the engine off, Blue started to growl. She heard loud laughter coming from inside the house.

"You sonofabitch, you. You owe me, man."

"The fuck I do. I bought this here bottle, didn't I? You hit the jackpot here, my man." More laughter.

Jess sat in the truck not knowing what to do. She didn't really want to go in and confront the situation. Every nerve in her body felt like it was on edge. She decided to avoid it as long as she could, started the truck again, and drove back behind the barn to unload the poles.

The job took her no more than fifteen minutes, but in that time, she calmed down enough that she felt she could deal with the problem in her house. Her house. She needed to remember that. Casey had been warned yesterday about coming back out here and not only that, he had brought his friends, and they were in her house.

Her house. She had to deal with it now. She drove the truck over to the gooseneck, stock trailer and proceeded to hook it up to the truck. When she was finished, she pulled around to the house.

Before she could change her mind, she got out of the truck, told Blue to stay, and went up to the front door, pulled it open, and looked at the group sitting at the table. The two beards were there as well as a tall, skinny newcomer. Casey sat at the head of the table as if holding court, his bad leg propped up on a spare chair. All the heads turned toward her as she came in. The first beard grinned at her. "Well, look who's here to join the party. Come on over and sit down. Hey, Bear. There anything left in that bottle? I think the little lady needs a drink."

Jess shook her head. "Casey, can you come outside for a minute?"

"Aww, you're goin' to make me get up just when I was gettin' comfortable?"

She beckoned to him and then stepped outside letting the door shut behind her. Inside she could hear him push a chair away, and then, "Better calm down the boss lady." Laughter, then the thump, thump of his bad leg as he limped across the plank floor. The door opened and he maneuvered his body through the opening. The door swung shut behind him.

"What can I do for you?"

"You can get that bunch out of the house. I don't want them here, and I don't want them or you to come back. Is that clear?"

"Whoa now. What's got you all up in a lather? We just figured you might want to party with that Mexican boy gone. You savvy?"

"Sorry, Casey, but you need to get out now. Before I call the sheriff. What you are doing is breaking and entering. You could face some jail time if I have to do that. You savvy?"

She was shocked when that came out of her mouth. Her dad had made her fear talking back to him, and that had been reinforced with Clint, but here she had done just that to Casey. She saw the flash of anger race across Casey's face. Flushed with the liquor already, his face looked like it would explode.

"Don't threaten me, missy. You don't know who you're dealin' with." He turned, and as he did, he swung his leg in an arc and clipped her leg hard as he opened the door to go back into the house.

Jess winced. The blow had been more a statement than an injury, but the effect had been the same. She turned away and got back into her truck

Once again, she found herself shaking as she started the truck and pulled out of the yard. It felt like so many times before where she had felt helpless and vulnerable. She hated feeling that way and wondered if she could ever overcome it. She took out her phone and called Mike.

When he answered, she told him what had happened.

"You're not still there are you?"

"No, I'm headed up to Flagstaff to pick up the fence boards. Look, Mike, I don't want Casey to get in trouble for this. I just want him and his buddies out of the house. Could you get somebody to drive by and just check and see if they've gone? I would really appreciate it."

"You're sure you don't want me to arrest them? I mean, this is breaking and entering." "No, really, I just think I want it to end. If he goes to jail, I'm afraid it will go badly for me."

"Alright, I think you're making a mistake, but I'll have a deputy in the area check for you. We'll talk tomorrow though. I think this guy is dangerous.".

When Jess pulled back into her yard late that afternoon, the truck was gone. Casey and his friends weren't in the house, but the house was a mess. She got back into the truck and drove around behind the barn again to unload. By the time she had finished, the sun had already sunk below the horizon, and only a sliver of red showed like a wound in the western sky. Even though it had been a relatively easy day, she felt incredibly tired.

Jess ate supper in the absolute quiet that descended on the ranch at night. She went out, checked on the horses, then took Blue and climbed the hill behind the barn and sat on a sandstone boulder at the top looking down at her ranch and the hills in the distance as they faded to blue-gray in the twilight. Sometimes she wanted to just hold onto these moments, these peaceful moments that came in tiny doses. They came more often than not as a result of her connection with the natural world around her. She also realized that they often were when she could be totally alone. She thought about Mike and his kindness and thoughtfulness and wondered how he fitted into her life.

Right now, all she wanted to do revolved around getting her training sessions going and figuring out if that could be her core business. She thought how funny it was that she had gone from high school directly into a business she had known nothing about, and now, here again, she would be entering another business where she didn't know anything about the business aspects of it. Her love of horses drove this idea though. Deep in her heart, she felt that somehow, she could make a success of it. As the moon began to rise along the eastern horizon, she stood and stretched. The sky began to fill with a swirl of stars as the darkness became complete. It looked to her like a Van Gogh painting. The thought of that made her smile and she headed down the hill to the house.

The next morning a breeze coiled around the corner of the house before dawn. Blue, who had climbed up to sleep with her in the middle of the night, took up half the bed. As she stirred, Blue licked her face. "Oh, buddy, you have some pretty bad breath. I think I need to get you some breath mints." She laughed and rolled out of bed. She felt like she needed a shower, but knew it would be futile to do that before the long hard day she had ahead of her. She settled for a quick wash up in the sink in the kitchen, then got breakfast together for herself and food for Blue.

Jess sat at the table for a while letting the morning settle around her. The excitement she felt was tempered by a certain nervousness. Here again, she had let a man she didn't really know, enter her life. She shook her head, stood up, and scraped the last of the eggs into a pile on her plate with the last piece of toast. She carried the plate over to Blue's food dish and pushed the last of the breakfast off her plate and into his bowl.

Now, her nervousness gave way to an intense excitement that almost overwhelmed her. Her dream of getting the round pen built was becoming a reality, and all she wanted to do was to get at it. She put the dishes in the sink to soak, went outside, and headed to the barn.

When she finished the morning chores, she came back into the house from the barn. Filled with nervous energy, she finished washing the dishes, and at eight, she heard the rattle of a truck and trailer on the road. She looked out to see a red F- 350 Ford pickup drive in pulling a flatbed trailer with a Kubota tractor on it. Mike followed behind in his pickup. She quickly dried her hands and went out to meet them. After they pulled in, Mike got out first.

"Good morning. I hope you got a good night's sleep last night. We have some work ahead of us." He smiled and beckoned to Jason to follow them. "You lead the way, Jess. Let's get these posts in the ground, eh?"

"I can hardly wait. I've been as excited as a little kid all night. Thank you so much for doing this, Mike. This is way above and beyond."

He smiled at her again as they walked around the barn. "It's nothing, Jess. I want to see you get a good start is all. Things have been tough enough for you. I have the time, so why not help you out? Working outdoors brings back my ranching days anyway."

"Well, my gain then." She laughed and punched him in the shoulder, then ran to the circle she had drawn in the dirt. He faked a chase then waved the truck in.

When Jason had the tractor unloaded, he got down and came over to them. Mike turned to look at Jason who had a big smirk on his face. "Jess, I understand you already met, Jason. Is that right?".

"Hey, Jess. Ready to get 'er done?" Jason took his hands out of his jeans pocket and reached a big, calloused hand out to her. She shook it and pointed to the marks she had put on the ground at every post location.

"These are where I want a post. I guess a couple feet deep ought to be about right unless you think they should go deeper?"

"Looks like you got ten-foot posts. I would go three feet deep and that will give you a nice high corral fence. What you plan to do with this?"

Jess turned to face him. "I'll use it in training horses. Because it's round, they can't get caught in a corner, so when I drive them, they never feel trapped, scared. That way they begin to respect me and eventually trust me. It's the first step in a long process of getting them finished and ready for whoever's going to ride them."

Jason nodded his head. "Sounds complicated to me, but sure sounds like you know what you're doing. It won't take me long to get these dug, then I'll help you and Mike to set the poles. That'll be all I'll have time for today, but it should get you guys well along anyway."

"That's more than enough. I really appreciate it, Jason. You let me know what I owe you when we are all done."

"Won't be a dime. I owe Mike for a lot of things he's done for me. Gotten me out of a few tough times. Anything I can do for him, I will." He turned and climbed up on the tractor and then started it up.

Drilling the post holes took less than an hour. Two more hours and the posts were all set in place and ready for the fencing and gate. Jess headed back to the house to get lunch ready. Mike came in right after. "What can I do to help, Jess?"

"I'm pretty well set. Why don't you get some plates out of that cupboard," she pointed "and I'll set everything out. Is Jason coming in?"

"He just finished putting the tractor on the trailer and was tying it down when I headed up here. He should be in shortly."

They chatted about the weather and local politics, and Jess chimed in when she could. She knew nothing about the news and thought to herself that she would have to start getting the local paper to catch up. When they were finished, Jason stood up and carried his plate to the sink. "I'd better get going, Jess. I promised my wife we would go to a movie this afternoon. I'm glad I got a chance to finally get to see you in your natural habitat." He laughed and Jess blushed. He went on. "Seriously, it's good to match up what you're really like to what this guy has said about you." He winked at Jess and started for the door.

Jess stopped him and gave him a hug. "I can't tell you how much I appreciate your help, Jason. It would've taken me days to get all those post holes dug. You and your wife will have to come out when it's all done and have supper." She paused and looked over at

Mike. "You, too, of course." Jason winked again, but this time at Mike.

"You hear that, buddy? Can't see why she would invite you, but there you have it, an actual invitation." He laughed as Mike threw his hat at him and waved as Jason went out the door.

"Okay, Jess. Let's get this thing finished. You ready?"

"Anytime you are."

The rest of the day they cut and nailed up the boards for the fencing with Jess doing the cutting. By late afternoon, they had fenced it, and built the gate, and were ready to hang it. When they got it in place, Jess stepped back and took it all in.

"It's really beautiful, Mike. It's exactly as I pictured it. Thank you so much. I don't know how I am ever going to repay you and Jason too."

"I already told you. There's no need to even thank me let alone repay me. It really was my pleasure. I just like seeing you smiling." He turned away, embarrassed. "I mean…" He hesitated. "I mean I just like helping you. If you need anything else, I'm always willing to help."

Jess hardly knew how to respond. "I appreciate that, Mike. You've already done so much for me. I couldn't ask you to do one more thing."

"Any time, Jess. Any time. I guess I'll pack up my tools and go now."

"Are you sure I can't make you some supper before you go?"

"Nope. I'm good. Couldn't eat another thing after that big lunch spread you put on."

"That was nothing. You'll have to come back for supper soon." She felt suddenly embarrassed. "I mean, it's the least I can do" She hesitated again. "I mean, and bring Jason and his wife too." She stopped now. It had all sounded so awkward, so personal.

"Ok. You take care of yourself, and stay in touch, will you?" Jess nodded and gave him a long hug. It felt good when he wrapped his arms around her and squeezed her back. The warmth of it brought back memories of the early days with Clint when everything had seemed special and romantic. When she let go, she stepped back and saw that he was staring at her.

"You're special, Jess Oliver. You know that? You're strong and brave, and talented. You're going to make good at whatever you take on. I'm glad I've had the chance to get to know you." He turned away, gathered up his tools, and took them to his truck.

Jessica stood there staring at his back as he loaded his tools. A warm feeling swept over her. Even when she had met Clint, she had never felt anything like this, and it confused and frightened her a little. She thought about how all her life she had sought after praise from her father, then Clint, and rarely found it from either of them. Here a man with no real connection to her praised her, thought she was special. She didn't know what to do with that. There had to be some kind of catch to it. She watched as he got into his truck, then waved to her as he pulled away. She hadn't moved. She stayed in place until his truck rounded a curve, and she lost sight of it. The road dust rose in a slow cloud over the fields, filtered the setting sun before it dispersed and disappeared.

Chapter 23

Jessica finished the feeding, and, as Blue lay sleeping in the hay nearby, she took time to brush each of the horses and take a rasp to their feet. By the time she had finished and headed up to the house, darkness already blanketed the desert. The skies had a magical quality that only the total darkness of the desert could expose. A giant, sweeping arc of stars and moonlight stretched from horizon to horizon. She stood for a moment looking up at the magical skyscape. Her mind drifted to the afternoon, and she smiled at the warm feeling of accomplishment and connection that she had felt ever since Mike left.

She shivered in the cool air and turned to head in. As she approached the house, Blue started to growl and the hair rose along his back. She reached behind her for the Glock, then remembered that she had left it under her mattress this morning since she would be spending the day with Mike. She opened the front door carefully and stepped inside. It took a moment for her eyes to adjust to the deeper darkness, and when they did, she saw Casey sitting in a chair facing the door. She turned on the overhead light. His face had a flushed glow to it and his eyes were sleepy and unfocused. An almost empty whiskey bottle lay on the floor beside him. He looked up, squinting into the light.

"Been waitin' for you. Out there most of the day with that cholo boyfriend of yours, eh? He a regular fixture here now?"

Jess didn't answer, but instead, called Blue with her, moved quickly across the room and into her bedroom, shutting the door behind her. She lifted the corner of the mattress and took the Glock and shoved it into her belt, pulling her shirt loose over it to hide it. Suddenly, the door opened behind her, and Casey stood leaning in the doorway. Blue growled and Jess grabbed hold of his collar.

Casey stepped into the room. "What do you think you're doing? You think you can just go in your bedroom and there's nothin' to talk about? I asked you a question. Is this cholo boy takin' my place?"

The old fear crept over her again. "Look, Casey. I had a lot to do before I get those horses. Mike is a friend. He offered to help me, and I couldn't turn it down." Bolder now, "And besides, we don't have anything more to do right now. I've paid you for all your time. I think our connection is over. I thought we had this discussion before. You can't just walk into my house like this. How did you get here anyway? I never heard you drive up."

"Sore leg or not, I can still ride. I came in the back way while you was out there fussin' with them horses of yours. And, I thought I meant more to you than just a hired hand. I thought we had a, I don't know, a connection."

He moved toward her now, and she tried to move away, but she felt the wall against her back as she did. "Casey, stay back. You don't want to make this any worse than it is already." Her hand under her shirt now, her fingers closed around the butt of the Glock.

He stopped. "What are you talkin' about? All I wanted to do was give you a little hug, just like old times."

"You've obviously been drinking again, so I'm going to cut you some slack, but you need to go now. Get on your horse, and go on back to Molly's. Nothing is going to happen here. You understand that?" Just then Jess's phone rang in her back pocket. She released her grip on the pistol and reached back and pulled out the phone, glanced at the caller ID. It was Molly. She clicked the receive button. "Look, I need to get this, so you turn around and get out of here, and don't come back. Am I clear?"

He moved toward her another step, and Jess tossed the phone onto the bed and pulled the Glock from under her shirt. Blue snarled and barked and tried to get free, but she had a firm grip on his collar. Casey stopped short. "Well, look at you, Miss Annie Oakley. What you plan to do with that pea shooter there? You goin' to shoot me?"

"Look, Casey. I don't want it to come to that, but I'm not going to let you just walk into my house and act like you own me. I've had enough of that in my life, so if I have to shoot you, I will." She felt her hand shaking now. She wasn't at all sure she could back up the words she had just said with action.

Casey hesitated a minute, eyed her as if assessing his chances, then took a step back. "Alright, alright, I get you. This ain't over though. You know that. I know you need me here. You can't handle this place by yourself. You should still keep that deal we talked about in mind, you know. We could make a real go of this spread, and I know you have feelin's for me that you just don't want to admit right now, but you'll come around." He backed out now, and

Jess heard the front door open and then close. She let go of Blue, and he dashed out into the living room barking.

Jess grabbed her phone and walked out of the bedroom. She sat down at the kitchen table and put the Glock on the table in front of her. She felt herself trembling again. How had she gotten herself into this situation? Another man in her life who wanted to control her. She didn't want to get Mike involved in this, but she had begun to feel that old fear that had driven her life for so long. She wanted to be done with that once and for all. First her dad, then Clint, and now Casey. She started to pick up the phone to call Mike but thought better of it. She would wait to see if she could handle it herself first. She decided to call Molly back instead, but when she picked up the phone to call her, she realized that Molly was still on the line.

"Hello?"

"Jess, are you okay?"

"I'm okay, but I've had my fill of Casey, that's for sure. Did you hear any of that?"

"I sure did. I was just calling to let you know that he had taken his horse and ridden off and to watch out for him."

"Obviously he was here when you called. He was drunk and got pretty aggressive. I actually had to pull my pistol on him to get him to leave." She hesitated a minute. She didn't know how much Molly had heard, how much more she wanted to tell her.

"Are you okay? You poor thing. I'm sorry. I guess we should never have had him help you. I feel like it's my fault."

"No, no, don't feel that way, Molly. I let him into my life. I needed help, and I hired him. He didn't seem like a bad guy at first, but I'm beginning to see another side of him now. I don't want him to think he can come around here anymore."

"Maybe you should talk to Mike. Maybe a little sheriff action would scare him off. I can talk to Casey too."

"No, definitely not. I don't want you to get involved. He has worked out as a boarder for you. I'll get this worked out. I may call Mike, but for now, I want to try to handle it myself. Calling in Mike might just make him madder, and I don't need that."

"Well, if you're sure… I don't want you taking any chances though. You call me if he shows up again. I will say something then."

Jess couldn't help but smile at that. Little Molly taking on Casey, quite a picture. She had no doubt that Molly was capable of it though.

"Thanks, Molly. I always appreciate you letting me bend your ear a bit. I better get something to eat. I'm about starved. Thanks again."

After she hung up, Jess made a sandwich and poured herself a glass of water from the pitcher in the refrigerator. She sat in the perfect quiet eating, thinking about the day. Despite the ending and Casey's drunken threats, she couldn't contain her excitement. Two days and she would begin her new adventure. She thought about all the ways she wanted to work with the horses, what she would need for the training, and then, her thoughts shifted to Mike and that warm feeling swept over her again. She smiled as she cleaned up the kitchen and put away the leftovers. Too early to be thinking about someone new, she told herself, but then the warmth of his embrace, his kindness filled her with as much excitement as her new business venture did.

When she was about to get ready for bed, it occurred to her that this would be the perfect time to take a shower. The water would still be warm from a long day in the sun and even though the night coolness had already started to settle in, the warmth before going to bed would feel wonderfully soothing after a long day of working hard.

Stars were her only light as she undressed on the little wooden platform outside the shower. She shivered as the night breeze touched her, washed over her. The shower felt exquisite as the warm water cascaded over her shoulders, rolled down her body. She washed her hair and felt the grime of the day rinsing away, felt the pure luxury of the act. When the water began to lose its warmth, she turned it off and in the still warm enclosure, dried herself off and wrapped the towel around her head. She pulled the curtain away and stepped back out onto the platform. As she had so many times before, she looked up at the dark hill looming over her, and there against the starlit sky, the dark form of the cougar stood silhouetted. Somehow, it didn't frighten her. In fact, she took a certain comfort in the creature's wildness as if it were merely a reflection of the wildness that had begun to awaken in herself. She dressed in her pajamas and gathered up her dirty clothes. When she turned to go into the house, the big cat disappeared over the ridge.

Jess rose early, still filled with the excitement of anticipation. She ate a quick breakfast and headed out to the barn. For now, she had nothing particular to do. Logan had called while she ate, and the horses would be delivered tomorrow. Today she could spend the day the way she wanted to, and what she wanted to do was take Faith for a ride. After feeding Mickey and Faith, she curried and brushed them both until their coats shone in the early morning sunlight. The simple pleasure of the act that she had done probably thousands of times, always surprised her. So many things she had to do repeatedly, had grown stale and boring for her, but this never had. Maybe the connection she felt kept it fresh, maybe an association with the best times in her life. She didn't know for sure, but it had been her meditation for years and had been the one slice of time during the Clint years that she could call her own, a time when she could feel safe.

When she finished, she tacked up Faith and led her out to the mounting block. Faith seemed distracted by something she sensed in the distance. She danced a little at the mounting block, something highly unusual for her. Jess settled her and made her stand after she mounted, stroked her neck, and whispered to her that it would be okay. Jess nudged her into a walk and they headed east into the sun that had fully crested the hills ahead. They passed below a massive rock formation to the South and passed from sunlight to shade, from warm to cool. The day felt cooler than the days before, and Jess relished the cool air. The sky, cloudless now, seemed to shimmer and radiate its own light. Jess pulled her Stetson lower to shade her eyes as she rode ahead. She started up the first of the series of hills that she would have to traverse to get to her destination, an intermittent spring-fed stream shaded by a willow grove. Halfway there she realized that she hadn't taken her pistol with her, and at first, thought about going back to get it, but she had already come too far. She put her heels to Faith's sides and pushed her into a long trot.

In a half-hour she crested the last hill before the brook. She stopped at the top and looked down into the valley below her. The willow grove appeared lush and cool from up there. She could see the trickle of water flashing in the sun as it danced over rocks and swept into the first bend. Jess nudged Faith forward and they headed down into the valley. They made their way through the desert landscape and between the boulders, tan and dry in the sun. Suddenly, they were among the willows and both of them felt the stark contrast. She slid off of Faith, took her down to the stream where her filly drank deeply, and then Jess led her up into the trees and tied her to a willow branch. A mossy strip along the stream bank called to her, and she went to it and laid on her belly and let her fingers dangle in the moving water, felt the stream cooling her, drawing the peaceful feeling back into her. She rolled over and lay on her back and watched the sky through the network of branches above her. This feeling, this peace, filled her and relaxed her. She closed her eyes and the soft sound of flowing water lulled her to sleep.

Faith's whinny awakened her. She opened her eyes, confused at first as to where she was, and then the willow branches above her brought her back to reality. Faith thrashed around at the tree, then broke free. With her reins trailing behind, she took off running through the trees and out into the open, headed for home. Jess jumped to her feet and ran after her, calling her name. As Jess broke free of the trees, she saw what had spooked the filly. The cougar lay on a rock a short distance away, its tail twitching rhythmically back and forth. Jess slowed, stopped, and then turned to face the big cat. Thirty yards separated them, and the cat lay still with only the slightest movement of its tail, its golden eyes staring at her. She was mesmerized, but somehow, again unafraid.

The cat rose and very deliberately stepped down off the boulder, glanced back at Jess, and disappeared over the ridge. Jess stood and watched the spot where the cat had lain as if she expected it to reappear. Suddenly, a Gambel's quail burst from the ground a few feet in front of her and broke the spell. Jess turned and climbed up over the hill and then took off running again, calling to Faith, hoping she had stopped somewhere so that she would be able to catch her. Jess didn't relish the long walk home.

When Faith trotted into the yard, Casey was sitting on the porch. "Now where in the hell did you come from? You lose that Jess girl somewhere?" He hobbled over to the mare and caught her, led her down to the barn, unbridled her, and put her in a stall. "I guess we'll just have to wait and see what happened, eh, girl?"

Afterward, he made his way back up to the porch to wait. A half-hour later, Jess limped into the yard. Blue ran out to greet her, and Casey stood up. "What the hell happened to you? You fall off that filly?"

Jess gave him a sideways look that said everything. "You really think that's what happened? You think I would fall off my own horse?"

"Hey, here you are walking, and the filly come in without you. What else would I think, Miss Expert Horsewoman?"

"Well, you'd be wrong. Cougar scared her while I was down by the stream in the willows. She broke loose and took off running. I never did catch her, obviously. Is she alright?"

"Yeah. The reins are a bit worse for wear, but she's fine. Knows how to take care of herself. Guess we need to eliminate that cougar, huh?"

Jess shook her head. "What do you mean "we"? And no, I'm not going to kill it unless it actually threatens the stock. It's beautiful."

"Have it your way, but if it comes near me, I plan on takin' it out. That's the way I handle those things."

The look of disdain Jess gave him wasn't lost on Casey. "Hey, and if you don't like it, that's too bad, little missy. I do what I want to do."

"That's pretty clear since I told you last night not to come back." Jess brushed past him and headed out to the barn. Faith paced restlessly in the stall. Jess haltered her and brought her into the aisle to untack her. She looked her over carefully, but Casey was right. No apparent injuries. She slid the saddle off, put it on the saddle rack, and let Faith out with Mickey. She didn't want to have to deal with Casey again just yet, so she sat on a bale of hay, took out her phone, and called Molly. Molly picked up after the second ring.

"Hey, Jess. I wondered how you were doing. I've been busy but was planning to stop over today and catch up. What's going on?"

"How about I come over there instead. Would that be okay?"

"You bet. You know my door is open for you anytime, girl. What time?"

"How about right now?"

"Perfect. I was just about to fix some lunch and I hate eating alone. See you soon."

Jess stood up, checked on the horses to see if they still had plenty of hay, and then headed up to the house. Casey still sat on the porch, but she said nothing to him as she got into the truck and left. Ten minutes later she pulled into the yard at Cal and Molly's place. Their dogs barely registered that she was there anymore. Just some tail wags as they lay on the porch. The screen door banged open, and Molly enveloped her in a big hug. "So good to see you. I take it from the look on your face that it isn't going well."

"Could be better."

Molly took her by the arm and led her inside. "Just sit down here, and tell me all about it while I finish up the lunch." She pulled out a kitchen chair for Jess.

"I don't know where to start actually. Casey showed up again this morning. He was sitting on my porch when I got back from taking a ride with Faith."

"I didn't see him take off this morning. He has sure become the sneaky one." Molly laughed. Then she turned back to Jess and saw that she wasn't smiling at that. Molly stopped what she was doing and sat down across from her. "Okay, start from the beginning, and tell me all about it."

Slowly at first and then more quickly as she got further into her telling, Jess described the days since Casey got hurt and the interaction with Mike. She started to cry. Molly came around the table, sat next to her, put her arm around her shoulders, and held her until the crying stopped.

"I don't know what's going on with me. I never used to cry, and now every time I turn around, I find that my darned eyes are leaking." She wiped at them with the back of her hand.

"Girl, you have been through a lot in the past month. You lost a husband, asshole that he might have been, took on a ranch by yourself, and now you're starting a new business, and to top it off, you have another asshole hounding you. I'd say you have plenty to cry about."

"The worst part is I feel guilty about him getting hurt and losing work. My feelings are all screwed up right now. I don't even know how I feel about Casey. I mean, I should kind of hate the guy. He is so much like Clint, but sometimes, when he is being nice, I get confused about it."

"First of all, from the little I know, accidents happen on a ranch. What happened to him was an accident, pure and simple. You couldn't have prevented it no matter what you did, so stop blaming yourself. And you need to really think about what you're saying. From what you've told me, I don't see how he is any different from Clint. Same actions, same guy. Is that what you want in your life again?"

"I know you're right, but there are times when it just feels familiar and familiar can feel comfortable, like I know where I stand. Do you know what I'm saying?"

"Look, Jess, I'm sure as hell no psychologist, but what you're describing sure doesn't sound healthy to me. Why would you want to put yourself through that again?"

"I don't know, Molly. I think because it's all I've ever known. I know you're right. I just don't seem to know how to break the cycle."

Molly gave Jess a tight hug and then stood up and went back to getting the lunch ready. "Okay, I think I know just what you need, and that is a good lunch to get you thinking clearly." A few minutes later she put some roast beef sandwiches, pickles, and olives on the table and poured them both a cup of coffee.

"Molly, I can't thank you enough for putting up with my woes all the time. I don't know what I would do without you. You've been a lifesaver for me."

"Oh, pfft. We're friends, Jess. That's just what friends do."

Jess smiled at her. She gazed off absently for a minute. She started again, her voice quiet. "I was a shy kid, you know. I didn't have a clue how to go about making friends. This is all new to me." She stopped and looked at Molly. "You've taught me a lot about what friendship is, Molly. Thank you for that."

When they finished lunch, Jess helped clean up then headed for the door. "I guess I'd better get back. There are a few things I need to get done before those horses get dropped off tomorrow. Thank you for lunch and for listening, Molly. I owe you big time."

Back at the ranch, Jess went straight to the barn. She had seen no sign of Casey when she got back, but his truck was still there. She really wanted to avoid him as much as possible. She had stalls to clean, and she wanted to set up an area where her horses and the new ones could get to know each other over the fence. There would be a lot of snorting and stomping. Hopefully, nobody would get hurt. Introducing a new horse into a herd was always dangerous. A lot of dominant behavior went on, and a kick or a bite could mean a horse incapacitated. She sure didn't need that with these expensive horses.

She headed out into the pasture to figure out her fencing situation. She had a half dozen steel fence panels that she had used before to separate new horses from the herd. She wanted to be sure they would be enough for the two new horses to have room and not get in each other's way. She had begun to set them up when she caught a movement behind her. Casey made his way into the area she had fenced off.

"You need some help with them panels, Jess?"

"No, I've got it. Thanks though."

"I don't know. I can hold up an end while you set them where you want them. Looks to me like you're strugglin' with them."

"No, I said I'm good, and I meant it. I've done this many times before. I don't need your help."

"Hey, I get it. You're still mad at me for showin' up here with the boys. I'm sorry, Jess. I know I was drunk, and I probably said some things I shouldn't have."

Jess just shook her head and kept working with the panels to get them set where she wanted them, Casey stood in the shade of the barn watching her. When she had finished, she had a separate pen in the pasture. Mickey and Faith both investigated it, quickly lost interest and wandered off to eat hay. She had used zip ties to bind panel to panel, and she walked the perimeter to test it. Sturdy and capable of holding two horses, she was sure of that.

When she turned back to the barn, Casey had disappeared. Jess went inside the barn and spent the next half hour sweeping the cobwebs down from the ceiling and then giving the whole barn a thorough cleaning. She wanted more than anything to give a good impression when Logan brought the horses. When she finished with that, she started to muck out the stalls.

Stall cleaning had a certain peaceful rhythm to it, and Jess fell into that rhythm quickly. She had done it so many times since she was a kid that it was like second nature to her. It always gave her time to think, to unwind. As a kid, it had been a way to pay for her riding lessons, but over the years it became something pleasurable, something she looked forward to, another way, really, for her to connect with the horses. When she finished, satisfied she had done everything she could, she went up to the house to prepare supper. Casey was again sitting on the porch.

"So, what's your plan? You know anything about breaking horses?"

Jess stopped. "I don't 'break' horses. I train them, and yeah, I do know a thing or two about doing that. Why do you think Mr. Miller wants me to do it?"

"Just sayin'. A lot more to it than most folks think. I think you should've stuck with what you know. Seems to me, you was doin' good with the cattle business. Why go and fuck that up?"

Jess just stared at him. "Casey, what are you still doing here? Whatever it is, I thought I made myself pretty clear. You and I, we're done. You're not welcome here anymore. You need to get into your truck, and go home."

Jess didn't wait for a response. She went on into the house. She heard the truck start up, and then he was gone, and a feeling of regret rose up and surprised her. She hadn't meant to be so rude to him. She just felt really confused about her feelings now. Later that night, as she lay in the darkness, she thought about what Casey had said. Maybe he was right. Maybe she was foolish to think she could start training other people's expensive horses. What experience did she really have anyway? Her own horses? Helping a friend or two with their problem horses? The old familiar doubts started to creep over her, started to make her feel inadequate.

After tossing and turning for the better part of an hour, the tiredness took over and she fell into a fitful sleep.

Chapter 24

In the morning, the fears of the night before seemed to fade. She had paid attention to the demeaning comments of others far too long. First, it was her dad, then Clint, and now Casey. She felt like she needed to finally trust herself. Deep down, she knew she could do this. If there was one thing she understood, it was horses, and expensive as these were, she knew that within a week she would have a good handle on what each one needed to get them to where she wanted them to be. She could hardly wait for them to get there.

She made a hurried breakfast for herself and fed Blue. As she washed the dishes, she heard a truck pulling into the yard. She dried her hands and went out into the yard to greet them.

The truck, a big, Ford 350 King Ranch dually, had pulled the fancy three-horse trailer up to the barn. Jess hurried down to help unload the horses. A short, chubby man climbed down from the truck cab and walked over to greet her. "Jessica? Logan Miller." He stuck out his hand, and she shook it.

"So nice to meet you, Mr. Miller. Can't wait to see the horses."

"Call me Logan. They are a good pair. I think you will enjoy working with them. I'm thinking I will give you two weeks, and then

I'll stop by and see what kind of progress you've been making. Does that sound fair?"

"That would be fine. I should be able to get a good start on them by then. They are my only priority right now, so they will get plenty of attention."

"Ok. Let's get them unloaded so you can see what you have to work with." He turned and walked around to the back of the trailer and lowered the loading ramp. He unlatched the right-side door and dropped the padded chain from across the back. He called to the horse to back, and a large, black and white paint rump started to make its way to the door and backed down the ramp. The quarter horse attached to the rump had perfect conformation and was beautifully put together Jess thought. She caught the lead rope hanging around its neck and led it off to the side. The horse circled her, straining at the end of the lead. This one, high strung for a quarter horse, would be a handful at first, but the possibilities of a horse like this, thrilled her. The second horse, a chestnut gelding, backed out, and Logan picked up the lead and followed Jessica as she led the paint into his stall. She directed Logan to the other stall she had prepared for the horses and smiled as she stood back and looked at them exploring their new space.

"I want to give them a little bit of time to settle in before I start, so they'll stay in here for a couple hours, and then I'll introduce them to my horses over the fence. I guess we're set here for now."

"I guess so. I'll leave some of the grain they have been on so that you can transition them to whatever you have been feeding. Good luck, Jessica."

"Just Jess."

"Okay, Jess. I'll see you in two weeks then." With that, he walked out to his truck, took a bag of grain from the passenger seat, and set it by the door of the barn. He got back into the truck and pulled away from the barn and out onto the main road.

Jess sat down on a bale of hay and watched the two horses as they started to eat the hay she had put in the stalls for them. She could hardly wait to get started and already had a plan in mind for the first lesson she wanted to work on with them. She was lost in thought when, Casey broke her concentration, startling her as he came into the barn.

"So, these are the million-dollar nags he wants broke, huh? Don't look all that special to me. Just jump on 'em, ride the buck out of 'em and give 'em back. Shouldn't take no time at all, I'd say."

Jess stood up and went over to the chestnut. The horse came to her, and she rubbed its face, played with its ears, ran her fingers over the velvet softness of its nose. She couldn't believe Casey had come here again. She had begun to fear that she would never be rid of him. "There won't be any buck if I do it right. These are smart horses. They're going to learn really fast, I can tell. And there isn't any 'breaking' going to happen."

"Says you. The only way to train is to break 'em down, let 'em know who's boss. They need to see that right off. That's the way I always trained 'em, and it always worked great for me. You go ahead and try your fancy training, and when that fails, I'll get 'em trained for you in nothin' flat. Hell, even with a bad leg, I could get them boys broke just like that." He snapped his fingers.

Jess kept her back to him. She felt confident in her abilities. She wouldn't let him tear her down, destroy her confidence. She thought about all the times her mother had let her dad do that to her, her mom, so quiet and kind and always made to feel less by her husband's comments. Jess had suffered that herself, but it was only now that she had begun to recognize what her mother had gone through too. It made her sick to think she hadn't recognized it before, but she'd been just a kid, her attention focused only on her own needs. What could she have done anyway? She made a mental note to give her mom a call to see how she was doing. She had been so busy the past few days, she had hardly any time for anything.

Suddenly, she felt a hand on her shoulder. "Hey, you ignorin' me? Come here and give me a good mornin' hug." He spun her around and, wrapped his arms around her, and pulled her to him. Jess tried to push him away, and when he wouldn't let go, she slapped him across the face. Casey grabbed her by the wrist and slammed his fist into her cheek. She fell back against a hay bale and bumped her head against the stall wall. She lay there dazed, afraid, and angry.

Casey stood over her, angry at first, and then reached down and took her hand and pulled her to her feet. Didn't mean to hit you so hard. Just a natural reaction when somebody hits me, I hit back. You shouldn't have hit me, you understand?" He smiled at her.

She felt the old fear taking over once again, but she knew she had to get out of this situation. "Look, Casey. I don't want you to think there is something between us. I'm not interested in any kind of relationship right now. I just lost my husband, and I'm starting a whole new situation here, so please, just be on your way, and don't come back around here. I have a lot to do in the next few months, and I just need some time to myself. Can you understand that?"

The smile disappeared from Casey's face. "You seemed to have time for that cholo boy."

"He's just a friend who did a couple of favors for me. Nothing else, and it really isn't any of your business. Don't make this anything nasty. I've appreciated your help with the cattle. I really have, and we've settled up." He stared at her.

"I don't mean nothin' to you?"

"It's not that. I appreciate all the help you gave me. I just don't want to be involved with anybody right now."

Casey stood staring at her for what seemed an eternity and then turned and walked out. Jess sat down on the bale again. She buried her face in her hands and then realized how much her cheek hurt where he had hit her. She wanted to cry again, but somehow, she held it in. She had things to do, and she couldn't let this stop her.

Today she would concentrate on the simplest thing. She would let the horses settle in and then introduce them to Mickey and Faith. She tried not to think about how much like a prisoner she had begun to feel again. She thought after Clint had died that the feeling would pass too. Now, with Casey, here it was again, and she didn't know what to do about it.

She stood up now and walked back over to the stalls. She realized that she hadn't asked Logan for the names of these two guys. She decided to wait until she started to work with them to give them her own temporary names to use while she worked with them. She knew from experience that horses tended to name themselves after a little while. Their personalities came out just like people's did, and from that, names seemed to come naturally. She smiled at the thought, and once again felt the pain in her cheek.

By eleven, she felt that the horses had settled enough to introduce them to her two horses. She first led the paint into the pen and then went back to get the chestnut. When she put the chestnut in with the paint, her horses that were at the far end of the pasture, looked up and then set off at a gallop toward the pen. Mickey approached the pen all arched necked and prancing. Faith came behind, softer, acting more curious than dominant. In the pen the two horses approached the fence, noses outstretched as they shared sniffs with first Mickey then Faith, followed by loud, high-pitched squeals and pawing, and then they all settled back into their own routines. The two new horses went about eating from the piles of hay Jess had put in the pen, and Mickey and Faith wandered away to graze. A non-event. Just what she had wanted. She would wait a day or two before they were in the same pasture, but so far so good.

By twelve, things were settled and Jess went up to the house to make some lunch. As she ate, she thought about Casey and remembered the anger in his voice, the bitterness. It reminded her so completely of Clint, that it sent chills down her spine. She began to wonder if she should stay here at all, or if she should pick up and make a new start somewhere where no one knew her. Her anger rose up again. No one could push her off this place. She wouldn't let them.

Chapter 25

At the El Palacio Mexican restaurant in Kingman, Mike and Jason sat at a corner table, both facing the door. They had just put in their lunch order. "So, how is it going with that Jessica girl? You go on a date yet?"

Mike had a pained look on his face. "I don't think either of us is ready for that. I don't know that it will ever happen."

"Come on, my man. That girl is a keeper, and you know it. What are you waiting for? Some guy is going to come along and sweep her right up. How is that going to make you feel?"

"Look, Jason, I don't know how I feel. Every time I look at her, I think of my wife, and I just don't think I can do that again. I mean, I like her and all, I just don't know that I'm ready to date anybody."

"But if you were, she would be the one? Come on, man. Give it a shot anyway. What would a date or two hurt?"

"Even if I were to ask her out, I don't know that she would accept. It's been only a few weeks since she lost her husband. Look how long it's been for me, and I'm still not fully recovered."

"Her husband was a colossal asshole, and you know it. It had to have been the best thing that could ever happen to her."

"Maybe, but I'm not going to push it right now. We can be friends and not go there. For now, that's the way we'll keep it."

"Suit yourself, but I think you're being just plain stupid. Don't let that girl get away."

The food came right then, and they both dug into the meal. When they finished, Mike sat looking out at the street through the front windows. "I'll think about it,"

"What?"

"You're right. She is special. I'll think about asking her out. Just don't bug me anymore about it, okay?"

Jason cracked a big smile. "Oh, my wife is going to love this." Mike elbowed him in the ribs.

...

Jessica decided to give the horses a few more hours to get acclimated. She needed a few things from the grocery store. Seligman was the closest, and even though the grocery there was small, it would be fine for the few things she needed to pick up. She got to town at two, drove by the Route 66 touristy displays and establishments until she pulled into the lot of the Seligman Grocery. Once inside, she quickly did her shopping. She hadn't eaten much for breakfast, and as she checked out, she realized she was starving. Seligman didn't offer a lot of dining choices, but she ended up picking a place called The Roadkill Café/O.K. Saloon. Inside, the walls were festooned with a variety of tchotchkes and examples of taxidermy set off by the pine paneling and pine ceiling. There was a homey feeling to it. There were three cowboys at the bar and a young couple at one of the tables, but otherwise, the restaurant appeared empty. She picked a table and sat down. A middle-aged and slightly overweight waitress came to her table.

"Hey, there. What can I get for you?"

She ordered a hamburger, fries, and a soft drink and sat studying the decorations and, more surreptitiously, the other patrons. She decided the young couple were tourists off Route 66. The cowboys looked like most of the Arizona hands, weathered and tough. She wondered if this was one of the places, Clint used to come to drink. She felt uncomfortable as she always had in restaurants. She flashed back to the scenes her father would make. The food was too cold or the waitress too slow or inattentive, the bill wasn't right. There was always an excuse. For her, it added up to just one more embarrassment to endure. Now, alone with no chance of embarrassment, she still felt the pain of it, the eyes on her from all parts of the room. She wanted to eat quickly and get out.

The burgers and fries came and she got up and got a catsup bottle from another table. She drenched both the burger and the fries in catsup and began to eat. As uncomfortable as she was, she realized that she had missed the treat of eating out. She quickly ate all of the fries first and then, just as quickly, ate the burger. She held up her hand and the waitress brought over the check. "That was fast. Did you want any dessert?"

"No. I'm good, thanks."

"Ok, honey. You can pay at the register as you go."

Jess dug into her purse and put a tip on the table, got up, and paid at the register. Moving from the dark restaurant into the brilliant outside light blinded her for a moment. She stood in front of the restaurant and felt the relief of being outside again. For a moment, the thought of how her unhappy past had shaped who she was swept over her and overwhelmed her. She realized that these moments of self-reflection had come more frequently since Clint had died. Each time the reflections happened had been a moment of epiphany that felt both good and painful.

She looked up and down the street. Seligman had a more touristy feel to it than Kingman. Much smaller definitely, but totally geared to the traffic off the famous Route 66. It surprised her that she didn't feel comfortable in any town anymore. She had grown up in the suburbs, but she had spent a lot of time in Boston and had never felt uncomfortable there. The past six years had changed her in many ways, but somehow, this was the most surprising. She got into the truck and pulled away. She opened the windows and let the warm air blow across her face, sweep her hair back and then send it forward again. The flow of it began to feel cleansing, began to free her again. She turned on the radio. "Letter to Me" by Brad Paisley poured out of the speakers and the lyrics struck her. If she had only known what she knew now when she was seventeen… and the tears rolled down her cheeks again.

When she pulled into the yard, a sheriff's vehicle was parked in the shade. She got out of her truck and walked over to it. Mike got out as she approached.

"Hey, Mike, what are you doing here?"

"Hey, Jess. I had a call out this way and just thought I would stop and check in and see how you were doing. I also put a new lock on your door. I hope you don't mind. I was worried about Casey showing up again and being able to easily get in the house." He handed her a pair of keys.

Jess smiled at him. "I'd been planning to do that and just hadn't gotten around to it yet. What do I owe you?"

Mike ignored the question as he walked closer. He was staring at her face. "What happened here? Looks to me like you got punched. Casey hit you, didn't he?"

Jess turned away. "It's okay, Mike. Just a one-time thing and he apologized. He got a little carried away, that's all. I'm fine. I can take care of myself."

"Look, Jess. It's not alright. No man should be hitting a woman. I don't care what the circumstances are. I don't want to see you getting hurt. The next time could be a lot worse. I see this all the time. Do you know how many domestic disputes we go to? It makes up a large part of our runs daily. All it ever does is escalate, or the woman has to hide, or if she fights back, she's going to get it worse." Mike hesitated for a minute, looked her in the eyes. "Is there something between you two? Do you love him? Because that complicates things?"

Jess found herself riveted by his gaze, unable to look away. "No, nothing like that." She turned away. "I don't know, Mike. He isn't a bad guy most of the time. He was there when I needed someone to help me with the ranch." She hesitated now, not sure how much to share.

Mike took her by the shoulders and turned her to look at him. He stood so close to her she could feel the heat off his body.

"Jess, I know this is none of my business. I just don't want to have to come out here on a call. I don't want to find you beaten to a pulp like so many of the women I've seen in these situations or, worse yet, dead. Why don't you let me put him away for a while? File charges, and I'll get him out of your life. This can't happen again"

Jess hesitated again, and then, "I told him not to come back. He keeps coming around here, and frankly, he scares me a little bit, but I don't want you to get involved. That will only make him madder, I think. I really need to handle this myself."

Jess felt the warmth of his hands on her shoulders, saw the concern on his face, but the immediate reaction she had to that touch was to guard herself against what might come next. Now as he stood there in front of her, she wondered at that. She felt comforted by him really. Nobody had ever made her feel like that before, and she felt the confusion rise up in her again. The Caseys of the world were the guys she knew, the ones she had grown up with, lived with. She knew where she stood with them. Mike puzzled her. He genuinely seemed to want to protect her, to take care of her, but hadn't she been protecting herself all her life? Hadn't she been the one to care for herself?

Mike dropped his hands from her shoulders, stepped back. "Okay. I sure can't force you to do that, and I know how capable you are. I just don't want anything to happen to you. You understand that I hope."

"I do, and I appreciate it. I really do. It's just a lot to take in is all. I have this new business, and I guess I have a lot of old business to figure out and take care of too. I promise if things get worse, or I think I can't handle it, I'll call you. And I really do appreciate you checking on me." She stepped up to him and gave him a hug, then stepped away. "I really should get to work. I want to get some progress every day with those horses, so I have something to show Logan when he comes out here again."

"I understand. Look, Jess, this may be out of line…" It was Mike's turn to hesitate now. He looked away, uncomfortable.

"What? Is there something I can do for you?"

"I don't know. I'm sure this is too soon, but the real reason I stopped by was because I was going to ask you to have supper with me. I understand if you want to say no. I just thought…"

She smiled at him, surprised to see him embarrassed, uncomfortable. "Sure, but why don't I make us a nice supper here. I owe you so much already, and it would really be my pleasure." She hesitated for a moment, then, "In fact, you should ask Jason and his wife to come too. It would be the least I could do for you."

Mike smiled at her. "I kind of wanted to do something for you. I didn't want you to have to go to more trouble."

"Listen, Mike. It isn't any trouble at all. I owe you, and this would be a little payback. If you don't mind, I'd like to invite Molly and Cal. They've been helping me too."

"Why don't you let me set a dinner up for all of us at one of the restaurants in town. I'll pick up the tab, and then you could just relax and enjoy yourself."

"Definitely not. I would never have you do that, and besides, and I know this will sound crazy to you, I hate going to restaurants."

"Really? Why's that?"

"Long story. I'll explain it to you some time. Let's just go with my plan. It will be a little party." She paused. "I'm sorry, would that be okay with you?"

"Whatever makes you happy, Jess, but I insist on coming out early and helping you prepare things. Would that be okay?"

Jess laughed. "If you insist. Do you have a special dish that you'd like me to make?"

"Nope. I've been eating my own cooking for the past four years since my wife passed. I'm open to anything home-cooked."

"That's good because for the past six years I've had to cook whatever Clint brought home since he did almost all the shopping. I'll try to find something special for everybody."

Mike smiled. "Okay then. You'll let me know when?"

"Later this week. You check with Jason and I'll check with Molly, and we'll find a time that works for everybody. Sound like a plan?"

"Sounds like a plan. I'll call you after I talk with Jason. I better go now and let you get back to your work. You take care of yourself and call me if you need anything. I mean that. I don't want anything to happen to you. Mike gave her that intense stare again, hesitated a moment, and then, "Okay if you're sure you're alright, I'll get back on the road. Check with me once in a while though, will you?"

"I will. I promise."

Mike went over to his vehicle and opened the door. "Looking forward to that supper." He smiled, took off his hat, and got into the patrol unit. He waved to her, started the engine, and pulled out of the yard.

Jess watched him go, the dust rising behind his car, drifting up and then away in an ever-thinning cloud. It made her think about how much they needed rain right now. This was the rainy season, and they had had almost none. It would be hard on the cattle. She turned back to the barn, and as she headed out there, began planning her first steps with her two new horses.

She had decided to work with the chestnut first and led him over to the new round pen. She turned him loose and began to drive him around the pen, a lariat in her hand the loop of which she would toss to drive him forward. He moved with power and grace, his good breeding showing in everything he did. She could hardly wait to get to the finer work, the actual riding and trust-building that she would work on over the next few weeks.

When he tried to turn back, she blocked him with her body position and the lariat until he kept going in the direction she wanted. After several circles to the right, she sent him back to the left. She worked with him for less than a half-hour and then stepped back and turned her back to him, took the pressure off. She looked over her shoulder and saw the behavior she had hoped for. He stood quietly licking and chewing. She turned to face him now and his ears went up and forward, his attention fully on her. She sent him off again but this time for only a couple rounds to the right and a couple to the left and then she turned away from him again and waited. A minute later she felt him close to her, and she turned and rubbed his face, talked quietly to him.   He stood next to her as she rubbed his face and ears, then she began to move around him, rubbing the lariat coil all over him, tossing the loop over his back and under his belly. His skin twitched and quivered at first, then he settled into it and relaxed completely.

The Paint reacted a little differently--more dominant and less willing at first-- so she had to work longer with him. She guessed he had been gelded later than she liked to see. It made him more stud-like, harder to handle at first, but she had also found that when you won over that type of horse, you got a courageous horse that would do anything for you. By late afternoon, she had finished working both of them and felt satisfied with how far they had come in such a short period of time. It all felt familiar, natural. She took great satisfaction in that.

All through her teen years, she had done this with other people's horses, and it had been her escape. She recognized that now. The barn, the horses, they had been a comfort, and as dangerous as it was to work with thousand-plus-pound animals, it had been her safe space. She always connected with the horses she worked with, so she had one thing in her life that her dad couldn't take away from her, one thing that she sensed she was truly good at, and it gave her confidence in that one tiny corner of her life. It had helped her survive all those years of yelling and criticism.

She had started the feeding and stall cleaning when she heard a pickup pulling into the yard. Jess headed up to the house. There on the porch stood Casey once again. She didn't want to have to deal with him.

"Hi, Babe. I brought some groceries and I thought maybe I would cook up a little supper for us, but looks like you got a new lock on the door. What's that all about?"

Jess brushed past him, unlocked the door.

"I'll get the groceries out of the truck."

"Casey, much as I appreciate the thought, you really can't do this. I thought I made that pretty clear."

"Aww, come on, Jess. Let it go. We've been a team. You don't want to let that go now, do you? Just let me cook you up a nice supper, and if you still feel that way, then I won't bug you anymore."

Here was the other Casey. Jess didn't know whether to fight it now, or try to get through today with him and hope that she could end it somehow afterward. She looked closely at him as he stood there by the truck. He seemed sincere, maybe contrite.

"Okay. Just this once. After supper though, you have to go. Is that clear?"

"Yes, Ma'am. Let's just have ourselves a nice little supper and see how that goes."

Jess shook her head. Casey looked over his shoulder, smiled broadly as he unpacked the groceries from the truck.

"Just a little payback."

Jess went back to the barn to finish cleaning the stalls while Casey made the supper. When she came back in, they ate the steak and potatoes Casey had prepared and talked about her horse training. A peaceful calm that seemed foreign settled over the house. Casey drank heavily from a bottle of whiskey he had brought. She worried about the drunk Casey she had seen before, but he seemed mellow and quiet, and Jess chewed both on the steak and on the thought that Casey had this other side. She would never have guessed that about him. She felt a tenderness toward him that surprised her. After supper, they worked together to clean everything up, and then Casey produced a little CD player and put in a CD of dance music. "How about a little dance with me? You up for that?"

"I don't think so. Not much of a dancer."

"That's okay. You're about to learn from the best." He took her hand and pulled her into his arms.

Jess couldn't help but laugh.

"I never had a chance to practice with anybody, so you're going to have to watch your toes." She smiled at him, and he wrapped his arms around her and spun her around. They shuffled together through the first song, and then he held her and just swayed with her as the next song started. His pelvis pressed against hers, and she could feel him getting hard. She tried to put some space between them. He pulled her back against him and leaned down and kissed her. She pushed back away from him and awkwardly bumped into the kitchen table, every nerve alert now.

"What the fuck? I make you a nice supper, and you can't even give me a little kiss? You really are a cold bitch. I guess everything Clint said about you is true. Surprised he didn't kill you instead of you killin' him."

Jess maneuvered away from him, put the table between them.

"What are you talking about? You knew him better than you said, didn't you? And what do you mean, I killed him? A broken rope killed him, a rope I told him to replace, but he was too damned stubborn to do what I asked him to do." She hesitated a moment, then, "Maybe you should go."

"Yeah, I knew him. We was buddies. He told me all about you, told me what a bitch you was. Now I seen it for myself. You're worthless. Nothin' but a pretty face and a skinny boy's body. What the hell did you expect? That I was goin' hang around here with you and not touch you?" He moved around the table now, and Jess circled away from him, moved toward the door of her room.

"We had a damned deal. Now you want to break it. We was goin' to be partners. With the way you been leadin' me on, I figured we was more than just partners, but you're nothin' but a damned tease." He moved quickly, but his injured leg slowed him enough for Jess to get into her room and shut the door. She flicked the lock but knew it wouldn't keep him out for long.

She ran to the bed and lifted the corner of the mattress to get the Glock. Gone. She ran through her mind the last time she had the pistol. Had she put it back? She remembered it clearly and, yes, she had put it away as she always did, but it was gone now. The door banged open, the frame and trim splintering, falling away in brittle pieces. Casey stood in the opening.

"What are you looking for, little missy? Would it be this?" He reached around behind himself, and when his hand came back into view, it held the Glock. "What were you plannin' to do with this? Were you goin' to shoot me? I seen that you had this thing the first week that you got it, so I knew it was here someplace. Just did a little diggin' to find it while you was out in the barn. Didn't want you hurtin' yourself or nothin'." He reached behind his back and tucked the gun back into his belt.

Jess tried to remain calm. "Casey, what do you want from me? I don't want it to end like this. Why don't you give me my gun back?"

"No, I think I'll just keep it for now. Kind of an insurance policy, you know." He walked over and sat on the end of the bed. "I think you need to treat me a little better, Jess. Hell, all I wanted was a little hug, maybe a kiss, and here you go actin' all dramatic. Not goin' to hurt you to treat me a little better, is it? Oh, and I picked up your phone you left layin' out there. I don't want you callin' that cholo boyfriend of yours. In fact, I think you should give him up. You got yourself a live-in boyfriend right here."

Jess stood, back pressed to the wall, unable to move.

"Clint told me how he treated you. I ain't goin' to do that to you. I can't see hittin' no woman unless she is just askin' for it. Now, why don't you come on over here and give me a little hug?" He stood and faced her, and then, in one quick step, he had her, wrapped his arms around her, and hugged her. Jess, knew fighting him would be futile. She put her arms around him and then felt the butt of the Glock. In an instant, she pulled it from his waistband and shoved the muzzle into his ribs.

"Let go of me, Casey." Her voice, calm, steady.

He released her and took a half step back. "Well, look at you. What are you plannin' to do now, shoot me? Well, you just go ahead." He stepped toward her.

She pulled the trigger, but nothing happened. Before she could react, Casey had taken the gun back from her. "See, here's the thing. This gun don't work without a shell in the chamber, and to do that, you have to work the slide, like this." He slid the slide back and let it go. "You see, now there's a shell in there ready to fire. Should I try it? He lifted the gun up and put the muzzle against her forehead.

Jess felt the tears start to flow, once again felt the helplessness she had felt so many times in her life. Casey, lowered the gun, put it away and reached out with one calloused hand, and wiped away the tears running down her cheeks. She felt the roughness, the thumb sliding along her face, and then he leaned in, kissed her cheek where the tear had been, took her chin in his hand, and tilted her head up. He stepped closer now, ran his hand through her hair, and then gripped the back of her head and kissed her fully on the mouth, the smell and taste of the whiskey, overwhelming. She didn't resist, couldn't really.

"Now, that wasn't so bad, was it? You behave yourself, and we can have a good time out here on this old ranch. What do you say? That work for you?" The words were more slurred now.

Jess glared at him. The tears were gone and the anger had risen in her, but for now, she would just have to do what she needed to in order to survive, the same thing she had done all her life. She knew how to do that, but she wasn't going to make it any easier for him than she had to.

"I need to wash up before I go to bed. That okay with you?

"Yeah, you do that. Smell nice and perty for me. But don't take too long. And I want to see you undress, so you come back in here to do that, you hear?"

Casey drank the rest of the whiskey as Jess left the room. She took her time at the kitchen sink, washing her face and then lifting the T-shirt to wash under her arms. All the while she listened carefully until she heard the light snoring she had hoped would come. Barefooted, she slid out of the house and ran to the barn. Blue rose up from a pile of hay when she ran into the barn, his tail wagging furiously. She grabbed a bridle from the rack and then whistled softly for Faith. Her horse trotted up to her, and she slipped the bridle on, hopped up on the mare's back, and rode out of the barn and into the night with Blue trailing behind. She headed cross country to Molly's.

The call from Molly brought Mike out to the ranch with a backup. When he got there, Mike studied Jess's face, still bruised and tear-stained and strained from the tension she had been under.

"Okay, tell me where he was in the house when you left. Is he armed?"

Jess explained about the Glock and that Casey had been drunk and asleep when she left. Mike went to the other patrol unit and briefed the officer behind the wheel, then turned again to Jess.

"I'll be back after we take care of this." They pulled out of the yard and headed toward her ranch.

...

On the way there, Mike called his partner. "Rick, we're going to come in, lights off, and walk in from the road."

"Roger that. Are we going to need the battering ram?"

"Negative. Jess gave me the key. We are just going to slip in nice and quiet and try to make this an easy arrest. No need for a standoff and having to call in a swat team. Clean and simple, that's what we want."

They turned the lights off a half-mile away and drove slowly through the quiet darkness until they were in front of the ranch. The place was lit only by a sliver of moon, a tiny, white split in the darkness. They approached from the side. There were no windows there, and they could get all the way to the house without being seen if by some chance Casey had woken up. The move across the porch would be the trickiest part. The wood, old and creaky, might give them away. Mike counted on the thick stone walls of the house to muffle the sound enough to keep their arrival a surprise.

They waited at the corner of the house and porch, listening for any sound that would let them know if Casey had heard them, might be waiting just inside the door, but the house gave no clue. If he waited for them inside, the thick walls, muffled any sound that might have given him away too.

They made their way as quietly as they could across the porch, Mike, key in his left hand, his service weapon in his right, led the way. At the door, he stopped and listened again. Nothing. He tried the door handle. The door wasn't locked. Mike dropped the key into his pocket, nodded at his partner, and motioned that he would go left and his partner would go right as they entered. Mike started a countdown with the fingers on his left hand and on three, threw open the door, and jumped through the opening. "Police! Come out with your hands up." He moved quickly across the room and through the open bedroom door, flicked on the light switch. Casey sat upright, leaned sideways fumbling for something on the side table.

"Don't touch that. Hands on top of your head, now."

Casey hesitated, the Glock under his hand, then slowly raised his hands and put them on his head. "What the fuck is this about? Where the hell is Jess?" And then, seeing who it was. "You? You're a cop? What the fuck did she do?"

"Keep your hands on your head. Get out of bed and kneel on the floor facing the wall. Now."

Casey stood up, clad only in a pair of boxer shorts. He stood, legs wide, defiant, and then as Mike moved closer, turned and knelt with his face to the wall. Mike stepped in behind him, moved the Glock from the table, and handed it back to his partner. He took his handcuffs from the leather pouch on his belt and snapped one of the cuffs on Casey's right hand and then twisted both hands down and to the middle of Casey's back before snapping the other cuff in place. With the cuff key hanging from his belt, he locked the cuffs in place.

"Stand up now and turn around. You're under arrest."

"For what? For livin' here with Jess? For helpin' her out all this time? This is bullshit, and you know it. I'll be out of there before I even get a free meal."

Mike said nothing, just took Casey by the arm and started to head toward the door. "Hey, wait a minute. Ain't you goin' to let me at least put on a pair of pants, my boots?" He nodded his head toward jeans hung over the bedpost.

Mike turned to look at his partner. "Rick, would you grab those pants? I guess we shouldn't offend everybody by exposing them to that set of legs bare like that."

Rick chuckled and grabbed the pants from the bed, checked the pockets, and threw a pocket knife on the nightstand. Mike pulled Casey back to the bed and pushed him down into a seated position.

"Rick, could you slip those on for the gentleman? I will make sure he doesn't try anything cute."

Casey stared up at Mike, a look of pure hate on his face. "I'll remember this. You'll be real sorry that you got involved here. You hear me?"

Mike shook his head. "Real tough guy, aren't you, especially when it comes to women."

Rick slipped the pant legs up and then had Casey stand while he pulled them the rest of the way up and fastened the belt. "Ok, Mike. Let's move him." As Mike took Casey out, Rick picked up some boots and a shirt from the floor and carried them out to the patrol vehicle. After they loaded Casey into Rick's car, Mike stood with Rick outside the car.

"Rick, I'm going back to the Websters' place and get Jess's statement tonight while it's still fresh. You take this scumbag in and book him, will you?"

Rick smiled. "Don't be spending too much time on that report now, buddy. I heard you was sweet on that girl."

"You've been listening to too much office gossip. Just get him out of here, will you?"

Rick grinned, got into his car and pulled out onto the road, and headed back to Kingman.

Mike drove the five miles to the Websters' as quickly as he could, and as he pulled into the yard, Molly, Cal and Jessica came out onto the porch. Mike got out of the patrol car and walked up to where they stood on the porch.

"No real problem. He was sound asleep when we came into the room, still a little drunk from what I could tell. You'll have to come in tomorrow and file a complaint. I'll send the impound people out to pick up his truck. We will have to keep your weapon as evidence. Do you think you can get by without it for a while?"

"I guess I will have to. I sure don't like doing this to him."

"Jess, he's a bad guy. He crossed the line, and now he is going to have to pay for it. That's not your fault. You know that, don't you?"

Jess nodded. "I guess. I just feel bad. He had his moments when he seemed like a nice guy."

"I'll bet your husband- Clint, was it? -was the same way. That's just the way these guys are. Don't worry about him. He made a really bad choice. His problem, not yours. Why don't you let me drive you home now? You can pick up your horse in the morning."

Jess suddenly realized just how exhausted she was. "Okay. Thanks, Mike. Thanks for everything."

Chapter 26

Jess slept late the next morning. The hot, morning sun lay across her arm until it felt uncomfortable and brought her fully awake. She rolled over and stared at the ceiling.

She thought about Casey in that jail cell, and a flash of regret shot through her. She wished that it hadn't come to that, but there really had been no other choice. It had become too dangerous, maybe even worse than her experience with Clint. She rose and made a quick breakfast, fed the horses, then quickly took a shower in the lukewarm water left over from yesterday.

By noon, she had saddled and ridden the chestnut. It had been without incident, and she felt proud of herself. She knew deep inside that this was what she was meant to do, that she had a gift. She wouldn't let anyone take that away from her now. She hadn't let her dad do that. She hadn't let Clint do it, and she sure as hell wouldn't let the remarks Casey had made about her methods shake her confidence either. She ate a lunch of eggs and bacon at noon, and as she ate, Jess felt the satisfaction of her morning overwhelm her. She had much to do still, and she knew from experience that there would be setbacks, but everything about her work with the horses felt right, felt freeing.

With the afternoon ahead of her, she decided to head into town. She could sign whatever she needed to at the sheriff's office as soon as Mike called her, and she decided that as long as she was in town anyway, she would buy the things she needed for the dinner party. She had never given a party, and in fact, had really only attended a couple when she had been living at home. She sat at the kitchen table and planned the menu. With her list ready, she headed into Kingman to do the shopping. The Safeway had few customers, and just before she got ready to check out, she checked her phone and realized it had been off all morning. When she turned it on, there were four messages from Mike. In the last one, his voice sounded anxious.

"Jess, we've held Casey as long as we can without a complaint. Can you get in here as soon as possible and sign the official complaint? Otherwise, he is going to walk."

She called back while she stood in the checkout line. When he answered, "Mike, I'm really sorry."

"I tried to call you, but your phone always came up out of service."

"I'm sorry. I think I accidentally left it off for a while. I'm just checking out of the grocery store now. I can be there in a few minutes."

"Ok. I have the paperwork ready for you. I'll be here when you get here to walk you through it."

Jess pulled into the station lot fifteen minutes later. She called Mike to let him know she would be coming in, and as she walked into the small lobby, the door to the back offices opened, and Mike stood there waiting for her.

"Good to see you, Jess. Come with me."

Jess walked into the office area and followed him to his cubicle. He pulled out a chair for her, walked around the desk, sat down, and picked up a single sheet from the top of the pile on his desk. He laid it down in front of her.

"I highlighted where you have to sign," he said pointing, "Here and here."

Jess looked it over. The page seemed to swim before her eyes, but what registered with her was the list of charges that seemed too long for what had happened to her.

She looked up at Mike. "Is this all really necessary? I mean this is a lot. Won't this put him in jail for a really long time?"

Mike leaned forward in his chair. "Jess, first of all, this isn't your fault. He got himself in this mess. Secondly, it isn't likely that he will be convicted on all these charges. Some will be easily provable. Some will be thrown out. I just want to cover our bases here. If there's anything you don't think is accurate, I'll change it, but I think it's everything you described."

Jess brushed a lock of hair back from her eyes. She leaned over the document and picked up the pen. A stab of regret ran through her like a knife, but she quickly signed the two spots and handed the paper back to Mike.

"I trust you, Mike, but I can't help feeling that somehow this is at least partly my fault."

"Jess, everyone has choices. He made his, and now with any luck, he's going to pay for it. Before you go, I need to get a picture of your face and the bruise." He stood and offered his hand to help her stand up. She took it, and he didn't let go as he led her over to stand against an open section of white wall. He let her hand drop and then took her shoulders and turned her so that the injured cheek would be clearly visible in the photo. Jess waited quietly while he set up the camera and then blinked when it flashed. She started to move, but he asked her to stand still for another shot. Another flash and then he stepped away from the camera and stood close to her.

"Are you okay? You look a little pale. Do you need some water?" All this in a low voice, his closeness more intimate than professional.

"I don't know. I think I'm okay. Just a little overwhelmed, I think. I feel like I've been in a blender lately with all that has happened." She hesitated a moment then looked up at him again. "Mike, thanks. I can't remember when anyone has been there for me like you have. I know it's your job and all, but I'm glad it was you who came out last night and not somebody else." As soon as she said it, she felt embarrassed. She turned away. "Is there anything else?"

"No, you're free to go. I'll see you next Saturday night then?"

"Yes. I'm not sure how this is all going to turn out, but I'm really looking forward to it. My little chance to pay back some of the kindness everyone has shown me."

"No need for any paybacks, but I'm really looking forward to it too. I'll be there early so I can help you with the prep if that is still okay."

She smiled at him. "Not necessary, but definitely appreciated."

He smiled back. "Okay then, I'll bring my unnecessary self out there at 5:30."

Jess laughed. "See you then, Officer," and she made her own way to the door and let herself out.

In the late afternoon, she worked with the Paint, and though he gave her a little more resistance than the chestnut, by the time she was finished, she had saddled and ridden him too. She wanted to talk with someone about it, wanted to share her joy of accomplishment. She really wanted to call Mike. Somehow, she knew he would understand, but she felt uncomfortable with the idea. He had already done so much for her, and she didn't want to bother him. She thought about saddling Faith and riding over to Molly's, but she didn't want to bother her either. Instead, she busied herself with chores around the ranch, the barn chores first, and then as the sun went down, she worked on cleaning the house. She ate supper after nine and then, still restless, decided to take a night ride.

She saddled Faith and led her horse out the back side of the barn and up into the hills with Blue trailing along. At the top of the hill, she stopped, and as she stepped up into the saddle, she heard the cougar scream in the distance. Although it sent a cold chill down her spine, it filled her with that sense of wildness that she now realized she had craved all her life. It made her smile.

She rode through the darkness as she had so many nights before during her marriage to Clint, but this time felt different. This time she rode for herself, not to escape from something, but to escape to something. She nudged Faith into a canter and, along a flat stretch of desert road that she knew well, she pushed Faith into a flat-out gallop. The wind coursed through her hair whipped it back behind her, ran its soft fingers along her face. In the distance, the big cat screamed again, and Jess answered with her own long scream as she rode.

Jess slept fitfully that night after she thought about all that had happened in the past two days. She hoped that it was over now and that she could concentrate fully on the horses. The horses were the key. Nothing else mattered except getting them ready, and she could hardly wait to ride them again.

In the morning, she began the basic training all over again knowing that much of what she had done in the past two days would be tested. The groundwork, the saddling, the riding went more quickly now, and she could feel the trust growing between her and the two horses. That was the key. They had to trust her to be able to do all she would ask of them. She wondered if that key could open the door to a relationship for her too, and who came to mind was Mike. She had never felt anything but safe with him. She hardly knew him, but something about him felt like he would never hurt her. She realized that her work with horses was based on her ability to recognize who they were, what they needed, their character. Was it the same with people? She wondered if she was beginning to have that same instinct with people too. Why couldn't she always sense the character in men the way she could so quickly sense it in horses? She instinctively knew a dangerous horse from the look in its eye, the way it moved. What characteristics did dangerous men possess that she should look for?

At ten, Molly's car pulled into the drive. Jess heard the horn honk and called that she was in the round pen. When Molly came through the barn and out to stand at the round pen, she seemed quiet, worried. "Hey, Jess. How're you feeling? You recovered from the other night?"

"Really good, Molly. I'm fine, and these are some really smart boys here." She nodded at the horses. "They pick things up quickly. I think Logan is going to be surprised and pleased."

"I have no doubt about that. You're talented, girl. Really happy for you."

Jess, let the paint stand as she talked with Molly about the supper she had planned as a thank you for all the people who had helped her.

"That sounds great. I know you're busy right now, so I'll let you get back to work. I just wanted to check on you. You look so much more relaxed today. That's great to see. You take care, Jess. I'll see you soon. Is there anything you would like me to bring?"

"Nope, just yourself and Cal and your appetite." Jess smiled at her and Molly laughed and waved as she headed back to her truck.

After Molly left, Jess once again felt the need to share her success with somebody, talk about what she saw in each of the horses, the subtle changes that were beginning to show up. She loved Molly, but Molly wouldn't understand. Not being a horsewoman, the subtleties of training would be lost on her. Suddenly, she realized that what she was really seeking was validation. Until now she had always sought validation from the men in her life, her dad first and then Clint. It had all been for nothing. They had torn her down, belittled her, made her feel less. But here in this place, in this moment, she suddenly realized that she didn't need validation from anyone. The horses proved her value, proved it to her, proved it to anyone who saw the results of her work. She felt the whole working with them, and now she needed to feel that in the rest of her life. It felt like part of the weight she had been carrying all her life had suddenly been lifted.

The afternoon went quickly. She took the chestnut out on a short open country ride for the first time. He spooked at a few things at first, but quickly settled in and relaxed. She crossed over a wash where a bit of damp sand filled a low spot, and she was surprised to see the track of the big cat. The track was clear, and fresh and seeing it gave her that familiar chill. She looked up at the rock outcropping above her to see if the cat had set up a spot to pounce on anything below. No sign of it. She turned the horse and headed back to the ranch, riding slowly and under control so that the horse didn't get the idea that it was alright to run back the barn.

By the time she got back, it was nearly dark, and so she did the feeding and stall cleaning then went back to the house to get some supper. The house was dark and somehow it made her feel a little lonesome. It was funny. She loved the night darkness out in the open, but a dark house made her feel sad. She decided that maybe it was because as a kid so often she had come home to a dark house when her dad would be working late and her mom would be sitting by herself with a single lamp, reading.

She made a small dinner for herself. Afterward, she took her coffee, went out to the porch, sat on the top step, and watched the moon rise. Blue came to her, licked her hand, and looked up at her. She rubbed his head, took comfort in his presence. She went into the house, called Blue in with her, and locked the door for the night. She went into her room and got ready for bed. As she lay down Blue hopped up onto the bed with her, curled up beside her, and promptly fell asleep. As she lay there in the darkness, she wished that she could fall asleep so easily. She tossed and turned for the better part of an hour before her fatigue got the best of her and sleep claimed her.

Chapter 27

They had decided that the next Saturday would be the day for the party. The days leading up to Saturday all seemed to blend together for Jess. She had a routine now that she hadn't been able to establish before. She rose early, did the feeding, ate breakfast, then worked for two hours with the new horses. She gave the horses a break until late then worked with them again for a couple of hours each, starting at three. By seven she was finished with the training, did the feeding, and made herself a late dinner each night. Logan would be there to check them out early next week, and Jess wanted to have them as polished as possible by then. They wouldn't be fully trained, but it would be enough for him to see what she could do, and that was all that mattered right now.

Evenings, she talked with her mom or visited with Molly, who in many ways felt like a second mom to her now. Jess began to get a feeling of what a friendship was really like with their talks, and when she went home, she felt at peace and accomplished in ways she had never believed possible for her. Even the cougar seemed to have disappeared.

On Friday morning, she worked with each of the horses, concentrating on having them respond to her leg cues. Jess felt pleased with how quickly they were learning. She worked with the paint first and then the chestnut. When she finished with the chestnut, she untacked him and then bent with her hoof pick in hand to pick his feet. As she did, her phone, which she had put in her shirt pocket, slid out and landed hard on the concrete floor. She picked it up, tried to restart it, but without success. All she could hope for was that it could be repaired. She stuffed it into her jeans pocket, finished with the chestnut, and turned him out.

She had two hours until she started training again, so she decided to take the phone into Seligman to be repaired. The heat mirages that rose from the pavement as she drove east on I-40 gave a dream-like quality to the day. When she pulled into the phone store's parking lot, she thought about how much had happened in the relatively short time since she had bought the phone. It seemed impossible that it had only been weeks and not months since that moment.

"Well, hello there," the same clerk who had sold her the phone greeted her as she came through the door.

Jess smiled at him. "I don't know if you remember me, but I bought this phone here a few weeks ago." She held up the now-dead phone.

"I do. Late afternoon, and I stayed late to charge it up for you."

"Yes, that's me. Sorry about that, by the way."

"What can I do for you?"

"I dropped my phone, and now it won't turn on. I was wondering if it is repairable."

"That depends on what was damaged. I have a repair guy who works evenings. He'll be in later today to pick up anything I have for him. You would have to leave it though. If it is a repair he can do, he'll have it back to me by tomorrow morning. Will that work for you?"

"I guess it will have to. Thanks. Do you need a deposit or anything?"

"No, if you want to check back tomorrow, I'll let you know if he could repair it and how much it is." He handed her a card with the business phone number on it, and she took it, but wondered what good it would do her since he would have her phone.

When Jess got home, she went back to work with the horses and so by the time she had finished, darkness had started to fall. She fed and watered the animals. She couldn't find Blue to feed him, so she left his food by the barn door so that he would have it later in case he was out foraging.

The house seemed eerily dark as she approached. For some reason, something felt off. She opened the door tentatively.

• • •

Molly's phone buzzed on the nightstand where she had left it last. In the living room, Molly had the television turned up while she was ironing and didn't hear it. The buzzing stopped, and a minute later, a message popped up on the screen.

• • •

Jess stepped into the house and switched on the light. Casey sat on the couch waiting. Jess froze, then started to turn to get out of the house.

"You stay right there, little missy or you're goin' to die before we get a chance to chat."

Jess half-turned back toward him as he rose from the couch. He had a pistol in his hand.

Jess called out the door, "Blue, Blue. Come here, boy.

"No need to call that mutt. He ain't comin'."

She called again. Again, nothing. She began to feel frantic, the smirk and the "ain't comin'" haunting her. She wanted to cry again but kept it inside, controlled the tears with a fit of anger she didn't think she had ever felt before.

"You ain't goin' to find that piece of shit dog of yours."

"What did you do, Casey?" Her voice quivering, her anger now at the surface. "What did you do?"

Casey moved quickly, grabbed her wrist, twisted her and spun her to the floor. He squatted down, knelt over her, the pistol in his hand again, this time pressed to her temple. Slowly now, deliberately, "You put me in jail. After all, I done for you around here, you called that cholo boyfriend of yours. What the fuck were you thinkin'?

The fear coursed through her like her own blood. She couldn't think clearly, couldn't speak. He grabbed the front of her shirt, dragged her to her feet, and then over to a chair he had set in the middle of the room. He spun her around like a rag doll and shoved her into the chair. With the pistol in one hand, he grabbed a roll of duct tape from the table next to her and began wrapping tape around her waist, attaching her to the chair. She tried to struggle against it, but he put the gun to her forehead again and she was forced to sit quietly, accept what inevitably would come. At last, she found her voice.

"What are you going to do, Casey? Are you planning to kill me? How is that going to work? Do you think somehow, you're going to get away with it? You're going to be the prime suspect."

"I don't give a shit. You understand that? You think I can stand being in prison? I would rather be dead, so if that's what's going to happen, I might as well take you along with me. But first, we need to have a little talk, so I want you to be a nice girl and just sit here and shut the fuck up. You got that? I have some things I want you to get straight. First, you need to do what I tell you to do. You think you know what needs to be done all the time, but I know best, so when I tell you to do something, you need to do it."

He was pacing now, walking back and forth in front of her, talking to her, but as if she wasn't really there. He seemed lost in his own rant, and he hadn't bound her hands and feet. When he turned away from her, Jess reached into her back pocket and took out her pocket knife. She slid it quickly under her leg.

Her mind was racing. She wanted to get out of there, to run as far and as fast as she could. Casey stood between her and the front door. The way to the back door was clear, but the back door never got used. She wasn't sure it would open even if she could get to it. Struggling with Casey for the gun seemed out of the question, but if it came to that, she decided she would fight with everything she had.

Casey had been continuing to talk the whole time, but she had tuned him out, intent on finding an escape.

•••

Molly carried a load of ironing into her bedroom and hung the newly pressed shirts in the closet. As she turned to go back to the living room, she noticed her phone on the bed and picked it up. It showed a missed call and a message from Mike.

"Hey, Molly, Mike here. I've been trying to get hold of Jess but no answer. Have you talked with her today? I need her to know that Casey made bail. He's out of jail, and she needs to be careful. Okay. I've been up in Flagstaff for a meeting. I'm heading back, and I'll stop at her place to check on her and let her know what's going on, but maybe you could go over there just to be sure. Okay, thanks," and the message ended.

Molly looked at the time the message had come in. Six o'clock. It was almost 7:30. She felt some panic. She practically ran back into the living room. "Cal, I'm going over to Jess's place. I think I need you to come along too. Casey is out of jail, and Jess isn't answering her phone."

"Okay, hang on a minute while I get some shoes on. Grab the shotgun out of the closet and that box of shells on the shelf."

"Okay. Hurry, please."

...

Casey had been preoccupied with his rant pacing back and forth, but now he turned back to her. "So, let's just take a look at what got you in this mess. You led me along like a little tease, made me feel like you had feelin's for me. We coulda had somethin' here, you and me. Good little life raisin' some cattle and livin out here with nobody to bother us, but no. You had to go and drag that Mex policeman into it. Now it's goin' to cost you." He had tucked the pistol in his belt now, and as he passed, Jess calculated whether she could get hold of it quickly enough to take it away from him. She wanted badly to try, but she knew that it would be a one and done, one way or the other. She would either get it and shoot him, or he would kill her. She wasn't sure, no matter what the circumstances that she had the stomach to shoot him, and then her chance disappeared as he pulled up a chair and sat down in front of her, the pistol now covered by his loose-hanging shirt.

"I say we go into the bedroom now and have one last little fling before I send you on your way." He took a knife from his pocket, opened the blade, and cut the tape holding her to the chair.

"Stand up and let's go." She didn't move, but clutched the pocket knife under her leg. He grabbed her shirt and pulled her to her feet. Just then, the roar of a truck pulling into the yard distracted him, and he turned away. Jess quickly opened the knife, and in one quick move, drove it deep into Casey's good leg. He screamed in pain, and stumbled back clutching his leg. Jess ran for the back door. When she got there, she pulled on the old door with all the strength she could muster. It swung open. The landscape, dimly lit by the crescent moon, stretched out before her, and she ran up the hill. She could hear Casey cursing and stumbling through the house, both legs damaged now, hardly a match for her two good ones, but nevertheless, from the volume of his voice, making good time. She heard a yell from the front of the house. Mike's voice came to her clear as the night air that carried it. She wanted to warn him, and despite her breath coming in short gasps now as she ran up the hill, she managed to shout, "Mike, he's got a gun."

She could feel Casey closing on her, no more than twenty yards behind now, his breath coming in gasps. She tripped over something soft, fell onto one knee, and looked down to see Blue's body stretched out across the slope. She screamed, stumbled again as she tried to get up and her hand landed on a fist-sized rock. She gripped it and scrambled to her feet again. She heard Mike's voice. "Casey, stop. You don't want to do this." And then she was over the top of the hill.

Below her, she heard Casey stumbling on the slope and then a shout and a groan of pain. She started to really run now, the ground open and flat before her, and she could feel herself starting to put distance between herself and Casey. Suddenly, she heard a scream. She stopped, turned to look back, and saw the cougar on top of Casey. She froze, torn. She didn't know what she could do. It seemed like an eternity that the big cat mauled him, and yet she knew it couldn't be more than a few seconds. Casey struggled for a moment, and then the cat had him by the throat, and it was over. Casey lay motionless. The cougar raised its head, looked up at her, and for a moment they stared into each other's eyes, connected, then the big cat was gone. She suddenly realized that she still clutched the rock. She let it slip from her fingers.

Jess went to Casey, knelt beside him in the blood and dirt. A deep slice cut across his throat and a trail of blood poured from the wound and onto the ground. His eyes had rolled back in his head. She felt sick and wanted to throw up. She heard Mike again.

"Jess, you alright?" He sounded to her like he was in pain.

"Mike, where are you? I'm okay. I think Casey is dead."

"I'm down here."

Jess slid down to him. He was sitting up and clutching his knee.

"My bad knee gave out trying to run up this damned rocky hill. I got a glimpse of the cougar. Is that what got him? I'm sorry I didn't get here sooner, Jess. I tried calling you to warn you that he'd made bail. I left a message with Molly, but she never picked up. I decided I had to get here myself to be sure you were alright."

"You got here at the right time. You were the distraction I needed to get away. Yeah, the cougar came out of nowhere and took him down. I don't know where it is now. Are you okay?"

"Yeah, no worries. It has done this a couple of times over the years. When I'm on duty, I usually wear a brace that keeps it in line. It'll be fine after I ice it. I want to get up there and check Casey though. Can you give me a shoulder, so I can get up?"

Jess moved in beside him. He looped his arm around her neck and shoulder and she helped him stand up. He winced at the pain, and she wanted to help him but didn't know what to do.

"Just help me balance. It's easing up already. That cougar could have done me a favor though if it had taken him down someplace flat." He chuckled to himself and then realized that he might have offended Jess. "I'm sorry. Cop humor can get a little rough sometimes."

Jess turned her head to look at him. "It's fine. I'm just glad it's over. He killed my dog, Mike. He killed Blue. I think he would have done the same to me." The last words caught in her throat choked out with a sob. The tears started to flow just as they got to Casey's body. Mike squatted down awkwardly and checked for a pulse, then stood up again. He took Jess in his arms and held her while she cried it out. He felt tears fill his own eyes, fought against it. Eventually, Jess seemed to settle quietly against his chest. The crying stopped, and she leaned back and looked up at him, in the moonlight her face tear-stained, tired.

"Mike, thank you. I don't think I would have survived without you. He planned to kill me."

"Hey, I didn't do anything. Just showed up. All I can say is that I'm glad that you're safe, Jess. That's all I care about right now. Come on. Let's get you inside so you can wash your face and lie down while I call this in and get the sheriff and the coroner out here."

Jess nodded her head. He squeezed her one more time, and then they made their way back down the hill to the house. As they got to the house, they heard another vehicle pull into the yard, and then a shout, "Jess, it's Molly. Are you okay?"

"Out back, Molly. Yes, I'm okay. Mike's here. We're coming down now."

Molly and Cal waited for them in the front yard, Cal standing with the shotgun draped over his arm.

"Oh, Jess. I'm so sorry that I didn't get the message until just a few minutes ago. Casey is out of jail."

Jess managed a smile. "Yeah, I know. He was here."

"What? Are you okay?"

"Yeah, but it's a long story. Why don't you come in? I'll tell you about it while we wait for the sheriff?"

Molly, Cal, and Mike waited with her in the house while the sheriff and the forensic team worked on the scene. Jess tried to tell her friends what had happened, but the strain had taken its toll, and she started to cry again.

Mike gave her a hug. "Why don't you wait. You're going to have to tell your story to the sheriff anyway. We can hear it then, and you can get yourself together for a while before you have to go through it."

When the interview ended and Casey's body had been removed, Molly and Cal stood up. "We should probably go. Are you going to be okay by yourself here tonight?"

Jess stood up and gave each of them a hug. "I'll be fine. Thank you so much for being there for me. I don't know what I would have done without you these past few weeks."

Molly gave her another hug. "Alright, you take care of yourself, and if you need anything, call. Oh, and get that phone back so you can actually call." She laughed and gave Jess one last hug before they left.

Mike stood up and gave her a hug. "I guess maybe I should be going too. Are you sure you're going to be okay?"

She leaned her head into his chest, felt the warmth of his arms around her. She suddenly felt more tired than she had ever felt in her life, and the tears began to fall again.

Mike held her for a while and then picked her up and carried her to the couch. He set her down, and went to the bedroom, and got a blanket from the bed. He carried it out and tucked it around her and then sat down beside her.

"Hey, you. I'm going to stay with you for a while until I'm sure you're okay."

Jess rested her head against his shoulder and closed her eyes. She spoke in a whisper. "Thank you, Mike." She paused and then added, "For everything."

Chapter 28

Jessica woke early on the morning of Logan Miller's visit. The sun still lay low on the horizon and the rays slanted through her open window. Lying on her back looking up she noticed flashes of blue light dancing across the ceiling. She rolled onto her side and studied the girl with the blue, glass balloon on her window sill. Hopefulness. That had even more meaning for her now. The thought made her smile at the prescience of Molly's gift. She really felt now like she was the woman with the blue balloon.

The sun had not yet fully risen when she walked into the cool darkness of the barn. She turned on the dim overhead lights and filled the feed buckets, first for her two horses and the blue roan quarter horse that had belonged to Casey. The morning after his death, she had found the roan tied up on the far side of the house, and so she had taken it in. She had agreed to take care of him until the court decided what would happen to him. After those three had eaten, she turned them out and brought in Logan's quarter horses.

When Logan's horses finished eating, she took them one at a time and brushed them, and combed out their manes and tails. After that, she tacked up the chestnut and sat down on a bale of hay to wait. She thought about the events of the past few days. When she woke the morning after Casey's death, she found that Mike had at some point carried her into the bedroom and put her to bed. She walked out into the living room and saw him sleeping on the couch, loosely covered with an old sleeping bag that he had apparently had in his truck. Even in his sleep, he gave off an aura of gentle calm. She had made them breakfast, and he had given her a hug, kissed her lightly on the cheek, and he was gone. She hadn't seen him since, but they had talked. Everyone had agreed to put off the dinner party until the next Saturday to give her time to recover.

Her new life. That phrase kept running through her head. What did that mean really? She knew that it meant living without constant fear, but that experience in itself seemed foreign. Did it include a man? She wasn't sure about that. Mike had been a steadying presence in her life in the short time she had known him, but she didn't want to rush into something else right now. She decided that she needed time to figure out who she was before she fully included someone else.

Just then, Logan's truck pulled up to the barn. He got out, and she went out to meet him. "Good morning, Mr. Miller."

"Logan, Jess. Just call me Logan. I feel old enough as it is without being a Mr." He laughed as he walked up to her and shook her hand. "So how are my two boys doing?"

"I think pretty well. They are smart and willing, and we've made a lot of progress in the past two weeks. I'll give you a little demonstration, and you can judge for yourself."

For the next two hours, Jess put the two horses through their paces. While she finished and untacked them, Logan stood by and watched her work with them, care for them. Jess felt nervous, but she felt proud too. The horses had performed well and were far along for the short time she had been working with them. She turned to him as she put the chestnut back into his stall.

"What did you think? Is this what you were looking for?"

"Jess, I have to say that I'm really impressed. It's always hard to find a trainer who really understands horses. You have the touch, no question about that."

Jess turned away, fussed with a bridle that she had hung on the rack inside the door. She felt embarrassed at the compliment.

Logan continued. "You finish these out, then I have four more that I want you to work with. I'll put the word out too, and I know you'll get a lot more work from people I know, but just remember, mine come first." He smiled at her as she turned back to him.

Her smile matched his. "Thank you, Mr., I mean Logan. I won't disappoint you. Another week and I'll start them on cattle. I'll let you know when I think they are finished, but you're welcome to come and see their progress any time."

"Sounds good to me, Jess. I'll stop by every now and then to see what's happening, but I trust you, and I have seen the work you do, so the evaluation period is over." He shook her hand once again, got into his truck, and drove away.

Jess sat down on the bale again. She felt both weak and giddy. For the first time in her life, she had worked at something that was totally hers, and the feeling it gave her filled her with a sense of accomplishment, contentment. She didn't have to depend on anyone else for income or praise. She had begun to know who she was. She was Jess Oliver, horse trainer. She decided that she would never again let someone else define her.

She stood up now, turned the horses out, and started to clean the stalls. As she did, the black box that held Clint's remains caught her eye. It had gathered dust back in the corner of the unused stall where she had hidden it a lifetime ago. She saddled and bridled Mickey and then tied a small T handled shovel to the cantle of the saddle. She picked up the box in one hand and then stepped up into the saddle.

She rode west into the hills and through the brush that she and Clint had crossed through so many times over the past six years until she got to a little rise that looked back on the ranch. She got down and ground-tied Mickey. She set the box aside while she dug a deep hole. When she finished, she took the black box and slipped it down into the earth. She stood for several minutes looking off toward her home. Her home. She had felt like a stranger there for so long, but now she could truly call it her home.

She looked down at the box in the hole. "You didn't do much for me, Clint, but you did this one thing. You brought me here, and you died so that I could learn who I really am. I'll always appreciate that. I hope you're driving cattle somewhere." She stood for a few minutes more looking out across the valley below. The desert had started its full bloom and the prickly pear blossoms spread their yellow, red, pink, and white blossoms out across the landscape below. She felt full of the beauty of this still wild country. She turned back to the grave and shoveled dirt over the box until it formed a mound. When she finished, she stuck the short shovel into the ground at one end of the grave, its handle forming a rough cross. She swung up onto Mickey and rode back down-home.

Acknowledgements

A special thanks to my editor, Maureen Dunphy, to my beta readers, Shannon Lynch and Shannon Weston, and to my wife, Kathy whose honest analysis always helps me find the right direction.